ORCHARD GROVE

ORCHARD GROVE

VINCENT ZANDRI

NEW YORK TIMES BESTSELLING AUTHOR

Copyright © 2016 by Vincent Zandri
Cover and jacket design by The Cover Collective
Interior formatted by E.M. Tippetts Book Designs

ISBN 978-1-940610-78-8
eISBN 978-1-940610-86-3

First hardcover edition: January 2016
by Polis Books, LLC

1201 Hudson Street, #211S
Hoboken, NJ 07030
www.PolisBooks.com

POLIS BOOKS

ALSO BY
VINCENT ZANDRI

The Dick Moonlight series
Moonlight Falls
Moonlight Rises
Blue Moonlight
Full Moonlight
Murder by Moonlight
Moonlight Sonata
Moonlight Weeps

The Jack Marconi series
The Innocent
Godchild
The Guilty

The Chase Baker series
The Shroud Key
Chase Baker and the Golden Condor
Chase Baker and the God Boy
Chase Baker and the Lincoln Curse

The Remains
The Concrete Pearl
Permanence
The Scream Catcher (Polis Books)
Everything Burns
When Shadows Come

For Laura

"[I]t was with a good end in mind—that of acquiring the knowledge of good and evil—that Eve allowed herself to be carried away and eat the forbidden fruit. But Adam was not moved by this desire for knowledge, but simply by greed: he ate it because he heard Eve say it tasted good."
—Moderata Fonte

"Down to the closest friend every man is a potential murderer."
— Henry Miller

PART I
FADE IN:

PROLOGUE

SHE slips on thick, white-framed sunglasses, and lies back on the chaise lounge, relaxing smooth long legs and a topless torso against the springy fabric. Snatching a green apple from the table beside her, she takes a bite out of it and stares directly up at the hot sun. She thinks, *How funny that houses now stand where once were apple trees for as far as the eye could see. Apples I'd picked and ate until I could eat no more. An apple orchard where I could run and hide and no one would find me.*

The trees are all gone now, but the memories aren't. The memories are still festering like open wounds.

Why in God's name did I have to come back here? Why, of all places, did we have to buy a house on this very spot of land? Maybe we bought the house because I wanted it that way. Because I can't forget what happened here all those years ago. Because I relive the memories every day and every night of that bright fall afternoon, not as if it happened thirty-six years ago but only thirty-six seconds ago. Maybe we moved back here because I had no choice but to come back home to Orchard Grove.

In her mind she's a girl again.

1

Her hair is long, blonde, and smooth as fresh linen. It runs down the length of her back, nearly touching the elastic rainbow colored belt that holds up her cut-off jeans. It's early fall, but unseasonably hot. Indian Summer. She shouldn't be running so hard. But she hasn't got much of a choice. She's running through the orchard, her breathing heavy and labored, tears falling down her face and into her mouth.

There's a man coming up on her from behind. A big man.

He's shouting her name. "Lana! Lana! Stop Lana!"

He's a man of forty. Strong from constant physical labor and bearing the wiry muscles of a farmer who works seven days a week. He's wearing filthy khakis and an even filthier denim work shirt with a couple of buttons missing. Lana is afraid of the man because of what he will do to her when he finds her deep inside the apple orchard.

"Lana, I'm coming!" he shouts, his voice cutting through her like the sharpest of paring knives. "You can't hide from me, sweetheart. I'm your papa, Lana. Your father." Slowing to a walk to catch his breath. "You hear me, sweetie pie? You don't run from the man who protects you."

But still she runs. Runs as if the devil himself were on her heels. But he is not the devil. He is instead the man who calls himself her mother's husband and because he is married to her mother, he is now her father. He is coming for her inside a fenced-in orchard that covers four hundred square acres. As frightened as she is, she wants him to chase her. That's the plan. She knows that soon she will not have the strength to carry on. But then, neither will he. She will have to cease running. And when she does, she will be ready for him.

Finally, she stops by a single tree that occupies a short incline.

Winded and covered in a sheen of cold sweat, she need not run any farther. This is the place, after all. The place deep inside the apple orchard where she intends to put an end to the long nightmare.

"I'm coming, Lana!" she hears. "You can't hide. You know you can't hide, sweetie. Not from me. Not when I love you so very much."

Reaching into her pocket, she pulls out the small black can of Mace. Glancing over her shoulder at the apple tree, she spots the meat cleaver she had placed there only last night. She's ready for him. Ready for the step-monster.

"Chill, Lana," she whispers aloud while breathing deeply. "Just chill out and get your stuff together. You'll get your revenge. But first you gotta relax."

He's closer than she thought.

Soon she spots him coming up on her in the narrow, grassy corridor formed between the linear rows of trees. Her heart pounds so forcefully, she feels she might faint right on the spot… right under the fully blossomed apple tree.

But she can't faint. Because what she's about to do this man… this monster… will require every ounce of her strength, agility, and courage.

When he catches up with her, he is breathing hard and perspiring, the sweat having stained the armpits on his shirt. Unbuckling his belt with one hand and running his opposite hand up and down his scruffy face, he forms a smile that is as far from happy as Satan is from sweet baby Jesus.

"I like it when you run away from me," he whispers in his gravelly, two-pack-a-day smoker's voice.

He's standing so close to her now, she smells the sweat on him. The body odor. She breathes in his tar and nicotine-tainted breath.

"Then maybe you'll like this too," she says, raising up the Mace can, aiming the nozzle directly for his face.

He grabs hold of her shoulders just as she presses down on the nozzle.

The clear spray shoots into his blue eyes.

Releasing her, he brings both fisted hands to his face, fiercely rubs his eyes as if they were on fire.

"You little bitch," he screams. "I'll get you for this."

She watches him squirming, crying, the snot pouring out of his nostrils, running over his lips onto his prickly chin, and she thinks, *Right. I'm the bitch… I'm the little bitch… Well, asshole, just look at you now.*

Set vertically at the base of the apple tree, its handle positioned upward at the blue sky, is the cleaver or, what's more commonly known in the trade as a meat-bone cutter. A thick blade that comes in handy for cutting up apples on the thick wood-slabs inside the cider house. The cleaver will kill the beast that has been ravaging her for months now.

3

She takes hold of the two-pound axe-like blade, feels its awesome solid weight in her hand. Feels its power. Cocking it back, she takes aim and swings.

But she's not fast enough.

Her step-monster grabs hold of her forearm only a split second before the sharp steel touches the skin on his sweat and filth-covered neck. He squeezes her forearm like he's trying to crush bone while digging his fingernails into her skin. Her hand opens and the cleaver drops to the ground, bouncing off an exposed tree root.

White-hot pain shoots throughout her body. She drops to her knees, screams.

Reaching down with his free hand, he grabs a fist full of T-shirt, rips it away from her chest, exposing two small breasts protected only by a flimsy white bra.

"Go ahead and scream," he barks, the tears streaming from his poisoned eyes. "Not a soul can hear you."

Pushing her onto her back, he takes a knee, unbuttons his pants, pulls them down. He then pulls her jean shorts down, pushing them past her knees. Positioning thick hands between her legs, he pushes them apart with all the ease of pulling apart a rotted log.

"Scream," he insists. "I like it when you scream."

He forces himself on her and she feels like her entire body will tear in two.

…*Patience, Lana… Be strong…*

Reaching out with her right hand, she uses her fingertips to feel for the cold steel blade. She knows that in just a matter of a few seconds, the blade will find its home buried in the step-monster's skull. Just believing that soon his blood will be spilling all over the orchard floor, makes the pain go away.

He thrusts himself at her like a rabid, wild animal. Rather than resist him, she concentrates only on retrieving the blade. It takes great effort to move the blade one micro inch at a time. But then suddenly, she finds the blade gripped between her index finger and thumb. That's when she shifts the cleaver around so that she can once more grab hold of the wood handle.

The cleaver back in hand she does something that agitates the step-monster.

She smiles.

"Are you enjoying yourself?" he pants, his voice gravel-filled and coming from a place south of purgatory. "Maybe I'm not working hard enough."

"Don't be angry with me, daddy," she says.

For a brief instant, he stops all movement. A single droplet of sweat falls from the tip of his nose to her pale lips. He shoots her a confused look like he's suddenly been teleported to another planet.

"What the hell's the matter with you?" he says.

"Please don't be mad," she says, swinging the meat cleaver around swiftly, burying the blade into the side of his head.

The cleaver impaled in his skull, his wet blue eyes wide open, staring down at her, he tries his best to speak. But all he can manage is to move his mouth without sound. He makes a gesture with his left hand, like he's swatting at a mosquito that's buzzing around his ear. Sliding out from under him, she bounds up onto her knees, pulls the blade out of his head, a stream of dark arterial blood spurting out of the wound. She could stop then, run home to her mother, call the police, explain everything to them.

But she does no such thing.

Instead she watches the blood pouring out of his head, and she watches his eyes rapidly blink and his mouth open and close like he's begging her to be heard. That's when she feels something come over her. A warmth that's different from the sun's radiation. More like the kind of warmth you feel when you set yourself down gently into a hot bath.

She's no longer scared. Rather, she feels empowered. If this is what it's like to play god, she loves it. She's god about to enact her vengeance on the devil.

Taking aim, she positions the cleaver at the mid-point of his neck. Then, cocking the blade back as if her arm were a coiled spring, she swings it against his neck, impaling it halfway through the flesh, bone, and cartilage. The surprising thing is that he's still balanced on his knees, his eyes still wide open, mouth still moving like a ventriloquist's wooden dummy. Still trying to form words. Pulling the blade back out like it were an axe buried in a wood stump, she takes one more swipe at the neck, this time severing the head.

The head falls to the ground, rolls until a couple of rotten apples prevent it from rolling any farther. Peering down at the head, she's surprised to see that the expression planted on her step-monster's face is not one of fear or surprise, but more like confusion. As if he's perfectly aware that his head is no longer attached to his body, and he has no idea how it got that way.

Her eyes locked on his wide open eyes, she's never felt more satisfied in her life.

She's happy.

After she's dressed herself and cleaned herself up as best she can, she calmly makes the half-mile walk back through the orchard to her white farmhouse. In the garage she finds a spade and a pickaxe. Waiting until dark, she heads back to the spot in which the step-monster lies in two separate pale pieces and she proceeds to bury him beneath the apple tree.

It will take some time, but she's seen enough episodes of *Hawaii Five-O* to know that sooner than later, he will be considered a missing person by the Albany Police Department. But she will always know the truth. His body will always reside beneath this tree while his soul rots in hell.

Later on, when the farm is sold for a new subdivision to be called, appropriately enough, Orchard Grove, all the trees will be cut down to make way for dozens of the cutest little cookie-cutter houses you ever did see. But one tree will grow back, its limbs distorted and ugly, its fruit rotten, poisoned, and inedible.

It will be a tree only Satan could grow.

CHAPTER 1

STARTED watching Lana Cattivo two months ago through my master bedroom window. You know the one what I'm talking about. The slider window that's located at the top of a seven foot exterior bearing wall and that's hell to open and close when it gets too hot outside and this thirty-six-year-old house warps and expands. The kind of slider window that seemed modern and hip back in the 1970s when the ranch house was constructed for twenty thousand dollars along with dozens of identical houses on what had been a pristine upstate New York apple orchard.

Thus the name, Orchard Grove.

The funny thing is, by the time I got around to buying this house, the twenty grand price tag had shot up to three hundred K. By no means a financial stretch for a somewhat successful Hollywood scriptwriter. Or so I assumed at the time. But now that it's in foreclosure, I've had no choice but to glue myself to my typewriter and hope for a sale of David Fincher or Angelina Jolie proportions.

It wasn't the writing part that had been hard for me lately, but the selling part. Seems I couldn't sell a script to my own mother if she were still alive, even if I put a knife to her neck and started slowly sawing. But as for the writing? Well the writing was still coming out okay.

Correction… the writing *had been* coming out okay, until recently that is. Until she moved in on June first.

The beautiful, blonde drink-of-water who moved in directly next door to my wife, Susan and me on Orchard Grove, as if this were the only place on God's great earth she could have possibly moved to.

Here's how I'd watch her.

I'd position myself directly to the left of a queen-sized bed that faced the east since Susan insisted a bed should always face the rising sun, and that by nine in the morning would be empty and made up with a blue satin bedspread and non-allergenic pillows covered in matching cases. With all the lights turned off in the bedroom on a bright sunny day like the kind we've enjoyed all summer long, no one could possibly see inside my bedroom from the outside, even with the shades wide open. The sun coming out of the east would create a glare that would blind anyone on the outside trying to look in.

At least, that's what I thought at the time.

I had it all down to a science. If I positioned myself with my aluminum crutches far enough away from the surface of the slider window, I could see her without worrying for an instant that she, in turn, could see me watching her. Problem was, all too often I could make out my reflection in the window. The unkempt hair, the three-day facial growth, the almond-shaped eyes, and a slightly crooked nose that I broke during a high school football kickoff return. No one wants to see their own face looking back at them when secretly staring out the window at a beautiful woman.

Sad truth is, I was housebound then, which sort of made spying on her easier since I wasn't able to go outside very often and risk a run-in with her. You see, I'd just turned fifty, and years of football, jogging, hiking, weight lifting, had taken its toll on my feet. Not all scriptwriters are sedentary sloths who eat three-hour lunches with famous directors and spend the rest of the day bellied up to the bar. Some scriptwriters prefer to be men of action. But that action had caught up with me down in the jungles of Peru where I'd travelled late last year on my dime to research what I hoped would be my new movie. The movie that would re-launch Ethan Forrester's career, even if he no longer lived in Hollywood, the land of broken dreams and shattered contracts…"Don't call us, we'll call you, fuck you very much."

But it was a script I would never get around to writing now that Lana had moved in next door. Her sudden presence in my life turned out not to be a distraction, but instead an obsession. A half-naked and beautiful obsession.

But allow me to back up a bit.

Because, let's be real here. An obsession isn't something that just pops up overnight like a boil on your ass cheek. An obsession takes time. It requires slow simmering. It needs to sprout and grow like a sapling into a sturdy tree with a healthy root system and leaves on the branches. It needs constant feeding and watering or it will die an early death. That said, maybe the right move for me would have been to cut off the food supply to my ever growing obsession which, of course, was none other than my watching her through the window. Maybe the right thing to do would have been to simply stop, concentrate on something else. Like a new script for instance.

It didn't help that my wife Susan had already gotten somewhat acquainted with Lana, having run into her at her local P90X workout class the two take together. Susan even carpooled with Lana. Since we're spilling truths here, I'll even admit that I got a special kick out of watching them get into Lana's red convertible, the two of them wearing not much more than workout shorts and bikini tops. One brunette and the other blonde. With their sunglasses on, they looked years younger. Like a couple of college sorority girls heading for the beach.

On more than one occasion since the Cattivo's moved in, Susan offered to introduce me to Lana, but considering the condition I was in, I steadfastly declined. I just wasn't myself any longer. My surgery had thrown me for a loop, and weeks of being off my feet made me feel fat, old, and insignificant. Not an easy thing to swallow for a man who was used to running three miles per day and training with weights for five out of the seven days.

Plus I smelled.

I hardly ever showered or bathed, and it was a struggle to work up the enthusiasm to shave. It didn't help that I hadn't sold a script in months…

Okay, scratch that... hadn't sold a script in years. Or that our house was in foreclosure proceedings, or that Susan who'd only recently entered full force into a new body-changing exercise regimen worthy a Navy Seal, was in the process of becoming a chiseled statue and just as hard. While her life changed for the better, mine seemed to know no bottom, as if in slicing open my foot and inserting four permanent screws, I'd allowed my life, my talent, and my confidence to spill out onto the floor.

There were other issues to contend with... issues that kept me from being formally introduced to the woman I watched in secret through the window. The main issue being that I'd become reacquainted with the bottle, so to speak. The bottle helped me out on two fronts. First, it helped me forget the physical pain that seemed a constant companion. And second, it helped fill the void left behind when I found I was far too occupied with Lana's presence to even type the words, "Fade in."

So I guess you could say the booze became like a friend to me after she moved in and all I wanted to do with my time was stand by that bedroom window, crutches holding me up, my brown eyes staring out onto the most angelic sight you ever did see living and breathing on Orchard Grove.

And sure, the liquor helped me cope with the guilt. Guilt that accompanied looking at her for even a few seconds. It wasn't just an invasion of her privacy. It was just plain wrong, and I knew it. Still, I found myself glued to that window while everything else around me seemed to fall apart. In all honesty, it made me feel good to look at her. Made me feel like I was still a man and that all the old private parts still worked.

It was the opposite of how I felt when Susan would return home from work or her P90X class. When she'd take a good look at me, a double bourbon gripped in hand, no pages typed on the typewriter, a three day growth sprouting on my face, she'd simply shake her head in disgust (or disappointment which was worse) and silently walk away.

LANA'S morning routine was almost always the same, and it was something I'd come not only to count on, but look forward to. She'd emerge through her house's rear sliding glass doors onto the attached wood deck at nine o'clock sharp. Always, and I mean *always*, she'd be wearing a silk, red and black robe with Japanese images printed on it.

What do they call them? Kimonos?

Delicate red cloth covered in Japanese letters and pictures of smiling, naked Geisha girls with their hair pinned up into buns, fanning men lying on their backs.

Her hair was lush and blonde. It also draped her shoulders, but most of the time it was pulled back neatly into a ponytail, while on other occasions she'd allow it to fall where it may, like a silken gold veil that would become swept up in the wind. Covering her eyes were big square sunglasses like the kind you might find the women wearing on Venice Beach or down on Fifth Avenue in the Big Apple while they shopped on a sun-drenched afternoon. The thick sunglasses allowed her to look straight up into what thus far had been a perfect summer of unrelenting sun, seemingly without pain and without damage to eye and iris, as if she were exempt from the laws of biology and nature. As if she weren't human at all, but some lovely creation I made up in my head out of desperation. A woman whose life I had just begun to script.

She wasn't a tall woman, but she wasn't short either. Her name (according to the mailman who'd also taken special notice of her) was Lana Strega Cattivo. The family name, Strega, no doubt originated from Italian decent. But, if I had to guess, her blonde, blue-eyed features screamed of northern Italy. Her body was Gold's Gym slim without being overly muscular or too thin so that it retained every ounce of femininity and, in fact, oozed with it.

Her bottom was heart-shaped for lack of a better description and it provided the perfect balance to a pair of breasts that reminded me of fresh peaches. Those delightful breasts were fully exposed when she removed her Japanese robe, gently setting it onto the empty chaise lounge beside the one she always occupied without fail.

The house her APD detective husband, who himself was a transplant most recently from the Poughkeepsie PD and prior to that, the LAPD (thanks again, Mr. Postman), purchased for her was also a ranch that, like I said before, was identical to my own. Its layout was precisely the same so that the locations of the rooms were a mirrored reflection of my own home. Mine and Susan's that is. The home she'd been paying for on her own. The home we were about to lose, unless that is, Hollywood came knocking at my door again, which didn't seem very likely seeing as I hadn't even begun my new script.

I guess, if nothing else, Orchard Grove was a cookie-cutter heaven or hell, depending upon where your architectural sentiments lie. But nowadays, the only thing that resembled an apple orchard around here was the name printed on the battered roadside street sign.

Sometimes at night, while lying beside Susan, my right foot elevated by two pillows stuffed under my heel, my body only inches away from the exterior wall that separated my home from the Cattivo's, I pictured Lana lying in her bed a mere two dozen feet away. Perhaps she was sleeping on her side, facing me, breathing in and out gently, maybe her sheer, satin nightgown having run all the way up past her waist to the very bottoms of her breasts.

As of late, I found myself dreaming about her.

It'd become a kind of recurring dream. *Together we're lying in a bed inside a room with no windows or doors. Naturally, we're both naked, but we have no clothing lying around, as if God put us in that room for us to discover and explore one another without anything in the way but our own nakedness.*

In the dream, we aren't making love so much as we've just finished the act, and now we're resting, she with her head on my chest so that I can smell the lavender scent on her blonde hair, our naked bodies covered in a sheen of sweat that glistens in a light that doesn't come from electric light bulbs or candlelight, but that seems to shine down from the ceiling, like moon rays.

The music begins softly at first, but then builds up. Arabic music with drums beating, cymbals crashing, horns blaring. The once bare room becomes a forest suddenly, our bed surrounded by thick trees, all of which bear fruit. Round red fruit just oozing with juice. In the dream, Lana always says the same thing to me.

"I know you've been watching me. Through the window. Your wife, Susan, told me that you spy on me." She smiles then, sits up, and plucks a piece of fruit off the tree. *"I like it when you watch."*

I don't respond because my throat has closed in on itself while my chest grows tight at the sight of a black snake that's emerging from out of the tree foliage, its long thick body coiled around the same tree branch from which Lana stole the fruit. A snake with black eyes and a pink tongue that slithers and hisses as it slips in and out of a narrow half-moon shaped mouth.

Watching that snake, I don't feel fear so much as I feel myself being aroused. Something Lana can plainly see and enjoy. Reaching out with her free hand, she takes hold of me, and begins to caress me. She bites into the fruit and laughs, while the snake lowers itself down from the branch, opens its mouth wide, exposing four curved fangs that impale themselves into my neck...

Sometimes after I woke up from the dream, sweating and breathing hard, Susan would be lying on her side, facing away from me. Although she was asleep, I'd consider rubbing her back, and maybe sliding my hand gently in between her thighs. But knowing she hadn't slept with me in more than a year, and that she had no intention of starting back in on our sex life now, I always pulled back to my side of the mattress.

Eventually, I'd silently go back to sleep, praying that my physical reality might once more turn back into my dream life. The life I preferred to live with my new neighbor, Lana.

Back to reality... if you want to call it that.

Standing before the window, the crutches positioned beneath the tender place where my arms met the shoulders at the sockets, I'd watch her beautiful tan body awash in the bright morning sunshine. Since my work had taken a serious backseat to lust, I might already have a drink going. And if I were feeling particularly nervous or edgy, a joint going from the pot-for-profit plants I was harvesting inside a small patch of thick woods located just beyond the backyard privacy fence (A Maxwell House coffee can filled with five emergency G's was also buried on the site).

But the drink was just a hobby and the weed a way to make some badly needed dough, not to mention, a way of numbing the pain of not working. The pain of the guilt, and of knowing that my lack of production over the past two months was just one more reason that Susan and I were not only about to lose our home, but on the verge of losing our marriage.

I knew I should peel myself away from the window, dump the whiskey, and at least try to get back to my typewriter, forget that this woman ever existed. But as much as I would try, the effort seemed impossible. The problem wasn't that I hadn't written a word since Lana moved in. The problem was that *I didn't want* to write a word. I didn't even want to make the effort. It didn't hold an interest for me, as if her presence had severed the synapse or vein inside my brain that connected the desire to write to the actual physical act of production. You could say I was a doomed man. Doomed from the start. All I wanted to do was look at her. It was as though her very half-naked presence had cast a spell over me, rendered me impotent and worthless as a scriptwriter while, at the same time, making me feel like a new man.

In a word, I'd become a slave. But a more or less, happy slave.

Since Lana Cattivo moved into Orchard Grove, all I wanted to do was stare out the bedroom window at her body and when nightfall came, all I looked forward to was laying my body down only two dozen feet away from hers, and dreaming about our bed inside the forest.

CHAPTER 2

BEFORE I go any further, it's time I explained myself.

Time to come clean, as it were.

I'm not what you call a creep, or a sex fiend, or a pervert, or even a voyeur in the classic sense of those creeps who like to expose themselves without having actual human contact with the female source of their obsession. The point here is that I don't want to give you the wrong idea.

Under normal circumstances, I'm not the type to spend my days looking out the window at an attractive blonde. As a child I was what your average eighth grade teacher might describe as a good kid, a real pleasure to have in class, cuts us all up from time to time with his humor, gets along with everyone, needs to apply himself more, yadda, yadda. I scored average grades, played Pop Warner and high school football, suffered through Little League baseball, didn't binge drink (until college), limited my recreational drugs to pot, and actively participated in the Boy Scouts.

As an adult, I'm a hard worker, a good neighbor, a loyal husband, I pay my taxes on time, hand over my pocket change to the Salvation Army Santa standing outside the door of the Shop Right at Christmas time, and I even part with a monthly donation to the Wounded Warrior Project. Why? Because I'm a true believer in good vibes versus bad.

I was raised by two loving parents in upstate New York who fought a lot for sure (what parents don't fight when the money gets tight?), but taught me right from wrong, brought me to church on Saturday afternoons, educated me in private schools, made me answer for my transgressions be they getting caught with a joint in my jeans pocket or taking the car out when I wasn't supposed to and who, in the end, did the best job they could.

Later on when I married only to divorce a half dozen years later, they wondered not where *I* went wrong, but where *they* went wrong. People stay in marriages for better or for worse. At least, that's the way it's supposed to work. My failure must have been something they didn't do right when it came to teaching me family values. But when they saw for themselves just how badly Hollywood was eating me up, they supported me in my decision to come back east. When I found Susan and they saw how happy she made me, they further supported me by being nice to her, and they both went to their graves believing I'd found peace in the form of my second wife.

They weren't far off.

For the ten years that Susan and I had been married, I'd always thought, *well, two's the charm*. We were friends as much as we were lovers who enjoyed experimenting in the privacy of our own bedroom. It made a difference not having children underfoot, I suppose. It meant we could tryout things with one another more than the average Orchard Grove couple who were always tending to the unending needs of their kids, or so we assumed. We could play every night with the candles burning, the music blaring, the doors open, or even invite another playful couple over if we wanted to. Or we could simply make wholesome white, Wonder Bread love under the covers as we turned in for the night or when we woke up bright and early in the morning.

For a period of many years, Susan and I did the things a couple who are in love, and in love for a long time, do. Ours wasn't a question of lust, as it had been when we were young and new. Ours was a matter of trust, respect, and love.

True love.

But as time went on and my success in Hollywood dwindled, Susan

16

and I grew apart. Her role as lover dwindled in direct proportion to the responsibility she had no choice but to take on as sole breadwinner. But even then, the bills were piling up alongside my rejection emails. Although we didn't fight a lot about it, it was a constant source of tension which invaded our veins like a bizarre variety of sickle cell anemia which in the end, resulted in, you guessed it, no sex… *"Don't even think about it, Ethan buddy!"*

But something improved for me when Lana Cattivo moved in next door. There occurred a sea change of sorts. It was like my skin had cracked open as easily and as fragile as an eggshell, my insides spilling out onto the floor. But at the same time, the void left behind was filled with something else entirely. I guess you'd have to call that something else, desire, since lust wasn't entirely accurate. But then, neither was love. Not by a long shot.

Desire…

A desire like I'd never known before or, more accurately rendered, hadn't known in quite a while. It was as if I'd caught a virus and no matter how hard I tried to shake it, it just wouldn't exit my blood and bone. In a word, I wanted Lana like I wanted no one else.

And as I finished my second drink of the morning, I'd decided enough was enough.

No more creepy spying.

I was either going to do the right thing and pull myself away from this luscious woman and force myself to get back to work. Or, I would do the wrong thing by hobbling outside on my crutches and introducing myself to her, naked face to naked face. My gut told me that the former would have been the most sensible, most responsible decision, and one that just might have saved our home from entering into foreclosure. That same gut told me the latter would be like opening a can of venomous snakes or, in Biblical terms, like taking a huge, near-choking bite of the forbidden Orchard Grove fruit. It was *that* wrong.

Naturally, I chose the latter.

THE brutal truth: I looked like shit.

For sure I smelled like it too.

In the six weeks since my "comprehensive foot reconstruction surgery," or so the doctors called it, I'd only bathed three times since the act of setting myself down into a tub of hot water was a project that required so much strength and balance, I couldn't possibly do it alone. That meant enlisting Susan. While she portrayed someone who was always willing to help, it was just easier to let the bathing go, opting instead for sponge baths. Take it from a scriptwriter, portraying the willing wife and actually wanting to be the willing wife are two different things entirely.

But even when I did bathe, I had to be careful. From what the doctors told me, getting any water on my incisions would mean infection. I also had a six-inch stainless steel rod that had been drilled through the bones of my index toe. A full inch of the rod now stuck out of the toe. One day when I was finally healed, the doctor would grab hold of the one inch piece of rod and yank the entire length out with a pair of common constructer worker pliers. In the meantime, should the rod become bent or misaligned in any way, it would not only cause severe pain, but it would require a second surgery to straighten it out.

No two ways about it: I was housebound, and smelly, and for good reason.

In the bathroom, I shaved and gave myself a sponge bath. Slipped into a fresh, plain black T-shirt and put on a pair of clean Levis. For footwear, a single, brown leather, Tony Lama cowboy boot on my left foot while the bandaged wounds and the exposed rod on my right foot were covered with a thin black sock and a knee-high, Velcro-strapped walking boot. Stealing a look at myself in the mirror, I smiled. It might have been the first smile I'd seen on my face in ages (who looks at their face all that much when they're not content?). Maybe my house was about to be foreclosed on, and maybe I wasn't working, and maybe my wife and I had drifted apart, and maybe I was in a great deal of pain all the time, but a big part of me felt like a teenager again.

"*Here's Johnny*," I said to my reflection. And then, for the first time in a long time, I made my way out of the house.

SNAPSHOT

SHE *lies back on the chaise lounge, feeling the sun soak into her face and her naked breasts, and she once more wonders how she got back here. To this place that holds so many horrid memories. Why purposely seek out a house that's been built on the property where you were hunted like a wild animal by a monster who called himself your stepfather?*

The answer is simple. This is no longer the place where she was hunted, but instead the place where she became the hunter.

Sure, she sees herself as a girl running desperately through the trees trying to hide from the step-monster. But she also feels empowered. She beat the son of a bitch and now, by returning to this place where the apple trees have been ripped out to make way for homes and cute little families, she's come full circle. It will become the place where she will beat another monster.

Meet the new monster... same as the old monster...

But for now, no one knows what happened on Orchard Grove back in the late 1970s and early Eighties, and no one ever will. Only she, her step-monster, an Albany Police Department Detective by the name of Miller, and the Devil know. And that's enough.

19

CHAPTER 3

BOLSTERED by my crutches, I stood as straight and upright as possible inside the dining room, my eyes looking out the rear picture window onto the backyard and the invisible pot patch beyond the privacy fence. I inhaled and exhaled to calm my nerves, like I was only moments away from picking up my date for the junior prom.

When I felt good enough about "me," I carefully negotiated the two steps down into the den and opened the sliding glass doors. I stepped out onto the deck, leaned my bodyweight onto the crutches, looked up to the sky, felt the good warmth of the morning sun shining down upon my clean-shaven face. It was then that I heard the distinct and pretty sound of chirping and I was almost ashamed of myself for having forgotten what for the past two springs and summers had become my, let's call it, fatherly duty.

Nested inside a small hole up over my head in the aluminum soffit was a pair of robins that had been coming to this house to birth their babies for years now. The robins were so used to Susan and me at this point, they didn't even fly away when we came outside onto the deck. Some of that had to do with familiarity and some of it had to do with the fact that I often fed them birdseed, especially when the momma robin was clearly with child. But since my foot operation, even a simple task like feeding the birds had become a project. Sometimes Susan fed the birds, but more often, she forgot all about it.

Susan was a working girl after all.

Now that I was outside however, I had no trouble with grabbing a scoop full of seed from the fifty pound bag that leaned up against a small metal shelf to my left, and reaching up into the round hole, gently depositing the food inside it, onto the flat interior aluminum panel. Almost immediately you could hear the robins pecking at the food, like I was their life savior, and I guess, in a way I was. But I'd grown to love those birds over the years, and who knows, maybe they loved me. This might seem a bit silly, but they are what we had in the place of children, and to be further honest, I sometimes worried about what would become of them when the day finally came for Susan and I to move out, and move on with our separate lives.

I wiped my hands off on my jeans and once more inhaled and exhaled.

Shifting my gaze over my right shoulder, I caught sight of her. With the wood stockade fence surrounding the perimeter of our property and a similar fence surrounding hers, I could only make out the upper portion of her body. The portion that enticed me the most since it was naked. The back of her head, the erect nipple-tipped left breast, her bare shoulders and arms.

My breath escaped me. It was all I could do not to pass out on the spot.

Shifting myself on my crutches so that I faced her property directly, I started to make my way across the wood deck in her direction. It was only a walk of maybe fifty or so paces, but it seemed like fifty miles.

By the time I got to the other side of the house-length wood deck, I knew I'd crossed the point of no return. Lana was not only sexy and alluring, but she was intuitive too. I'll say that for her. Because my deck was a good two or three feet higher than hers, it allowed me to peer over the tops of both privacy fences, down on her. All the time I had been hobbling my way across the deck, I sensed she knew her morning sunning routine was suddenly about to be intruded upon. It was as if I could see the fine hairs on her pretty little neck standing up at attention the closer I came to the edge of my deck, and the fence gate just beyond it.

Then, just like that, she lifted up her head, rolled over on the chaise lounge, and looked up at me. Even though both our fences and a narrow strip of grass in between separated us, the distance between us could not have been more than fifteen feet. I was that close, but considering the relative difficulty of using the crutches on uneven ground, I was also that far away.

Quickly, but somehow gracefully, she snatched the Japanese robe from off the empty lounge beside her, and tossed it over herself. Sitting up, she tied the drawstring around her narrow waist. Did it in one fluid, natural, if not panic-free motion.

"Can I help you?" she said loud enough for me to hear over both fences. When she spoke, a slight smile formed on her face. I took the smile as part embarrassment, part taken-by-surprise, part happy for the unexpected company.

"I'm sorry," I said, my now sweaty palms squeezing the rubber-gripped crutch handles. "I didn't mean to startle you." Which is to say, our relationship began with an apology of sorts. My apology for sneaking up on her.

She raised herself up off the lounge, stood up on the deck looking as smooth and beautifully shaped as she did lying down.

"You'll have to pardon me," she said. "We lived in Southern California for ages. I'm soaking in the sun while the getting is good."

"The sun has been shining on you ever since you moved in," I pointed out. I started to laugh nervously, and I felt the blood's warmth as it filled my cheeks and made them blush. "I hope you don't think I've been spying on you."

She casually crossed her arms over her chest. "Well, have you been?"

I felt a slight start in my pulse.

"Me?" I said. "Not a chance."

"You're the screenwriter. I've met your wife Susan. She's very attractive."

"You both attend the same sweat shop, or so I'm told."

"P90X," she said. "Susan knows how to use her body, let me tell you." I sensed her shooting me a wink under her sunglasses. "You're one lucky boy."

Reaching with both hands around the back of her head, she pulled out the rubber band that was holding her hair in a tight ponytail, allowing it to fall to her shoulders. Running both her hands through the thick hair, it came to veil her face.

She added, "I just assumed I was the only one on Orchard Grove who stayed home during the day."

"Used to be *I* was the only one."

"So you get to hang around the house all day and ahhh, spy on the new neighbors?"

Another start in my heart. More intense this time. Already, she knew how to play me.

"Screenwriters always work from home," I said. Then, looking down at my black-booted right foot where it rested on its heel on the edge of my wood deck. "I've tried the Starbucks thing and it just doesn't work."

"You step on a landmine in some faraway war zone?"

Her question took me by surprise since I was sure she couldn't see it from where she was standing. But then, I'm sure that at some point during the many weeks she and her husband had been living on Orchard Grove, she'd seen me getting around on a rare venture outside with my crutches. Or, more realistically, perhaps Susan had let her in on my operation.

"Nothing so romantic, I'm afraid," I said. "Hammer toe and bunion surgery. Plus a crack in the foot plate."

"Ouch, that sounds worse than a landmine injury."

"You make it past forty, the parts start to wear out. One by one."

"But once you replace them all, the vehicle is as good as new. Besides, from where I'm standing, the body looks as though it's still in mint condition."

Her compliment sent a wave of warmth shooting up and down my spine. Thank God for the sun shining down so brightly on our backyards, because otherwise, she might have noticed how red my face must have been by then. I don't think I'd blushed over something a woman said to me in ten years. But in the span of two minutes, Lana made me blush twice.

"But where are my manners?" she said. "I'm Lana, and I was just about to grab an iced coffee. Would you like one?"

Thought she'd never ask.

"I'm Ethan, Lana," I said, gingerly making my way down the deck stairs, then hobbling toward the fence gate. "It's really great to meet you, and if it's okay with you, I like my coffee hot."

"Like my women," I wanted to add. But I didn't want to seem too forward to a woman I'd already fallen head over heels for.

CHAPTER 4

ONCE I'd made it across the narrow strip of brown sunbaked grass without falling on my face, I entered into her yard by way of a wood fence gate that was identical to my own. It was then that I was able to capture my first up-close and personal glimpse of her. She was even more stunning from only a few feet away. But there was something else that made being in her presence so much more special than staring at her through the bedroom window.

It was the way she smelled.

The scent was distinctly lavender, like the scent I smelled in my dreams, and it was carried in my direction by the light breeze that blew from out of the west against my face. It was as if she'd washed her entire body in lavender before coming outside to sun herself on the deck. She held out her hand and smiled warmly. I was able to catch a quick peek inside her robe then, as it opened and parted when she moved.

As I stood there, propped up on my crutches, I began to imagine her naked body bathing in a tub of hot steaming bathwater and lavender scented bubble bath. I had to watch out or I would give away my enthusiasm for my new neighbor by growing hard in a place that would not only be noticeable considering my rather snug fitting Levis, but also considerably more embarrassing than a face that was once again, blushing bright red.

Looking into her deep blue eyes, I wanted to drown inside them. It felt strange sharing the same air with her, but it also felt marvelous. Sensual even. I took her hand in mine. It was soft, petite, and warm. Together we focused our eyes on our hands as they joined, my hand the larger and her hand the more delicate and frail. Like a child's. I have to admit, I felt electricity pulsing in my synapses, as though she were in the possession of far more energy than the average woman. It was an energy that she was able to transfer not onto me when we touched, but into me. Deep, into my bones, heart, and soul.

"Would you like to come in while I make the coffee?" she asked politely.

"Sure you don't want me to wait out here?"

"A man who answers a question with a question," she said. "How did I know you would be like that?"

"How do we know anything about the people who live only a few feet away from us?"

"You're doing it again. " She laughed. "Come. Keep me company while I make coffee."

Pressing my lips together, I nodded.

Opening the sliders, she stepped inside with her bare feet and me right behind her with my crutches and bad foot. Like I already said, the layout of her house was the same as my own, so that as soon as I stepped on through the door into the television room, I looked to the left for the dining room and beyond it, the kitchen.

I stood there for a second or two, resting my shoulders on my rubber-padded crutches, while I took a quick survey of the pinewood paneled walls. There wasn't a whole lot to see, but what I did see spoke volumes about her cop husband. Occupying the long far wall so that it was the first thing that drew your eye's attention, was a series of framed photographs of the Albany Police Detective.

The wall was like a "This Is Your Life" layout of the officer's career thus far.

Besides at least a half dozen framed diplomas and citations for marksmanship and courage in the line of duty from Los Angeles Police

Department, there was also a picture of him as he graduated from the police academy. He was a young, wiry, black-haired new recruit who enthusiastically shook the hand of a much older formal-uniformed cop who was wearing white gloves and handing over a diploma.

Then there was the picture of the young officer book-ended by an American flag and the California state flag, a bright but cautious smile planted on his face. The photo beside that one was of the now maturing detective dressed in plain clothing with thinning hair and a face having become ruddier and puffier as will often happen when you drink a little too much whiskey day in and day out. He was standing in front of an unmarked cop cruiser, his sidearm prominently clipped onto his belt buckle, arms confidently crossed. The plates on the car were New York State and the signage mounted to the glass and brick building behind him read, Poughkeepsie Police Department.

There was a wet bar set up against the wall directly below the pictures. Several bottles of whiskey occupied the bar-top, along with a bottle of vodka, one of gin, another smaller green bottle that contained vermouth, and an empty decanter beside those.

Lana must have noticed me noticing her wall because as she reentered the TV room with a mug of hot coffee in one hand and a tall glass of iced coffee in the other; she also turned to view the wall.

"John's wall of fame," she commented, along with a distinct exhale. "He's worked very hard to get where he's gotten."

"I can see that," I said. "He's done well for himself in a hard, dangerous business. He's got the plaques, the house in the burbs, and the beautiful wife to show for it."

She turned quick, caught my eye.

"You say the sweetest things, Ethan," she said, "even if you won't make many feminist friends with that kind of talk."

"I try," I said, "even when I'm not trying. If you get my drift."

"Oh, I get your drift. You must be one hell of a writer."

"I'm sorry. Sometimes I'm too frank. You're allowed to kick me in the shins whenever I get out of hand."

"If I had shoes on, I just might. In the good leg, of course."

"You're not wearing much of anything."

27

"Does it bother you?"

"Not in the least."

She bit down on her bottom lip, nodded slowly, thoughtfully.

"What do you say we take our coffees outside," she said after a beat. "I'm missing the sun. Hope you like black, no sugar because I'm fresh out of dairy and sweetener. Later on I'm heading to the grocery store so I can make some cookies for the neighborhood kids. It's kind of a pet project of mine. Would like some?"

"Cookies or kids?"

"Cookies, silly," she said, giggling. Then, "Now, can we head outside before I drop this stuff and make a mess?"

"I'm right behind you," I said.

"Lucky you," she said, strutting herself to the already open sliding doors. "Lucky me."

CHAPTER 5

OUTSIDE we sat as a round stainless steel-topped table that was empty other than her smartphone, sunglasses, and the remnants of a Granny Smith apple that she'd probably munched on for breakfast. We sipped our coffees and looked at one another and smiled self-consciously. At least, I did.

Lana put her sunglasses back on and positioned her face up toward the sun so that she could soak it in while we chatted. We engaged in small talk mostly. I asked her the usual questions you ask anyone who has just picked up, lock, stock, and barrel, to move to a new city where everyone is a stranger. I asked her why her husband decided to come to Albany, and she told me he was offered the job by the APD Chief of Police himself.

"It was a deal he couldn't possibly refuse," she said, making quotation marks with the fingers on both her hands when she said the word "deal."

I asked her how she felt about it, or was that too personal a question. She didn't mind telling me that she'd originated from Albany and to be truthful, hated like hell to have to come back to its forever-long winters. What she truly wanted was to be back in LA, but John wouldn't hear of it. They'd first met in LA, in fact, when he was still a young officer for the LAPD. She was waitressing at the Venice Ale House down on the boardwalk when he came in with his buddies. He didn't stop pursuing her until she agreed to spend her life with him. That kind of attention and love doesn't come around so often, she pointed out. So she married him, despite the fact that he's five years her junior, and would always be five years her junior.

"How unusual," I said, sipping some of the coffee, squinting in the sun's rays, wishing I hadn't forgotten my Ray Bans. "Robbing the cradle." Then I told her that I used to frequent the Venice Ale House. That I lived not far from it in a duplex on the beach road. Back when I was actually selling scripts.

"Maybe we've met before," I said. "But then, I think I'd remember a woman like you."

"You're a lucky boy and Susan's a lucky girl," she said. Then, after drinking some of her iced coffee, "Why do you say it's unusual I married a younger man?"

I cocked my head, scrunched my brow.

"I don't know," I said. "I'm just more used to the traditional, man marries the younger woman, dies a lot earlier. Then the wife remarries and pisses off the adult kids who are in debt up to their ears and depending sorely upon the dead dad's inheritance... an inheritance that may now go to the new husband."

She laughed. "Well back then, John and I were both in our twenties, so my being older than him didn't really seem to matter. But now that I'm in my forties, it seems to matter."

"How so?"

She raised up her smooth, bare legs, relaxed her feet on the empty chair beside her, lowered her head just enough to get a look at me through those thick square sunglasses. Just the sight of her made my breathing labored.

"Aren't you the nosy one," she said.

"I'm a film artist. It's my job to be nosy."

Slowly, thoughtfully, she raised her eyes back up to the heavens. "In that case, I'll suggest you use your imagination to guess how the flame with John has diminished in its intensity over the past few years."

I felt yet another electric spark jolt my body. It seemed to originate in my stomach and spread out from there, like the waves from a pebble tossed into a pond. I focused on her. Her bare neck and the suntanned skin on her chest, the sweet spot in between her two pert breasts.

My spell suddenly broke when her phone rang and vibrated at the same time, making the entire table vibrate. She leaned up straight, not like her phone was ringing, but more like an alarm had gone off. She picked up the phone, looked at the number, bit down on her lip.

"John," she said.

"Aren't you going to answer it?" I said.

She shook her head. "No." Then she pressed something on the phone that made it stop ringing. Tapping in her entry code, she checked something else. Her texts, or so I assumed. Still biting her lip, she put the phone down, but her hand knocked into her coffee, nearly spilling it over. Some of the coffee shot up and out of the cup however, and stained the sleeve of her robe.

She stood up fast.

"Crap," she said, staring down at the wet fabric. "Coffee stains. Excuse me for a second, Ethan." She quickly disappeared into the house.

I sipped my coffee and stared at her phone. A little voice filled my head. It told me to quickly pick the phone up while I had the chance, check out her texts. Maybe there would be something interesting on there. Something that would shed some light on precisely who Lana Cattivo really was without my having to drag it out of her.

I could hear the water running in the sink in the kitchen. The sink faced the dining room. She would have no way of seeing outside onto the deck while she was scrubbing the stain out of her robe sleeve. In a mere moment, the phone would lock up and my chance would be gone forever.

I reached out, took hold of the phone.

There were too many apps for me to take in all at once, so I went to the most obvious. The WhatsApp text message service. I opened it. There was a long list of photos. Faces from men and women whom I had no way of knowing. That's not entirely right. I recognized the face of her husband. There was a text beside it. It said, "Working late. Wait up anyway." Nice guy. The date was from two nights ago.

I scrolled down.

No one single face popped out at me.

Then she turned off the faucet. My heart pounded and adrenalin filled my brain.

I was about to quickly place the phone down on its face, when I saw a name. It said, "Susan." I glanced at the photo that went with the name. It wasn't a photo I'd ever seen before and since it was so small it wasn't easy to make out. But for certain the Susan in question had long, thick brunette hair. If the Susan in question were my wife, I wouldn't be entirely too surprised since they'd been sharing rides to the gym. I looked at the final message in a series of messages set beside the name. But it wasn't typed text. It was instead, a voice message created by Lana.

I heard footsteps crossing over the kitchen. In a matter of two seconds, Lana would be back. I hit the voice message anyway. The word, "Baby…" came out of the speaker. But it was all I could make out before I had to press the command that made the screen close and quickly set the phone back down in the same place where she'd set it a moment ago.

I'd barely pulled my arm back when she reemerged out onto the deck.

She stopped in her tracks.

"Everything okay?" she said, her eyes veering from the phone to me and back to the phone again.

"Sure," I said, swallowing. "All good."

She nodded, grinned and sat herself back down.

"I'll bet you're just dying to know everything there is to know about me, aren't you, Ethan?"

I was certain then that she'd seen me sneaking a peek at her phone. But then, if she had, she didn't seem angry about it. She seemed suspicious and that's all. The name "Susan" flashed into my brain. A Susan with dark hair, just like mine. How many millions of Susans were there in the world with black hair? Countless. A Susan whom Lana called, "Baby…" It could never be my Susan since the two only knew one another as acquaintances. You don't refer to an acquaintance as "Baby" and you don't refer to her as "Baby" if you're another woman. Generally speaking anyway.

"Yes," I said, lifting my coffee, taking a sip, praying my hand wasn't trembling too much. "I would love to get to know you more."

She licked her lips.

"We'll just have to see about that," she said. "Maybe, if you're lucky, we can be the bestest friends ever on Orchard Grove."

SNAPSHOT

SHE'S *calmly listening to this man with the horrible looking foot and the screenwriter brain lie through his teeth about sneaking a peek at her phone messages. Maybe he already suspects something about Susan. About she and Susan. Or perhaps it's just his intuition speaking to him... what do writer's call it? Their built-in shit detector. The detector telling him that something isn't quite what it seems on quaint, suburban, Orchard Grove.*

But then, she knows for certain that he is madly in lust with her. It's possible this lonely, has-been is falling in love with the fantasy he's been watching from out of his bedroom window for weeks now. If only he knew the truth about Orchard Grove, about all the boys and men who also fell in lust and love with her all those years ago. If only he knew about their fate, he might not only think twice about sharing an innocent coffee with her, but also about spending so much time watching her. Christ, if he only knew the real truth, he'd pack the house up tonight, grab Susan by the hand, and move as far away from Orchard Grove as humanly possible.

If only he knew the bloody truth.

She sips her iced coffee, stares out at the old apple tree that occupies a slight

34

incline, just beyond the fence-line. Miraculously, the tree still bears fruit. She recalls how her step-monster breathed his last only a few feet away from that tree. But then, she also recalls the next man. Was his name Brian? Or was it David? Just a thin, lonely, middle-aged man who arranged a date with her via the classifieds in the local arts and entertainment give-away news rag. It had been so easy.

With only a few weeks to go before the trees were scheduled to be cut down to make way for the new Orchard Grove subdivision, she arranged to meet him there, to walk with her amongst the trees one final time.

She packed a picnic lunch for him. Nothing special. Bologna sandwiches on sliced white bread slathered with ketchup. Bags of Lays potato chips. Homemade Toll House chocolate chip cookies… junk a thirteen-year-old girl likes to eat. She even included a can of Miller beer for him and a Tab for herself.

At the time, she wasn't entirely sure why she included the meat cleaver and the thin black can of Mace in the basket… what force or inner voice propelled her to place the items there. But soon after they started making out, he tried to put his hand in her pants. Instinct took over, and she took hold of the Mace and sprayed his face. He began to choke, his eyes wide and red and burning. He held out his hands as if to choke her, but she grabbed hold of the cleaver and chopped his left hand clean off.

As soon as she chopped off the right hand at the wrist, her body became enveloped in that warm beautiful feeling, and for certain, she knew precisely why she brought the Mace and cleaver.

They were instruments of her destiny.

CHAPTER 6

"**B**UT what about you?" she said after a time, repositioning her feet onto the chair beside her, focusing her face up toward the sun to catch the maximum amount of rays. "What movies have you written?"

"Hasn't Susan told you?" As soon as I posed it, I knew that the question was moot since Susan rarely if ever, talked about my writing anymore.

She shook her head.

I told her about the films and also about the one novel I'd written. A mystery that was quickly remaindered. She'd seen the films or most of them, but never heard of the novel. Which didn't surprise me in the least.

"Shouldn't you still be living in LA?" she said.

I admitted that I'd lived there with my first wife all throughout the Nineties and into the new century, but when the Internet shrunk the world, I figured I could make my move back east which I preferred. But what I didn't tell her is that after my divorce and the hangover that followed, I could no longer afford Hollywood. I also left out the part about what a mistake it had been for me to separate myself from the studios and the agents who'd been buying my stuff for nearly ten years. Even optioning the scripts that often wouldn't be produced. Maybe novels could be written from anywhere in the world, but screenwriters… serious scriptwriters and show runners… still needed to be in LA to make the deals and seal them, face-to-face.

"How long have you and Susan been married?" she pressed on.

I drank some more of the quickly cooling coffee. "Ten years, no kids. But then, Susan has probably told you that already also."

"Truth is, we haven't talked much at all. We've discussed our P90X class and the asshole jock who runs it, if you'll pardon my French. But that's the extent of it. I'd really like to get to know her better."

I felt somewhat relieved that Susan hadn't yet opened up about us… about our trouble as of late. "You married long?"

"Long enough to know better," she said. Then, as she stared up at the sun, "And the fire still burns for you and the missus, Ethan Forrester?"

There it was again… the image of the name Susan on her WhatsApp. The name, the face and the long brunette hair.

"You want the truth? Or the sugar-coated version?"

She laughed. "So that's why you spend your day staring out your bedroom window at the scantily clad wife of a top Albany cop?"

I felt as if all my blood were about to spill out the fresh wounds in my foot.

"Snagged," I said. "Red-handed and red-nosed. You've seen me?"

"You want the truth or the sugar-coated version?"

"Very funny. How'd you know I was looking at you?"

"Hard to miss you with your face pressed up against the glass like that."

"Hey, wait a minute. I've been trying to be careful about such things. At least, that's what I've been telling myself, Lana."

Another giggle, not like we were discussing my voyeurism and hers, but as if we were talking over Toll House cookie recipes.

"Don't worry yourself over it," she said, taking on a sly grin. "I kind of like it."

More of that electric jolt I'd been getting since first laying eyes on her inside her own backyard, as if she had her hand on a video-game-like controller and kept pressing the trigger.

"Glad to be of service," I said. "If you'll excuse the cliché."

She drank some iced coffee, then gently set the glass back down on top of its own condensate ring. For a time we sat in silence. But with the insects buzzing around us and the gentle wind blowing the leaves on the trees and a dog barking in the near distance, it wasn't all that silent.

"Tell me," she said after a long slow beat, turning so that she was once more staring at me through those dark sunglasses, "how many times per day do you rub that cock of yours when you're staring at me?"

The electric jolts now became a firestorm that erupted inside my entire body. Using the crutches as leverage, I stood up. Supporting myself with only one crutch shoved under my right arm, I shifted myself around the table, until I stood directly over her.

"Careful, Ethan Forrester," she said looking up at me. "I wouldn't want you to hurt yourself."

I took a good look over my left shoulder and saw nothing but empty backyards, half blocked out by the fence. It was the same view over the other shoulder. Behind us, nothing but tall trees and scrub and my pot patch. I knew that if I didn't make my move then, I might never get another chance.

Taking hold of her arm, I lifted her out of her chair, took her in my arms, pressed my lips against hers. Her robe flew open as if she fixed it to happen that way, and I pulled my mouth away from hers and kissed her neck and her chest, until I took an erect nipple into my mouth, tasting the warm, sweet, sun-drenched skin.

Pushing back her phone and coffee glass with my free hand, I balanced myself on my good leg and picked her up, setting her down onto the table. I reached out with both hands and grabbed hold of her black silk panties. I was pulling them off when I heard the distinct sound of a vehicle pulling up into the driveway.

"Oh no," she said from down on her back on the table. "John's home."

CHAPTER 7

EVEN with her husband about to barge in on us, it took all the strength I had left inside me to pull myself away from her while precariously balancing almost the entirety of my weight on one foot.

She slid off the table, quickly rewrapped her robe around her waist, and tied the belt into a neat bow. As I stood there watching her, heart beating in my throat, something told me this wasn't the first time Lana had been unexpectedly interrupted by her husband while she, shall we say, entertained another man.

She sat herself back down in her chair and grabbed her glass of iced coffee. I also sat down, careful not to break the plastic-backed chair as I thrust myself into it, my bad foot extended before me. Luckily my coffee hadn't spilled either, and as I was putting the mug to my lips, a man threw open the sliding glass door and walked out onto the deck.

"Hope I'm not interrupting anything!" he barked.

He was a man slightly taller than average height. Maybe an inch or so taller than me. But I pegged him for ten years younger and built with the powerful neck, shoulders, and arms of a weight lifter or former college fullback. For certain he was the man whose photographs occupied the far wall in the house's TV room.

He was wearing a black Oxford button-down that fit snuggly to his waist. Despite the obvious hours spent in the gym, his beer gut was even more obvious as it protruded beyond his brass military style belt buckle and pressed against shirt buttons that seemed on the verge of popping. I often wrote about cops in my scripts and I most definitely wrote about them in my one crime novel, so I was no stranger to their love of the bottle. This man was no exception.

Like I said, he was ten or so years younger than me, but aging more rapidly than the average bear. He had a full head of dark hair and his face was scruffy while sporting the pink tint not of a sun worshipper like his wife, but instead of a daily alcohol abuser as opposed to an all-out dysfunctional alcoholic.

With my hands wrapped around my now cooled coffee cup, I gazed up at him and neither smiled nor frowned. What he didn't know was that I was holding onto the cup so that he didn't notice them trembling. What I wouldn't have given right then for my sunglasses to use not against the sun, but as a mask. Stealing a quick glance over my left shoulder, I could see that Lana had pressed her lips together to form a kind of odd smile. But it looked more like the expression someone would wear while a doctor repaired a hangnail on their big toe.

He barged through the door with his blue jacket pushed far enough behind both his elbows for me to make out the inverted black grip on his 9mm Smith & Wesson service sidearm. With a broad but now very happy smile on his face, he approached the table and stopped just short of slamming into it with his thighs.

Turns out he wasn't alone.

He was accompanied by a younger man who was both taller and thinner, but with a neck that looked like a tree trunk. He was also packing a sidearm which was holstered and clipped onto a black belt that held up gray slacks under a matching gray jacket. His hair was black and neatly cut and he was sporting an equally groomed mustache and goatee. His eyes were hidden behind aviator sunglasses so that I had no way of seeing what color or shape they were. But I did sense for certain they were looking not at me, but into me.

"Hello, Carl," Lana said to the man. Between the low-toned voice and the dead-pan way in which it was delivered, I could almost taste the tension between the two, as if in the short time the Cattivo's had been in town she'd already managed to develop a history with this city cop, however short and sweet or sour.

"Lana," the man mumbled in an equally telling tone.

"Aren't you going to introduce me to your friend, Lana?" John said, his blue eyes locked not on his wife's, but on mine.

She cleared a frog from out of her throat.

"John, this is our next door neighbor, Ethan," Rachael said. "He's professional writer. A real screenwriter and a novelist too." And then, "Ethan, this is my husband, John, and his partner, Carl Pressman."

John noticed my crutches and the black boot-splint.

"Don't bother to get up," he said.

I held out my hand from where I was seated and John took hold of it. He shook it briskly and tightly not as a welcome, but purely as a demonstration of his strength, power, and dominance over me both as a man and an officer of the law. He held the hand for a second or two longer than men usually spend on a handshake, all the time locking eyes onto my own. When finally he released his grip, Carl leaned in and took my hand. His grip was firm but not as firm as his partner's. As opposed to John's show of strength, Carl's was more of an *I don't give a shit who you are because I won't remember your name or face in a few minutes* kind of shake.

"Listen, John," Carl said, "I'll wait for you in the Suburban. I've got a bunch of calls to make that just can't wait." He nodded at me, and smiled at Lana. She smiled back at him, but the pleasant exchange was about as phony as the plastic chair I was sitting in. He left the way he came in, back through the sliding glass doors.

"So a real screenwriter," John said, pulling out the chair closest to him, sitting down. "You mean like a I'm-hoping-to-sell-a-movie-someday kind of real screenwriter, or you actually make money at what I consider a hobby for drunks and addicts who don't want to work for a living? You know how many screenwriters I busted for DWIs down on the Strip alone? Goddamned West

Coast freak show."

"Don't be rude, John," Lana said. "You don't even know him."

He turned to her quick. "And you do, sweetheart? Or were you planning on getting to know him better when I'm not around?"

To say I was sensing some real tension in the air was putting it lightly. It didn't take an Einstein or an APD detective to see that the Cattivo's were having a little trouble with their marriage these days. Dawned on me suddenly that the trouble in question might be the real reason behind their move upstate.

Lana added, "I think we've seen a few of Ethan's films, back when we lived in Venice."

"That so," John said. "How come you're not living in West Hollywood on the corner of Gregory and Peck like the rest of those jerkoffs?"

"John!" Lana snapped. "Please."

He shot me a smile again, as if to portray himself as happy when, in fact, he was seething inside. Seething because his half-naked wife was hanging out with scriptwriter from next door, and by the looks of it, John had had a bellyful of scriptwriters as a Santa Monica cop. Can't say I blamed him.

"Just your luck, huh?" I said. "You move all the way to the east coast to start a new life and you land right smack next door to Hollywood in all its glory. Must be serendipity."

I wasn't about to tell him my scriptwriting career was just about non-existent these days. That was between me and the God of Tinseltown.

"Listen, Hollywood," he said. "Lana was just about to fix me some eggs and bacon, weren't you Lana? Maybe you'd like some, Hollywood. Or let me guess. You probably eat egg whites and kale. And hey, I can show you my gun collection. You like guns don't you, Hollywood?"

"Gun collection?"

"Fifty pieces. Each and every one of them in perfect working order, including an original Colt .45 Model 1911, official army issue. How's about them apples?"

"I'd love to see it," I lied.

"You must have people who shoot other people with guns in your scripts, Hollywood."

"Sure."

"But I can bet you dollars to dicks you don't get it right. None of you writer types get it right when it comes to guns. You call a revolver an automatic, and a pistol a machinegun, and you always forget to thumb off the safety because you don't know it's there to begin with… You can't help but fuck it all up."

"John, please," Lana once more scolded.

Releasing my coffee cup, I stole a quick look at my wristwatch as if I had some place important to be other than back to my bedroom window.

"Jeeze, look at the time. I really gotta go. My typewriter gets upset when I ignore her." Awkwardly, I pulled myself up and out of my chair with the use of my crutches. Then, to Lana, "Nice meeting you, Lana. Thanks for the coffee." Turning back to Cavitto, I once more offered my hand. "Nice meeting you too, Detective. Thanks for the firearms advice. Let's hope we never have to do business together. Cop to criminal."

Once more he took the hand in his, squeezed it hard. A little too hard so that I not only felt the tension of his tight grip, but his sausage thick fingers proceeded to crush my more mild-mannered digits. Glancing down at out interlocked hands, I could also make out the purple veins that shot out of the skin on the back of his hand.

"You'd have to commit murder for that to happen, Hollywood," he said.

My eyes shifted to Lana. She caught my gaze but then quickly turned away. It might have been warm and sunny out. Hot even. But something cold and unsettling coursed through every vein and capillary in my body, as if I'd been injected with ice-blue Freon.

"You don't plan on murdering anybody, now do you, Hollywood?" John went on. "Let's hope you save that shit for the movies."

He released his grip and I greedily took back my hand. But somehow, I still felt his hand wrapped around my own.

"Murder is easy when you do it only for the big screen," I said with a smile. "If you know what you're doing."

"Well, let me assure you," he said. "There's nothing funny about murder. Because you see, Hollywood, a dead man looks really fucking dead when he's dead. Understand?"

"Somerset Maugham," I said. "Modified, of course."

"Excuse me?" he said.

"Doesn't matter," I said, shocked he was be able to quote the great British author of *The Razor's Edge*, but not surprised he had no idea. "Welcome to Orchard Grove and if there's anything I can do to help you settle into the neighborhood, please don't hesitate to come calling."

Cattivo pursed his lips, ground his teeth.

Lana tossed me a smile and quick wave befitting of a professional Orchard Grove soccer mom. A scantily clad one, I should say. She then turned and began to stare off toward the back of the property and the narrow stand of woods. It was as if she spotted something in the pines or beyond the pines. Something that wasn't there at all but was instead, in her head.

Turning, I began hobbling across the Cattivo's deck in the direction of the gate. I couldn't get the hell away from there fast enough. Correction... I couldn't get the hell away from the detective fast enough.

"Oh and, Hollywood," he called out just as I was about to lift the metal latch on the gate.

I stopped. Leaning myself atop my crutches, I turned to face him. "What is it?"

"Since that little marijuana patch just happens to be located on the opposite side of your fence," he said with a smile and a wink of his eye, "I'm going to pretend it doesn't belong to you."

"Is this the hard-ass cop talking?" I said. "Or the concerned neighbor?"

He said, "You haven't met the hard-ass cop yet."

A wave of panic swept up and down my body. Now I knew what Lana might have been looking at, even if it was hidden from view, behind my privacy fence.

I pasted a smile on my face, however false.

"I wouldn't know about any pot garden," I said. "I never go back there for anything and I never touch the stuff. Bad for the lungs."

He let loose with a belly laugh that I thought for sure would pop the buttons on his shirt.

"Good answer," he said. Then, bringing his index finger and thumb to pursed lips, he made like he was inhaling off a fat joint. "Smoke a little for me, Hollywood."

I turned back to the gate, lifted the latch.

"Nice to see us getting off on the right foot," I said as I opened the gate, stuck my surgically raw foot through the opening. But either Cattivo didn't hear me, or maybe he was just pretending not to hear me, like some washed up actor in a cheap B movie.

CHAPTER 8

BACK inside my house, I immediately went to the bedroom window, looked out onto my new neighbor's back deck. Lana was no longer there. But within seconds she suddenly reappeared, this time with a can of beer in her hand. She set it down in front of her husband who immediately picked it up with the same meaty fist that nearly crushed mine twice in just a few short minutes, and by the looks of it, drained half of it in one sitting.

I took a quick look at the time. It wasn't yet noon, but I supposed it had to be noon somewhere in the world. When Cattivo sat his beer can back down again onto the table, some of the white foam jumped out of the opening. Lana shook her head in what I took to be disgust. That's when they began to argue.

I couldn't really hear what they were saying through the glass, so I had to concentrate as hard as possible on their lips, which wasn't easy either because John was facing the backyard, making it impossible for me to see his mouth unless he happened to turn in my direction. I could make out Lana's mouth okay, but she didn't seem to be saying a whole lot.

In the meantime, if I were to shift my line of sight to the right, I was able to make out the black, unmarked GMC Suburban that occupied the Cattivo driveway. Big mysterious Carl was planted behind the wheel. He was smoking a cigarette while speaking with someone on his smartphone, which I guessed to be an iPhone. His goateed face looked tight and unhappy. Maybe he hated coming here while his partner, and from what I could gather, department superior, drank on duty. While he argued with his wife. Maybe the only reason Carl came to Orchard Grove at all was because he had to come here. Or maybe, like me, he took advantage of every opportunity, no matter how small, to get a look at Lana.

Reaching out, I slowly slid the window open just enough for me to make out the Cattivo's angry voices. Did it without their noticing. In my mind, I was imagining their exchange as if I were reading it off a script I'd typed up only minutes ago.

JOHN

You're starting in again, aren't you?

LANA (exhaling, frustrated)

I don't know what you're talking about, John.

JOHN

We're not here one month and already you're getting cozy with the guy next door. What's his name, Hollywood. A screenwriter for Christ's sakes. I feel like we're back in Santa Monica and you're fucking some waiter who's convinced he's gonna be the next George fucking Clooney.

JOHN (raising his voice)

And what the fuck is going on with Carl? I see the way you two look at one another. You fucking him too? My partner?

LANA (folding her arms)

I'm going to ignore that thing about Carl, because that's insane. As for Ethan, I invited him over for a cup of coffee after I saw him feeding his birds. And please stop calling him Hollywood. It's demeaning.

JOHN (laughing)

What? You serious? He feeds the birds? You can't be serious. Hollywood the fruitcake. Maybe I don't have anything to worry about.

LANA

He's not gay, and I think you can see he's not gay.

JOHN

Okay, then I don't want you having coffee with him.

LANA

What's the harm in coffee?

JOHN

Dressed like that? You're half naked, woman.

LANA

We're all adults here.

JOHN

That's what scares me.

LANA

He's a nice man, who takes care of a pair of robins nesting on his back deck, and who also claims to be happily married. Nice to see a sensitive man in action for a change.

JOHN

No one's happily married. I'll believe it when I see it.

For some reason they decided to stop tossing verbal jabs and instead turn in unison toward my house. Maybe a glint of sun shone off my watch-face or even the whites of my eyes. Whatever the case, my immediate reaction was to duck down, as if John had drawn his weapon and fired it at my head. But with my bad foot, the response was delayed just long enough so that I'm certain they caught me spying on them. In fact, for a split second, two sets of blue eyes met my own brown eyes.

As I rolled over on the floor, pressing my back up against the wall beside the foot of the empty bed, I could only pretend that they never saw me, and that the glare from the almost high-noon sun would have prevented their seeing my face through the glass.

I sat there listening, but hearing nothing.

After some long tense beats, I used the crutches to pick myself back up. From there I went to the kitchen, opened the fridge, found a cold beer, and popped it open. I drank it right there, propped up on the aluminum crutches while standing inside the open refrigerator door, feeling the cold mechanical insides cooling down overheated skin. Like I said, it had to be noon somewhere on God's earth. What was this? My fourth drink of the day? Who the hell was I to judge John Cattivo?

For a brief moment, I considered drinking a second beer, but I knew it would lead to a third and a fourth and then more whiskey chasers. What I really wanted was to head back over to Lana's as soon as John went back to work. But that would be one hell of a bad idea. And of course, the more I drank, the more my inhibitions would melt away like an ice cube left out on the blacktop. It was important to stay in control.

Cattivo might have been a gun-carrying cop who'd made a vow to serve and protect, but that didn't mean he wouldn't hesitate to shoot me if he caught me in the act with his woman. Shoot me, then make it appear to be self-defense. Who would a judge believe in the end? A cop with a stellar record or a loser of a scriptwriter who drank too much and maintained a pot patch in his backyard?

Then came the sound of the Suburban starting up. Shutting the refrigerator door, I quickly hobbled back into the master bedroom, went to the window. Standing a few feet away from the glass pane, I shifted my line of sight to the front of the Cattivo property and saw Carl backing out of the driveway, so that the only vehicle left parked on the macadam was Lana's convertible. I had to strain my neck to see it, but when the unmarked Suburban was fully backed out onto the street, Carl thrust the transmission into drive and peeled out, burning rubber. It was an unusual sound for sleepy Orchard Grove, but then, John and Lana were not the usual Orchard Grove couple. Not by a long shot.

As time went on over the course of the next couple of days, I would discover just how dangerously unusual they truly were.

CHAPTER 9

FOR the moment anyway, Orchard Grove was cop free. I made my way back out onto the deck, past the robin's nest, and then out the west-side fence gate. Following the wooden fence all the way down to the woods, I bushwhacked the short distance to my pot patch. While balancing myself with my crutches, I squatted and harvested several fistfuls of fresh bud. Maybe it would be a bad idea to drink my day away, but a little smoke might be just the right medicine for calming both my nerves and tempering my ever growing obsession for Lana. And what the hell, there had been times in the past where smoking a little bud stirred up my creative juices. Was it possible I might actually write something today?

Time would tell.

Transporting it back to the house, I rolled a thin joint of the green weed then set the rest out onto the counter beside the sink to dry. When it was ready, Susan could sell it to some of the student teachers at her preschool for a thousand bucks or so, providing us with enough under-the-table cash to keep the bank at bay for the time being.

Firing up the joint I took a careful toke and prepared for the throat burn that always accompanied smoking green pot. But this was powerful stuff, and after this morning's adventure, I needed something to calm me down before I tried to write.

After a few short minutes, I felt the pot going to work on my nervous system and, for the time being anyway, I felt all the little creative creatures form front and center inside my brain. A writer far more famous than me once said, we are all we are ever going to be at the present moment in time. At present, I was a scriptwriter who was not writing because a woman had moved in next door. And that woman was dominating not only all my attention, but also all my emotions. My life had become worthless. I was a slave, locked inside a cell that contained three bedrooms plus one and a half baths. Lana made me feel special again. Alive. Young. Virile. But then, maybe after meeting her husband and the danger he posed, the obsession would take a back seat to my writing, even if for only a little while.

Sitting myself down at the typewriter, I leaned the crutches against the table beside me, easy access, and then I placed a fresh sheet of white paper into the spool. For a beat, I stared at the white paper hoping that suddenly, I would somehow hear the familiar clickety-clack of typewriter keys and magically see words appear on the page.

But today my luck was bad. Thus far anyway.

The muse wasn't there for me or, at the very least, she was being stubborn. I felt empty inside. I had no story to tell at a time when I was desperate for one. As I sat there staring at the stark whiteness of the page, I not only felt like the words wouldn't come, I felt exhausted at the thought of writing anything.

Back when Susan and I first met, nothing could have been further from the truth. I was newly divorced from my then wife of ten years and had just moved from Hollywood to upstate New York and a one bedroom apartment in the north end of downtown Albany. Up to that point in my life, I'd been lucky. I'd moved to LA fresh out of writing school to stake my claim and at thirty-four years old, managed to nab some gross deals on a few big budget films right out of the gate. I was making more money in a single month than my dad was making in a single year running his dry cleaning business. But it all went bad in the worst kind of clichéd way possible when my wife started sleeping with her personal trainer… a situation that was so common in West Hollywood as to be considered an almost right of passage.

Naturally we divorced, but when it comes to right-is-right in the California divorce courts, it doesn't really matter who beds down with whom since it's usually the one who has the most money who pays. In my case anyway, my wife's lawyer was able to prove she gave up her best years to support her down and out scriptwriter husband while he struggled through writing school, full-time. When I showed up in court drunk as a skunk and, at the same time, threatened to kick said lawyer in the nuts (that is, when they weren't stuffed in her mouth), the female judge saw fit to award my ex not the standard fifty percent of my estate but seventy-five, plus ninety-percent of the gross points I retained for the perpetual video sales of my films. She then ordered me behind bars for ninety days on behalf of making a mockery of her court.

Not my finest hour.

In the end, no studios would touch me after that incident and what money I had left, I wasted on lawyers, booze, and a plane ticket back east so that by the time I met Susan at a local west-end gin mill called Ralphs, my fortune had dwindled to a fraction of its former glory. But what I did still possess was relative youth and ambition, and no one… not my ex, not a black-robed judge, not the money changers at the big Hollywood studios… were going to prevent me from pulling myself back up from my bootstraps and making another three or four million.

That's pretty much the way I put it to Susan not long after I slipped onto the stool beside her at the otherwise empty bar. She was a few years younger than me, not yet thirty. She had shoulder-length black hair and a tall, but not skinny build that I found sexy and attractive. Her jeans had tears in the knees and fit her snuggly, accentuating a perfect heart-shaped bottom. She wore a white V-neck T-shirt that showed off enough of her breasts to keep me interested long after the first couple of drinks were history. Although she was still in grad school to become a certified kindergarten teacher, she told me she'd always been fascinated with screenwriting and, of course she loved the movies. Would I perhaps be interested in giving her some writing lessons?

"I'll pay," she said, shooting me a smile and a wink.

"How?" I said, winking back at her.

"Money of course, silly."

That's when I suggested she pay me in another way.

Her face beamed with big brown eyes and perfect luscious lips.

Checking the time on her wristwatch, she said, "I have to get up early for school tomorrow. No slack for the teacher's aide."

"I'm hot for teacher," I said.

She laughed and placed her hand on my forearm, giving it a squeeze.

With that, I paid the tab, and we took off for my downtown Albany writing studio.

We weren't through the door before we were undressing one another. We barely made it to the bed where we spent the next couple of late night hours rocking and rolling and loving one another's bodies even though we barely knew one another's first names.

By the time the clock struck midnight, she was getting dressed again. I signed a copy of *Break Up*, my one and only published novel for her, inscribing it, "With love." Four months later we were married by a Justice of the Peace in the white-marbled city hall on State Street in downtown Albany. Susan finished grad school and continued to teach pre-school while I kept up my daily writing routine like a man possessed, but only managing to sell my scripts to indie studios while the major outfits continued to shut me out. Oh well, I knew the situation wouldn't last forever. That as long as I was swinging the bat, eventually I'd nail a homerun again.

What all this meant of course, was that I wasn't making nearly the money I had been in LA, but what the hell, this was Albany and living in this city of less than one hundred thousand souls wasn't nearly as expensive, or sunny, or glamorous. Christ, you couldn't even find a decent restaurant in Albany. But what was important was that Susan and I were building a life for ourselves, having slapped some of the indie movie cash I'd managed to hoard away down on a ranch home in the sleepy, but oh so stable suburb of Orchard Grove in North Albany. Humble beginnings for sure, but it was also an idyllic time too when you really thought about it.

But the idyllic turned out to be a flash in the pan. Or perhaps not a flash but a slow roast.

After nine years of marriage, nothing bad had penetrated the invisible fortress we'd managed to build around ourselves. Trust ruled the day, meaning we didn't go around seeking extra-circular affairs, unless of course, getting together with some friends for a little wine, dancing, and swapping counts which it most definitely does not (swapping is consensual *and* sensual). We did not argue over money since we had enough coming in to pay the bills plus more than enough left over for some vacation time in New York City, Cape Cod, Miami, and even a two week trip through Italy and France as a belated honeymoon five years back. We drank responsibly, and did not do drugs other than the occasional recreational weekend stuff when the friends popped by or we visited them. We did not suffer from depression, or food addictions, or even allergies. No boredom, no sad pillow talk of *shoulda-coulda-woulda*. Not even sickness had managed to snake its way into our lives. We also did not get pregnant even though we did not consciously try to prevent a child from coming into our lives. It simply didn't happen, and on the occasions I tried to talk with Susan about it, she shrugged the whole idea off as something that would happen if it was meant to happen. Case closed.

In a word, Susan and I were happy with our lives… Happier than most anyway.

Until recently… over the past year… when even the contracts with my indie film companies began to dry up and we had no choice but to turn to selling pot to make ends meet. Unless, of course, I was willing to give up my writing for a proper job. I had always run as a man who wrote scripts, and I was convinced that I was just going through a sales slump was all. That eventually it would pick up. I was writing, and that's what counted.

But then the Cavittos moved in next door, even the writing stopped.

From the looks of it, whatever was left of Susan's and my impenetrable wall was about to crumble into so much dust and charred rock, just like Sodom and Gomorrah, when God destroyed the lust-infested city with brimstone and fire, sending the inhabitants straight to hell.

I sat at a dining room table that contained only a wood bowl filled with store bought apples and my typewriter, a sea-green Olivetti/Underwood Lettera 32. I sat as still as a stone, my eyes glued to the white paper and waited for my muse to speak to me the way she always had, until Lana arrived and my concentration became entirely focused on her. For a time, it seemed like my muse would no longer come to me. That she was jealous of my affair with Lana. Perhaps more jealous than Susan could ever be. But then you have to still be in love with someone in order to be jealous.

But then something began to happen inside me. A series of words didn't fill my head, but a face did. Let me correct myself… In my head I saw a series of faces flash by, like I was sitting all alone in a four-walled room with the shades drawn and projected one-by-one on a big white screen before me, were the still faces of the people who now dominated my time and my thoughts.

I decided to begin only with a name. Positioning my fingers on the keys, I typed…

LANA

She's a lovely apparition, and she knows it. A seductress without purposely trying to seduce. A heartbreaking beautiful attraction without trying to make herself attractive. A voice calling to me without her having to make a single sound or utterance.

Lana just is.

Blonde, or what some might refer to as strawberry blonde, she is of average height for a woman but her body and her being (her presence) is anything but average. She has no qualms, moral or otherwise, about sunbathing topless in a quiet suburban neighborhood like Orchard Grove, and while she knows that I have been watching her, I'm not so sure it turns her on so much as it is something that she has come to expect from a man like me… a man so easily and hopelessly drawn into her web.

She claims to have been born and raised in Albany, but from what I can glean, she hates it here and wishes only to be back on the beaches of Venice and Santa Monica. For the life of me I cannot understand why anyone would want to spend any more time in that plastic place than they have to. Land of sun, lies, false promises, and flavors of the month, be it a brand of frozen non-gluten yogurt or a never before heard of movie starlet with a Pepsodent smile to die for.

I can only wonder what her life was like there… who she seduced, and how many lovers she kept at one time. Judging from what her husband said about her already "starting in" in Albany, it was a lot.

Lana is a take-no-prisoners kind of woman.

I can see that from a mile away. A sultry character played by Sharon Stone if this were a Joe Eszterhas "Basic Instinct" kind of script. If I had even an ounce of strength left in my post-op body, I would throw a drape over the bedroom window and forget she exists. It might make a great opening scene to this script even. But then, my dreams would haunt me, and I would wake up wanting (needing) only one thing: Lana… her ass, her breasts, her hair, her mouth.

Lana, I love you, I lust you, I hate you, I don't even fucking know you. But I need you like a junky needs a fix.

To Be Continued…

JOHN

A hopeless case. But a dangerous one at that. Like a powder keg set beside an open flame. You never know when the damn thing is going to explode. Beguiled by a wife years older than him, he might have made one hell of a good cop at one time judging by the framed photos hanging on their den wall. In those photographs, you can almost taste the goodness in his eyes… the eagerness to please. The spit and polish. The I'm-gonna-be-the-one-to-finally-make-a-difference quality to his deep, blue, alive eyes. Eyes that, when I looked into them for the first time just an hour ago, had become flat, bloodshot, lusterless, and tired.

Rather than hope, there is rage boiling up from his bulbous belly. Mark my words, if John Cattivo doesn't kill someone someday (and I'm not talking about a dangerous criminal who's shot at him first), he will either kill himself or be killed by someone who hates him. His ending will not be a happy one.

To Be Continued…

ORCHARD GROVE

CARL

I'm guessing he's a Carl with a C rather than Karl with K like Karl Marx. The latter would suggest parents with an intellect, a sense of irony, and uppitiness for lack of a better word. But the former suggests quite the opposite. Average parents who gave him an average upbringing in an average city like Albany where nothing too good or too bad happens. I'm guessing he was super jock in high school, a chick magnet (maybe the girls gave him a nickname like "God" or something), and maybe quarterback of the football team, but not quite big or fast enough to make the squad in college, meaning that by the time he'd been handed his high school diploma, his life had already peaked.

He attended JuCo for two years before deciding to be a cop since, in his rather simple mind, it was as close as he could come to his high school football glory days without going back in time. Not a leader, but a follower who hates Cattivo's guts but will follow the superior officer's orders without hesitation or question nonetheless. A man who believes in the concept of team and refers to his fellow officers as "brothers in arms."

Is it possible he's in love and lust with Lana as much as I am?

Another bewitched man reduced to a useless emotional pile of rags and bones. I'm guessing that when I saw him on the phone behind the wheel of the black Suburban, his face in distress, lit cigarette dangling from his lips, he was leaving Lana a long message about how he can't possibly live without her. That's the way I'd write it anyway. A message that will only be listened to half way through before she deletes it and makes herself another iced coffee.

Should I be jealous of Carl?

Not in the least. I'm just as pathetic as he is.

To Be Continued...

CHAPTER 10

THE doorbell startled me out of my writing daze.

Shooting a glance over my shoulder through the big living room picture window, I spotted the big brown UPS truck parked up against the curb at the end of the drive. Standing on one foot, I shoved the crutches under my arms, crossed through the living room to the front door, opened it. The stocky young man was dressed in his summertime brown shorts and shirt. He held a small package in one hand, and a clipboard in the other. Looking down at the box, I could see that it was from Victoria's Secret.

"Looks like the wife is trying to cheer you up, pal," he said, handing me the electronic clipboard. "Sign on the dotted line," he added.

I signed and he handed me the package.

"Thanks."

"Enjoy yourself," he said, tossing me a wink. "Careful of the foot."

Shutting the door, I stared at the box. It was addressed to Susan. I didn't think a whole lot about it since my wife was always ordering things online. Clothes that we couldn't afford, for the most part. So some new underwear came as no surprise.

Shoving the box under my arm, I carried it with me into our bedroom, set it down onto the small antique dressing table that Susan used when she made up her face and also to do her bills or write the occasional letter. It was then I noticed a few new additions to the tabletop. A brand new bottle of perfume, for one. Also, a new leather-bound notebook filled with expensive paper. Like something an artist would carry into the woods for sketching.

Why hadn't I noticed the new items by now?

Maybe I'd been far too busy looking out the window and, at the same time, ignoring Susan's table. After all, it was none of my business what she kept on top of it or didn't, and for all I knew, the notebook and the perfume had been there for more than a year. After a while, you stop noticing certain things in a marriage.

Still, I couldn't stop my curiosity from getting the best of me. Picking up the notebook, I opened it to the first page. That's when I saw her name. Lana, scrawled in blue ballpoint in feminine cursive. Below the autograph was a simple XO and directly beside that was a lipstick red kiss made from Lana's actual lips pressed up against the page.

My heart pumped.

Only an hour or so ago, Lana told me that she and Susan hardly knew one another. That their only connection was the P90X class. I thought about the WhatsApp message on her phone. The word "Baby." Did Susan and Lana know one another better than she was letting on?

I took another look at the Vic Secret box. In all the years I'd lived with Susan I'd never once opened her mail. That is, unless she asked me to. Did I start now just because I sensed a deception in the works?

I felt the slight, almost featherweight of the package in my hand. Felt my fingers pressing into it. Then, just like that, I was tearing it open. Inside I found a pair of thong panties. Pink and, as far as I could tell, made of pure silk. Expensive stuff.

There was a note that came with it.

A small pink envelope about the size of one you might get along with a dozen roses. Susan's name had been written on the envelope in blue ballpoint.

I opened the envelope.

"How nice it would be to see you in these," it said. It was signed, "You know who."

I felt my pulse beating in my temples. Returning the note to the envelope, I put the package back together as best I could. When Susan came home from work, I would have no choice but to lie to her. Tell her it arrived this way. "You know how the mail can be sometimes," I'd tell her.

I set the box back down onto the table and ran the possibilities over in my mind. Either Susan and Lana were far closer than I thought or some strange man who referred to himself as "You-know-who" was sending my wife sexy underwear. Maybe she'd been seeing him for some time. It's only been the past year that Susan and I started to drift. It's possible she's been conducting an affair for that entire time. But then, why was my gut telling me that *you-know-who* was Lana?

It's precisely what I was mulling over in my mind when I made out the automatic chirping that can only come from a car lock being electronically opened. Sure I had other neighbors, but by now I'd learned to recognize the sound of her particular vehicle exclusively. The sound of its locks engaging or disengaging, and the gentle purr of its motor sounded like a thousand other vehicles in Albany alone. But somehow, hers was different. Everything about her was different and unique in ways that might not have been immediately discernable judging from her outwardly appearance. But she was unique all right, and that uniqueness could only be measured in terms of my growing obsession.

Turning, I started not for the bedroom window, but the window in the full bath located off the front hall vestibule. It would give me a better view of her driveway.

Crossing over the living room as fast as my crutches could carry me, I jammed my bad foot into the door jamb. The collision of swelled, surgically lacerated foot with the solid wood jamb nearly sent me through the roof. But still, I kept moving, knowing all the time that the real pain would be delayed. It was more important that I catch a glimpse of Lana as she was getting into her car than it was to perform a damage check on my foot. Just that one simple glance could make or break the remainder of my day.

The single slider in the bathroom was identical to the one in the bedroom. I stood maybe a foot or so away from it while I watched a now fully clothed Lana get behind the wheel of her red, two-door, Ford Shelby GT500 convertible. As the electric pain travelled from my toes to my brain and back to my toes, I focused my gaze on her as she adjusted the rearview mirror to just the right position, and then slipped on the same pair of sunglasses she'd been wearing out back.

She was sporting a black satin button-down shirt that was unbuttoned low enough to expose just a hint of red pushup bra, and both her wrists were supporting at least a dozen different silver bracelets. Her lips were painted bright red and her cheeks were tanned golden from the many mornings spent sunning on her back deck. Her hair hung down against her shoulders, but a colorful silk scarf was wrapped around it. From where I was standing in pain and no doubt bleeding, she looked every bit the Southern California transplant, which was something foreign for Orchard Grove. Didn't matter that she was born in Albany. Everything about her exuded California confidence and sexuality.

My foot began to throb with every pulse of my heart… Not a good sign.

Looking quickly down at it, I could see that the index toe had indeed begun to bleed. The pain was so bad my brow had broken out into a cold sweat and I felt vaguely nauseas. As my knees grew weak, I also thought I might pass out.

But I didn't care.

The pain was worth every second watching her power up her sports car, and back out of the driveway. But once she was gone, I was again filled with an emptiness that was far greater than my pain, more disturbing than the blood soaking into my thin black sock, more confusing than knowing my wife and Lana were quite possibly striking up a secret friendship.

Obsession… it had invaded my flesh and bone like a cancer.

What the hell was happening to me anyway?

Ten years ago I was a successful screenwriter living the kind of life any writing student would kill for. I had talent, money, notoriety, and the respect of my industry peers. But then, it all went bad because of a few bad choices drowned in booze and the tears that can only be shed by a husband whose wife is getting her orgasms elsewhere.

But the tears dried when I met Susan. It's true my career was still in a tailspin, but at least Susan had become my rock, my love and my happiness. But then, she left me too. Sure, we still lived together. But in many ways, she was already gone.

And now that Lana had entered into our lives, all I could think about was being with her. Making love to her. Could she make me happy? Could she love me more than Susan ever could? Could she be the muse that I'd been looking for?

Maybe my foot was a bloody mess, but I had become a very sick man. A man sick with love and lust. What I didn't realize at the time was that my disease would turn out to be terminal.

CHAPTER 11

INSIDE the medicine cabinet, I located a box of Band-Aids, set them on the edge of the sink. Seating myself on the lid-covered toilet, I undid the Velcro straps on the black, plastic and nylon, knee-high splint, pulled it off and then gently peeled off the now bloody sock. The long incision that ran the length of my second toe (the index or Morton's toe) had been reopened. The metal pin inserted into the very center of the toe, where the surgeon had drilled vertically through the bone, was now slightly bent so that it hooked upward at a thirty-degree angle. When the time came for the doctor to pry it out of my foot… and they would do so with a pair of workman's pliers, or so I was told by the assisting nurse… it would hurt like a son of a bitch. No two ways about it.

But just looking at the foot made my back teeth hurt. It looked like a long, narrow, chunk of newly butchered beef.

I did my best to clean the entire foot with warm soap and water before applying a Band-Aid to the tip of my toe and over the inch and half of exposed, bent, metal rod. Then, I applied an additional two, wider bandages to the incision that had been reopened. I slipped on a clean sock I'd taken from my underwear drawer earlier, put the splint back on, making sure the Velcro straps were tight but not too tight so that I didn't cut off the circulation on the swelled foot. The last thing I needed was to encourage the formation of a blood clot. A blood clot meant instant death.

Taking hold of my crutches, I went back into the kitchen and downed four Advil with cold tap water that I drank right out of the faucet. Then, I sat myself back down at my typewriter, refocused my eyes on the words I'd typed only moments ago, and I waited... waited to once more hear the sound of Lana's car pulling back up into her driveway.

Maybe a half hour went by.

But I couldn't be certain. Time had become warped since Lana's arrival in Orchard Grove. I measured it now not by the seconds or minutes that clicked away on the stove clock in the kitchen, but by the steady and consistent throbs of electric pain that would begin at the tip of my index toe, shoot at lightning speed up into my brain and then back down again to the tip of my toe.

I thought about having another drink or maybe reigniting that green joint. But in truth, too much dope made me paranoid. I was already paranoid or neurotic anyway. Better that I stick to the booze in order to curb the pain. Something strong, like Jack. But then, what the hell was I doing? I'd already talked myself out of drinking anything else, earlier. As a result, I'd gotten some writing done. Maybe not a lot, but it was a start.

Pulling the sheet of typed paper from the typewriter, I set it to the side with the others, and fit a clean sheet onto the spool. I sat there at the dining room table, staring at the newly typed pages, knowing that I should have been adding words to the new sheet. I'd done enough characterization study for one day. Now would be the time to begin my story. Maybe I would begin with a man staring out of his bedroom window onto a most beautiful apparition. A blonde beauty who'd just moved in next door with her cop husband, and who sunbathed on her back deck in the nude.

I raised both hands, extended my index fingers, and typed, FADE IN.

I was about to set the scene when the doorbell rang.

CHAPTER 12

THE sudden noise startled me, as if someone sneaked up behind me and screamed "Boo!"

I laid my hands flat onto the tabletop, pressed myself up, took a look over my shoulder out the living room picture window. I couldn't see anyone, but then that made sense since whoever was ringing the bell was hidden behind the closed door.

Fetching my crutches, I lifted myself up from the table, made my way through the living room to the front, solid wood door. When I made out Lana's face through all three of the small clear glass panels embedded into the door, my pulse picked up, and for a brief moment anyway, I forgot all about the pain in my foot.

Unlocking the deadbolt, I then twisted the opener counterclockwise. In order to open the door, I had to hop backwards on my good leg.

"Don't fall," Lana said as she carefully stepped through the door, her lavender scent once more filling my senses.

"I'll try not to," I said, feeling my throat constrict, and the center of my chest grow tight. "At this point, I might elect to have the whole damned foot amputated."

"Pain?" she said, brushing back her hair with an open hand, as if she were staring not into my eyes but into a mirror.

"You have no idea," I said, glancing down at the foot, seeing the small round spot of fresh blood that had formed on the new white sock that covered it. "Please come in, Lana."

She stepped into the vestibule and crossed over into the living room. I closed the door, locked it. But before joining her in the living room, I took the time to peer through the wooden door's top most pane of glass onto the driveway and the Orchard Grove road beyond it.

"Expecting somebody else?" Lana inquired. If I were writing this for my script, I would have said her voice sounded more sarcastic than inquisitive.

"Just looking out for your husband. I'm in enough hurt as it is. I don't need a bullet in my back."

"Oh, John wouldn't hesitate to shoot you in the face while staring you down."

"I'll take your word for it."

"You heard us arguing earlier?" she said. "Or couldn't you hear us well enough through the bedroom window once you cracked it open?"

I could feel her sly smile as if she'd squirted me with a squirt gun filled with holy water. Turning, I hobbled into the living room.

"I'd make a real crappy spy," I said.

"Yes, you would, Ethan. A very bad spy indeed."

I noticed then she was holding something in her hand. A copy of my novel, *Break Up*, it turns out. There was a scantily clad, busty blonde woman depicted on the paperback book cover. She was aiming the barrel of an automatic at a desperate man who was down on his knees, his arms raised to the heavens. The look on her face was one of fierce determination and hatred. You didn't have to read a single word to know that the man was as good as dead.

"You've been doing some shopping at the used bookstore," I said. "I could have provided you with a copy for free." Releasing my hand from the crutch grip, I pointed to the bookshelf pressed up against the far windowless wall in the living room directly to my right, the top two shelves of which contained copies of my one and only novel.

"I wanted to support the author with my five-fifty," she said.

"You're only supporting the used bookstore owner," I said. "That book was remaindered years ago, almost as fast as it was released. But that's very kind of you and your husband."

She held the book out for me. "He has no idea. Now would you sign it for me?"

I gazed into her blue eyes, until I ran my eyes up and down the length of her body. She was wearing the black button-down shirt that I recalled from an hour earlier, and a worn jean skirt that barely covered her thighs. For footwear she wore Cleopatra sandals, the thin leather straps to which wrapped around her ankles. I guess I never noticed it before, but she bore the blood red tattoo of a broken heart on her left ankle. Three red teardrops were crying, or bleeding, from out of the broken heart.

She noticed me staring down at the tattoo.

"Do you like my heart?" she asked.

"I didn't notice it earlier," I said. "Out on your deck."

We both gravitated out of the living room and into the attached dining room, where my typewriter was set beside the bowl of apples.

"You were looking at other things." She smiled again. "Until we were so rudely interrupted."

"Yes," I said, my eyes locking on the pages I'd written that morning, seeing the name "LANA" on the top page in capital letters. "Interrupted by your husband who's a top cop, carries a big fat gun, has an ill-tempered partner, and sports a nasty attitude about life." Slipping my hand from the crutch, I gently took hold of the pages, turned them over on the table.

That's when she took a step forward, coming even closer to me, apparently without noticing my maneuver with the pages. Or just not caring perhaps. She came so close that her lavender scent became almost overwhelming. It seemed to fill the dining room like a vapor. It made my throat constrict even more than it already had, and my stomach tie itself into knots. Christ, I felt like a teenager again gazing upon his first crush. That's the kind of power she had over me. When I focused my gaze upon the portion of her cleavage that was exposed under the unbuttoned portion of her silk shirt, I began to grow hard, and I didn't care in the least if she noticed. In fact, I wanted her to notice.

Again, she ran a hand through her thick hair, and when she lowered it, it brushed against her breast, arousing her nipple so that it immediately became erect through her thin bra and shirt. If I weren't on crutches, I would have stepped into her then, kissed her on the mouth. Hard. But she must have been thinking the same thing. Or wanting the same thing anyway. Because she came at me, not only with her mouth, but with her free hand, grabbing hold of my arm. We stood there for a while, over my typewriter, kissing and petting, until she pulled back to come up for air.

"Did I take you by surprise?" she said, her voice a hoarse whisper.

"A little," I said, wiping my wet mouth with the back of my hand.

She was still holding onto the book. I glanced at my watch. I knew that Susan would be home in one hour. But I didn't care. Or, at least a part of me didn't care. I hadn't felt this good about myself in ages. Not since I'd left LA.

"Let's have it," I said, holding out my hand for the novel.

"I almost forgot," she said, her breathing still labored.

She set it into my hand. Looking down at the novel, I could see that it was in very good shape for a used book. No dog-earing. Maybe the previous owner hadn't read it at all.

"I have a pen right here," I said, setting myself down hard in my chair before my typewriter, and placing the book on top of the pages I'd written earlier. At the same time, I leaned the crutches up against the table to my left-hand side. Opening the book to the front title page, I picked up the pen that was set in between the typewriter and the bowl of apples, and brought ballpoint to paper.

I had a choice here. I could either write a profound, authorly inscription. Or, I could keep it short and sweet and to the point. Knowing in my gut that Lana was going to turn out to be as much trouble for me as that blonde on the cover of *Break Up*, I went with the latter and penned …

For Lana,
For a wonderful fruitful life on
Orchard Grove.
Love Ethan
XOX

Maybe "Love" and "XOX" was a little over the top considering I barely knew her. But what the fuck. Closing the novel, I handed it to her.

Turns out, she was one of those people who had to gaze lovingly upon the inscription only a split second after you've written it. Being a scriptwriter who'd only penned one novel, and not a very popular one at that, I hadn't had the good fortune of signing a lot of books, but I'd signed a few. And truth be told, I preferred fans who chose to read the author inscription later on when they got home.

In my mind, Lana seemed the type to enjoy her instant gratification however, and she did nothing to prove me wrong. Her face lit up when she read it. You could almost identify the very moment she eyed that XOX as if it were an open invitation for her to jump me inside my own home. Inside a home-sweet-about-to-be-gone-baby-gone-home I shared with a woman I loved. Even if we had drifted apart over the past year. A woman whom I'd never cheated on, as God as my judge. And I might not have been a church going man, but I believed in God, or something like Him. I also believed in good and evil and that we had a choice when it came to embracing either one.

Setting the book gently down on top of my typewriter, Lana smiled. She held out her hand, grabbed an apple, brought it to her mouth, took a bite. Without uttering a single word, she held the apple to my mouth, as if I had no choice but to take a bite. As I bit into the apple, I realized that she didn't need to speak. That her actions spoke far louder than words ever could. They were the actions of a woman who wasn't the least bit in love, not with me necessarily, but any man. A woman who, more than likely, had never experienced a single day of love in her entire life. They were instead the actions of a lust-filled woman who also lusted power. Power over a weaker man like me, and a man like her husband. A man who only pretended to be strong.

But that's not right either.

Lust was one thing, but hatred was another. If hatred was her motivation, then lust was simply a tool or a weapon that she used for seizing power over a pathetic man like me. I've lived long enough to recognize pure hatred when I saw it, and Lana Cattivo possessed more than her fair share of it. I could see it in her blue eyes, smell it in her lavender scent, see it in the way she chewed and swallowed that apple. And the hell of it is, it made her all the more attractive and alluring. For her, hatred wasn't just a base emotion, it was a physical substance that, if need be, could be manipulated, like clay or, in this case, blood. You could feel it and taste it. Like the apple she made me bite, you could ingest it and digest it. It was the force behind her, her motivator, and in some ways, it was the primal source of her charm and ultimately, my unstoppable attraction to her.

It didn't come as a surprise when she set the half eaten apple back down onto the table, dropped slowly down to her knees, helped maneuver my legs out from under the table so that she faced me directly. I spread my legs apart a little to give her the room she required, and she began to undo my belt and unbutton my jeans.

Pulling her up, I began to unbutton her shirt and pull down her bra, exposing her suntanned breasts. Lifting up her skirt, I felt for her panties but she wasn't wearing any as if she'd scripted it that way.

I pushed her back onto the dining room table, but I didn't enter her right away. Instead I became filled with an insane desire to taste her first. Kissing her breasts, I shifted my way slowly down past the area where her jean skirt had gathered. I never moved an inch as her hips gyrated, the warm wetness pouring out of her body and into my mouth. My world was Lana and nothing mattered at that very moment in time on Orchard Grove.

Or did it?

Out the corner of my right eye, I sensed movement immediately outside the big living room picture window. I managed to steal a quick look. There was a person standing in the window watching us.

I couldn't be entirely certain. But for a brief and frightening instant, I swore that person was my wife, Susan.

CHAPTER 13

SOMETIMES you can't help but believe your own lies.

Especially the ones that you tell yourself over and over again. Like when you purposely distrust your eyes, accuse yourself of seeing things, all because you're getting your rocks off and holy Christ almighty, you just can't seem to stop yourself. Maybe you think I stopped myself as soon as I saw Susan in the picture window, looking in. That I immediately jumped away from Lana. Maybe you think I grabbed hold of my crutches, told Lana to get dressed, get the hell out, and never come back. Maybe you think I put my tail between my legs, hobbled to the front door, and opened it to face not an angry Susan, but a seething Susan. Maybe you think I'd beg for her forgiveness. Do it from down on my knees, if only it were physically possible.

But I did no such thing.

I just kept going. Kept making love to Lana like my life somehow depended upon it. Such was the power Lana had over me. Such was the serpent's spell.

But something else kept me going. When I took a quick second look at the window, the person was gone. Vanished. It led me to believe... rather, it made me *want* to believe... that a person wasn't there in the first place. That the face I had taken for Susan's wasn't hers at all. That I'd only imagined my wife standing there outside the picture window, seeing everything we were doing only a few feet away on the dining room table. Imaged her perhaps, out of fear.

Yes, the lies can be sweet sometimes. But they are still lies.

But I'm not so sure I would have stopped even if I hadn't been lying to myself. I wasn't going to stop until Lana had enough of me and I'd had enough of her. That moment came just a few seconds later when she let loose with a scream that would have woken up the entirety of Orchard Grove if this were the middle of the night. Raising herself up onto her elbows on the wooden table, she demanded that I enter her, her voice deep, throaty, and insistent, like I had tapped into the beast that lived in her soul, and only now was being swallowed up by it, becoming one with it.

Regardless of who or what witnessed me selling myself body and soul to this beautiful Satan, I proceeded to do exactly what she insisted.

CHAPTER 14

I didn't take long to finish.

Didn't take me long anyway. When it was over, we paid no mind to hugging, kissing, cuddling, or engaging in pillow talk of any kind. The sexual act or should I say, process, at that point, was an academic fact. Nothing more. What we were left with was shared bodily fluids that needed to be wiped away and the feeling of having sunk so low, that not even hell would take me. But I knew the feeling wouldn't last. That soon, I would want Lana all over again. And when I did, the want would be as obsessive and overwhelming as it ever was.

I stood up, more or less balancing myself on one leg, and she slid off the table, pulling her jean skirt back down with all the clinical indifference of a patient immediately following a physical. It was all very business-like and ordinary for her, which I suppose should have scared me to death.

But then, what the hell was I saying?

Lana was too good to be true, and too bad to be believed. It's not like I was in danger of falling in love with her. It's not like I was about to leave Susan, regardless of our problems, and declare my undying devotion to the new girl next door. I was in lust with her, and in lust I would remain, until whatever it was I was going through, ran its horrid course.

More lies?

Maybe.

As she continued gathering herself together, buttoning up her shirt, straightening out her hair, applying a fresh coating of lipstick, she suggested that perhaps it would be prudent if she took her leave through the back sliding doors. I knew that if she stayed even a minute longer, the demon would return and I would want more of her. I was just about to tell her what a good idea it would be to go now, when the mechanical sound of a key being inserted into the front door lock snared our collective attention, as if a bolt of heavenly lightning had just burst inside the front vestibule.

We both nearly broke our necks turning to see the door open and a woman step inside.

The woman, who was my wife, smiled.

"I didn't know we had company," she said.

SNAPSHOT

THE *memories come to her in snippets and flashes, like a vaguely remembered dream. Rather, the remembrance of only part or parts of the dream. The most important part. The part that woke you up from out of a sound sleep, your body covered in a sheen of sweat, your breathing labored, your heart pounding.*

Sex was always the catalyst for these vivid interior snapshots, as she liked to call them.

Snapshots that, to her, were a lot like speeding through the old pictures pasted to the pages of a photo album, back in the days before everything became digital, and you looked at your life on a computer screen.

Brian (or was it David?), was so shocked when she cut off his hand at the wrist, the stub spurting crimson blood, he never uttered so much as a peep when she took the other hand and then, of course, his head.

She met the truck driver who delivered heating oil to the farmhouse at the hotel-no-tell of his choosing at a time when she could not have been more than thirteen to his forty or forty-five. He cried real tears when she Maced him, and when she struck him with the cleaver smack dab in the forehead, he made the

76

gentlest of exhales, like a little baby having just fallen into a deep, peaceful sleep.

She added a little variety to the mix as she grew older and the apple trees were all cut down to make way for the houses. For instance, there was the grade school principal who hid from the student body and the PTA his affection for young women or, more accurately, girls. She consented to sex with the principal in the back seat of a Subaru wagon in the after-hours school parking lot with all the triviality and coldness of performing an everyday chore like carrying out the trash. The next morning, when the maintenance man found the body in the car in two separate parts, no one would ever suspect that the cute, innocent, athletic, peppy blue-eyed, blonde-haired step-daughter of the still missing man who once owned North Albany's last apple orchard could possibly be to blame.

For the longest time, it seemed as if she were free to seduce and murder anyone she wanted. In a word, she was God.

CHAPTER 15

SHE was all smiles.

My wife of a decade was bright-eyed, friendly, and eager to greet Lana… the woman she sometimes shared a ride with to her P90X class. A neighbor whose sunbathing habits she was well aware of since she too had witnessed Lana in action out on the back deck during the occasional day off from her work at the pre-K. The neighbor who might be communicating with her on WhatsApp. The neighbor who could be sending her presents. Or was that just my imagination getting the best of me? My writer's mind scripting out a nefarious plot. What did Hemingway once say? You wanna beat fear, you've got to learn how to turn off your imagination.

As Susan stepped from the vestibule into the living room, I could almost feel the anxiety pouring out of Lana's pores. Correction: the nervousness was coming from me and me alone. Because even if Lana was sweating bullets, she was doing so with the utmost grace and casualness, which told me, she really wasn't sweating anything out at all. The casualness of a professional maybe. She held out her right hand while approaching Susan.

"Hey there, Susan," she said with a friendly face befitting that of a true,

God-fearing Orchard Grove neighbor. "I was just trying to get your famous husband to sign his novel for me. How exciting it must be to be married to such a gifted artist."

Susan brushed back her brunette hair, crossed over the living room floor into the dining room, and politely took Lana's hand in hers.

Her big brown eyes focused on me, she said, "Well, like I might have already mentioned, Lana, it's not always that exciting." She laughed. "Ethan writes scripts for a living, and his hobby is writing scripts, and in his free time, he likes to write scripts."

"Wish I could say I've got a big movie premiering soon," I said with an exhale.

"Oh no," Lana said, making a pouty face that made me want to pick her up and toss her back down on the dining room table even with Susan standing in the room. "Dry spells can be dreadful. I recall some of my screenwriter friends in Venice, Hollywood, Malibu, Santa Monica, you name it... How desperate they would become when they couldn't sell their work. Half of them waited tables at the restaurant just to make ends meet."

I nodded, sadly.

Susan took her hand back so slowly, it was almost like she wanted to continue holding Lana's hand. While I couldn't blame her one bit, it made me uncomfortable.

"You'll get the big sale, Killer," my wife said to me, her voice surprisingly friendly. "You always do." Then, turning to Lana. "You just can't kill off a bad guy like my husband. That's why he was making the big bucks then and will no doubt make them yet again."

She leaned into me, kissed me gently on the cheek. The kiss took me by surprise and I had to wonder if she could smell Lana on my face. I wondered if she could feel and hear my heart pounding. When she pulled away, she didn't give me the least indication that she noticed anything out of the ordinary about me. In fact, she appeared more chipper and happy than when she first walked in a few minutes before.

Susan in the window... I had to have imagined it after all...

Lana grinned, nodded, like she also believed a big Hollywood score awaited me around the corner.

"Listen to Susan," she said. "A wife can always tell if their man is on the right track."

"And hound the man when he's riding the wrong set of rails," Susan added.

As always, Susan looked wonderful and sexy which, at the same time, saddened me, since we weren't as close as we once were. It never ceased to amaze me how fresh and put together she looked even after a full day of caring for a room full of screaming kids. She was wearing a blue and white-striped Russian sailor shirt over a pair of faded Levis that she purchased right out of grad school and that still fit her perfectly. She was a great fan of cowboy boots. Cockroach killers to be precise, and especially black alligator skin boots, like the kind she was sporting right now. The boot heels gave her already above-average height a boost so that she stood just a hair under six feet. With my upper body hunched over my crutches like a common cripple, she towered over me. Somehow I think she enjoyed being taller than me. It made her feel dominant.

Her hair was long, clean, and dark brown and it veiled a face that couldn't have been more perfect had a sculptor chiseled it out of pure Italian marble from the Dolomite Mountains. Her deep-set eyes were always alive and inviting and her lips were not thin or cosmetically puffy but succulent all on their own. She wore no makeup because her smooth healthy skin required none. But what she did wear was cologne and when its aroma finally registered with me, it gave me a slight shock. The smell was lavender and it was identical to what I smelled on Lana's skin. Identical to what I smelled in my dreams and now, for the first time, I knew precisely why.

"It's refreshing to see a married couple get along so well," Lana said after a beat, her eyes locked not on me, but on Susan. "What's your secret?"

"There is no secret," Susan said. "Only honesty, and of course, one tries to keep things interesting."

"In the bedroom," Lana said. "Or am I being too forward?"

Susan locked eyes with our new neighbor, and I saw a slight blushing in her cheeks.

"Especially the bedroom," she said. But it was a lie or, should I say, a gross exaggeration. I wanted to add, *We haven't made love together in over a year.* But I decided to go along with the sudden pretend change in our lovemaking status. The welcome change, I should say.

That's when Lana did something I never would have expected. She raised up her hand, touched Susan's forearm, and gently ran the tips of her fingers down the smooth exposed skin all the way to her hand. It was a subtle, but somehow sensual gesture shared between two women of the same sex.

My head was spinning by now because I was standing only inches away from a woman I'd desperately fallen in lust with… a woman who was, only moments ago, pressing her naked body against mine on the very table we stood over so that the rich scents of our physical exchange had to be hanging in the air almost like a fog. This, I also must admit: The devil that had so very recently taken up residence inside of me was thinking how wonderful it would be if I were to have both Susan and Lana in my bed at the same time. It was a thought that came to me with all the ease and instinct of breathing.

Susan smiled and giggled like a high schooler.

"It's not so easy being married to an artist," she said. "But it does have its advantages. Free movie tickets, for instance. In the time Ethan and I have been married, he's had a string of independent movies produced, and I never had to pay a single dime to see any of them at the movie theater."

"You make it sound so romantic," I said, not without sarcasm in my tone. "Gee whiz, free movie tickets."

Lana shared in the moment by adding, "Hey, I'm a cop's wife. I don't get free anything."

Then Susan said, "Lana, how would you and your husband like to come for dinner tomorrow night?"

Something cold and painful surged through my veins. It was the same sensation you get when you step off the curb unaware of the truck that's speeding past and narrowly missed creaming you by a few inches. Only in this case, you really do wish you'd been hit by a truck and put out of your misery.

"Susan," I broke in, "the Cattivo's are only just getting settled. Give them some time."

"Nonsense," Susan said, reaching out, setting her hand onto Lana's shoulder. "I'm insisting."

She did something peculiar then. Like Lana just a moment prior, Susan allowed her hand to slide down almost the entire length of our new neighbor's arm. If I didn't know Susan any better, I would have said she provocatively ran her fingers down Lana's arm.

"Might be nice if someone else did the cooking for you for a change," my wife added.

Lana's eyes lit up.

"We'd love to come," she said.

Then Susan suggested a time and Lana said she'd bring wine.

"Red and bloody," Susan said, locking her eyes on Lana's.

"Bloody is my favorite," Lana said with a wink of her left eye.

Cradling her novel against her breasts, Lana began heading for the front door.

"I'll see you out," I said, following close behind with my crutches.

"Oh, and Lana," Susan called out.

The source of my obsession stopped in the middle of the living room, turned. I too, turned to face my wife.

"I look forward to meeting Mr. Cattivo," she said, a crafty grin forming on her face. The gravity of her statement did not go unnoticed. In fact, it felt a little like a punch to my stomach.

"You're going to love him," Lana said while turning back for the vestibule. "Maybe see you in class tomorrow morning. Or let me know if you want a ride."

"I'll be there with Spandex on," Susan said.

When we came to the door, I reached around her waist while holding myself up with my crutches and opened the door for her.

"Thanks for coming by, Lana," I said, polite and loud enough for Susan to hear. Maybe too loud, too polite.

"Thanks for signing my book," she said, stepping out onto the concrete landing. Then, just before descending the three steps to the asphalt walk, she turned to face me once more.

"She knows," she said, with all the indifference of a snake that's just swallowed its lunch whole. And then she disappeared across the front lawn to her new house on Orchard Grove.

CHAPTER 16

BACK in the house, heart pounding, I crossed over the living room to look for Susan.

But she wasn't there.

"Susan," I called out.

She didn't answer. Glancing at the table, I saw that the apple core I'd set there only minutes ago was now gone. Susan must have tossed it into the trash in the kitchen. I called out for her again. Louder this time.

"I'm in here," she answered.

Her voice was coming from the master bedroom, which seemed odd seeing as it was only a little past three on a bright and sunny summer afternoon. It's possible she was changing into a pair of running shorts and T-shirt for a quick jog... an exercise regimen she clung to lately when she missed out on her morning exercise class. But my gut told me something else was happening instead.

My crutches under my arms, I limped my way across the kitchen floor, over the narrow hallway and into the master bedroom where I found my wife. She was lying on her back in bed. In the short time it took to say goodbye to

Lana at the front door, she had stripped down entirely. All she wore, if you want to call it that, were the pale skin outlines of her swimsuit bikini bottom and top, which not only highlighted nipples that were pointing toward heaven, but also a very dark, yet neatly groomed sex.

"It's been a year," I said, knowing that she must have been undressing as I was saying goodbye to Lana at the front door. "Why now?"

"Don't ask questions," she said, as she brushed back her hair with her open hand. Then, "Well, aren't you coming for me, Killer?"

"I can't write dialogue that good," I said, suddenly realizing that as difficult as things had been for us over the past year, I still very much loved my wife.

In my head, the image of Lana and I on top of the dining room table, a face in the living room window staring at us…

Unbuckling my belt for the third time that day, I hopped over to the bed, climbed on top of it, and proceeded to ravage Susan for the first time in far too long.

CHAPTER 17

WHEN we were finished, we lie on our backs, a sheen of sweat covering our naked bodies. After a silent beat, Susan got out of bed, went into the kitchen. When she came back in, she was carrying two bottles of cold beer. Coming around my side of the bed, she set the tall-necked bottle down on the nightstand. Then, her beer bottle in hand, she knelt onto the bed and, careful to maneuver herself over my bad foot, crawled to her side of the bed. I couldn't keep my eyes off of her. She looked like a beautiful jaguar.

She drank some beer, wiped her mouth with the back of her hand.

"You only came once," she said. "Have you been pleasuring yourself all day, Killer?"

I felt a spark in my pulse.

"Very funny," I said. "Sixteen was a hell of a long time ago."

I was doing my best to make light of the situation. But in my head, I couldn't get the image of a woman standing right outside my living room window while I rolled around with Lana on the dining room table. That woman in the window being my wife. Had she truly caught me in the act of adultery? Was this her way of dealing with my infidelity? By pretending she didn't see it at all and, in fact, inviting the woman I was with for dinner? She *and* her husband? Then following up the invite with our first sexual interlude in a year?

None of it made sense.

As I sat there, back pressed up against the headboard, my black-splinted foot doing its dull painful throb in time with the beating of my heart, I grabbed hold of my beer and took a deep drink. In terms of pure logic, I could only come up with one conclusion: that the woman in the window was a figment of an overstressed fictional mind. That I was literally seeing things in all my lust-filled passion for Lana and all my guilt over stabbing Susan, my wife of a decade, in the back.

Susan drank some more beer, exhaled. "You usually aren't satisfied until you've cum twice. Maybe age is catching up with you after all."

I laughed, even though nothing was funny. I'd just had sex with the woman I loved mere minutes after having sex with a woman I hardly even knew. By all that was right with the world, I should have been hating myself or, at the very least, coming clean with Susan. But in all honesty, I was too afraid… Okay, I'll say it… too cowardly to do something like that.

But then, what if something else was happening inside our bedroom? What if Susan saw everything going on in the dining room and was now torturing me? Maybe this was one big test to see if I'd confess. A test I was sure to fail.

"This is beginning to sound like a Cialis commercial," I said, after a time. "Fifty is the new thirty. Or so I'm told."

She set the beer bottle onto the nightstand, then turned over onto her side, facing me directly.

"How old do you suppose Lana is?" she asked.

There it was again. The spark in my pulse, this time accompanied by an electric jolt in my stomach. "Why do you ask?"

She reached out, set her finger onto my chest, caressing the light patch of black hair that shaded my sternum. "Do you find her attractive?"

Turning to her, I worked up a slight smile. "What are you getting at, Susan?"

"If you could, would you have sex with her?" Her hand was no longer caressing the patch of hair so much as it was slowly tickling the tight skin on my belly, then lower onto my trimmed patch of pubic hair. "Would you slowly undress her if you could? Put your hands on her?"

Listen, Susan was my wife. She was gorgeous. A knockout. A head turner. But she was also a highly educated woman who came from a sturdy Jewish background with loving, well to-do parents and an older sister who doted on her like she was still in kindergarten. What all this equated to, of course, was a sense of strong family values, and a personal moral bar that Susan had set very high for herself.

But that didn't mean she wasn't naughty from time to time.

If it wasn't for Susan, I wouldn't have known what great sex, as opposed to passable sex, was. I wouldn't have known anything could possibly exist beyond the standard foreplay, missionary position coitus, roll over and fall to sleep. As controlled as Susan was, she also had a fiery, out of control side to her that showed itself at the oddest of times. Rather, at times when I'd least expect it. She was the kind of woman who could gently take a crying child aside in the classroom, whisper something encouraging and sweet into his ear, and before you know it, the tears would be replaced with a smile and laughter. But she was also the kind of girl who would pick up a bottle of red for us on the way home to share in bed. At least, that's the way it *had been* for us not so long ago, before my career took a nosedive.

In a word, Susan was predictably unpredictable, and once upon a time, I loved her for it.

Her hand shifted now. South. She began to stroke me. I was no longer seeing Susan in the window. I was instead seeing Lana lying on the dining room table. I was seeing her moist, naked skin glistening in the sunlight that leaked into the room through the dining room and living room windows. I saw the soft but still firm flesh on her thighs and I was feeling her all over again.

"Would you do things to her while I watched?" Susan added as she picked up the pace of her stroking. "Or better yet, Killer, would you like it if I did things to her while *you* watched?"

My mind was on fire. Mind and body. Susan's actions and words were that much of a turn on. That potent. There was still love between us. Love *and* lust. I felt myself sinking into the softness of the mattress while Susan raised herself up onto her knees and straddled me.

"Please," was all she said, her voice having achieved a kind of rich deepness to it, as if it wasn't the Susan I married who was speaking to me, but an imposter who'd taken over her body. "Please, please, please…"

Only seconds after I entered her, she came with a loud scream. Looking up at her face, I realized she wasn't watching me while we made love. Instead she was peering over her shoulder, out the slider window onto the Cattivo's back deck and the blonde beauty who was surly out there sunning herself in the hot, sultry, afternoon sun.

CHAPTER 18

AS dusk approached our home on Orchard Grove, Susan and I finished another beer apiece and got dressed. I didn't mention the name Lana, and neither did she. Yet, our blonde-haired neighbor might as well have been standing in the same room as us. She was not a white elephant, but instead, a white devil.

When Susan entered into the bathroom to clean up and fix her hair, I hobbled over to her dressing table, picked up the perfume bottle, smelled it.

Lavender.

Susan was wearing the same perfume as Lana. Should I confront her about it? Or simply chalk it up as a coincidence? In the end I decided to do something else.

"Darling," I said through the closed bathroom door. "Did I mention you received a package from UPS today? Something from Victoria's Secret."

The water stopped and silence replaced it.

"Victoria's Secret," she asked, her tone one of surprise. "I don't recall ordering anything."

The door opened and she stepped out, looking fresh and put together, like she'd just woken up. She eyed the torn package set out on the table.

"Who opened it?" she said, her brows raised at attention.

"Arrived that way," I said.

Slipping my hand off the crutch, I grabbed the package and handed it to her.

She hesitated.

"Aren't you going to open it?" I said.

I noticed then a distinct tightness in her facial muscles.

She said, "Sure. Why Not? It's already opened anyway."

She pulled off the paper and opened the box. Reaching in with her fingers, she pulled out the thong underwear.

"Wow, nice stuff," I said, trying my best to act surprised. "You really are making an effort at pulling our marriage back together."

She tried to work up a smile, as if going along with my reasoning was just fine and dandy by her. That's when I leaned into her, kissed her gently on the cheek.

"What's that for?" Susan said, surprise in her voice.

"Thanks," I said. "For what you're trying to do… for us."

She bit down on her lip, nodded.

"It's good to know the spark is still there," she said. "That love is still there… even if the money isn't." She bit down on her bottom lip liked she'd caught herself. "Excuse me, the *work* isn't there."

I couldn't help but feel a slow burn at the money-*slash*-work comment. But that didn't prevent me from feeling good about the spark she so aptly mentioned. I made like I was about to turn away, get on with my life, such as it was, when I once more eyed the package in her hands.

"Is there a note stuffed inside?" I said.

Susan's face turned red. The note was hidden under the underwear, which meant she was able to pretend it didn't exist.

"No silly," she said. "Why would I send myself a note?"

I laughed, but it was entirely forced.

"Exactly," I said. "You'd have to be your own secret admirer."

THE shades on the slider window were now drawn so that there was no seeing in, no peering out. If you listened hard enough, you could hear the voices of Lana and her husband while they enjoyed their cocktails and barbequed out on the deck. Or maybe enjoy was too strong a word for it. Because the voices were not always kind. They were, more often, filled with acid.

Susan went back into the bathroom, this time with the Victoria's Secret package in hand, closing the door behind her. After a few seconds, I heard the toilet flush, and although I had no way of knowing it for certain, I imaged that the pink note card from "You know who" was now on its one-way trip to the Albany water treatment plant stationed along the Hudson River.

I went to the window, stood still and listened. While John accused Lana of spending her day with her new friend, Hollywood, and she defended herself by replying, "Just because I have a man who is a friend and an interesting person, doesn't mean I'm fucking him."

She was right of course. And also, very wrong.

It was all very strange.

By all means, I should have been shaking with fear considering the nature of the Cattivos very audible argument along with the fact that her husband was a hothead cop who carried a gun. When Susan came out of the bathroom for the second time, she was holding the underwear in her hand, the paper package and the box it protected now apparently tossed out. Opening up the drawer under the table, she set the underwear inside, then closed the drawer back up.

I was quite certain she could make out the war of words being waged by our new neighbors, but for some reason unbeknownst to me, she decided not to comment on it. Instead, she headed into the kitchen, picked up the phone, and dialed the local Chinese restaurant.

"Do you want wanton soup with your sweet and sour pork, Killer?" she called out.

"Sure, baby," I said, my gaze shifting from the slider window to the bathroom. "Whatever you say."

Hobbling across the bedroom, past the dressing table and into the bathroom, I peered into the wastebasket. The torn packaging material and the Victoria's Secret box had been tossed inside it. Bending down carefully, my left hand holding to the crutch for balance, I quickly rummaged through the box and the paper. The note was gone. My gut could be trusted after all.

Susan had disposed of the note, like so much waste.

SNAPSHOT

BY today's artificial intelligence standards, her method for attracting victims would never be considered very scientific. It was the 1980s after all. The pre-digital age. There were no personal computers. No Match.com. No Facebook. No Craigslist. You had to do things the old fashioned way, which meant posting want-ads in the "personals" section of the local newspapers and freebie news rags.

Looking for a date? was one headline that could always be counted on to produce.

Another was, **Young lady is sooo very lonely**.

But the go-to atomic bomb of headlines...the one that always generated the most responses from the sex-starved middle-aged pervert crowd... was **Lady looks sixteen!**

Of course, she was sixteen at the time, which is why the last ad always proved the most effective, especially when the potential client requested she send along a snapshot. You'd be surprised how easy it was to lure an adult male into a meeting at a strange motel and how easy it was to dispose of him once she was able to Mace them, and/or tie them up to the bedposts (usually at the victim's *request).*

But soon she became bored with the middle-aged crowd. How many time could she be expected to enact the ultimate revenge on her step-monster over and over and over again? Not to mention the chances she was taking by leaving the bodies behind for the police to discover. Sure she was careful about prints, but it was only a matter of time until someone at the APD or FBI picked something up off the surface of a chair, a bed sheet, a lamp, or the bathroom toilet.

Now that a young police officer... a tall, slim, Clint Eastwood look-alike detective by the name of Nick Miller... was working the case, she decided to switch gears. From now on, her victims would be much younger. Much stupider, and far more innocent.

They would be teenagers, just like her.

CHAPTER 19

THE next night, the Cattivos arrived right on time. I was sure I smelled booze on John's breath the moment he came through the door. He was wearing a yellow IZOD polo shirt that seemed out of place for a cop who carried a gun on his hip at all times. Because the skin on his thick arms was exposed, I couldn't help but take notice of a tattoo he sported on his left interior forearm. It was a heart that was dripping or, crying, blood. It matched precisely the tattoo that painted Lana's ankle, but with one slight difference. Written across John's heart was the name Lana, in big bold black letters.

He noticed me noticing it, so he lifted up his arm, more to show me his bulging bicep than the tattoo. Or so it seemed.

"I got drunk one night, came home with my heart on my sleeve. The usual story." He belly laughed.

"Looks like Lana's," I observed, but immediately wondered if I should have said it.

"Good of you to notice, Hollywood," he said. "What else have you noticed about my wife?"

Lana stepped forward as if to intervene, or at least change the subject. She was holding a bottle of wine in each hand. She turned to Susan.

"Red and bloody," she said, handing my wife the bottles. "Just like you ordered."

The funny thing was how Susan and Lana were dressed alike, almost like they'd consulted with one another before getting together at the appointed seven o'clock hour. And maybe they had. Both were wearing V-neck T-shirts and short skirts. They were also wearing similar brown leather sandals. Maybe the color of their clothing differed (Lana wore all red and black, while Susan's skirt was plain yellow, her T-shirt white), but they seemed to complement one another. Both took the time to pick out some nice jewelry for the evening. Susan's choice for a necklace was a silver broach shaped like an angel over her neck. Lana wore a simple string of pearls, which I guessed were real and very old. Both sported an eclectic assortment of silver bracelets around their wrists.

A smiling, if not beaming Susan began carrying the wine across the living room floor to the dining room and then down the two stairs to the already open slider.

"Who's having wine?" she asked.

"We all are," I said, following her with my crutches.

"Let's get loaded," John said walking beside me. Then, taking hold of my arm with what felt like a vice grip so that I nearly went over onto my face. "Let's get the girls drunk," he said into my ear. "I'm already there. You got any beer, Hollywood? Or don't screenwriters drink beer? You probably drink something all stuffy and shit, like brandy from out of snifter."

Somehow I managed to work up a fake laugh. "Plenty of beer on ice out back."

I pulled my arm away from him, rebalanced myself on my crutches. I knew in my heart that I already hated his guts. But I had to get through the night without showing it. I'd worked in Hollywood for a lot of years. I knew how to play the game. How to suck up to people I hated. People whose egos surrounded them like a thick, plastic, translucent bubble.

He took pulled his hand back, slapped me on the shoulder. Just a little too hard.

"You be a good man, Hollywood," he said. "Crack me one of those beers and maybe I'll let you hold my gun."

CHAPTER 20

WE ate the usual summertime fare. Burgers, hot dogs, potato salad, corn on the cob. For desert, Susan put out a bowl of ripe apples and a red Jell-O mold, neither of which anyone touched. Mostly, we drank. We drank a lot, as if seeking our own separate escapes. When the two bottles of red that Lana brought over were finished, she went back to her house to retrieve two more. When those were gone, the girls started in on gin and tonics. Meanwhile, I drank beer. One for every two that John was chugging. When he pulled out a plastic baggy of weed, I thought I might be seeing things.

"You know what they say?" he said, while proceeding to roll a big fat bomber of a joint. "Cops always have the best dope." He refocused his eyes so they were aimed at the fence at the far end of the perimeter. "That shit you're growing down there is for teeny boppers, Hollywood."

"Still don't know what you're talking about," I said, a cold chill shooting up and down my spine at the thought of him snooping around my property.

When he smiled, the edges of his thin mouth went vertical, making his presence even more sinister. The scruff that surrounded his mouth made him look like a pipe cleaner with big arms, big legs, and a big gun. I could not understand for the life of me what a hot woman like Lana was doing with him. Why she would have agreed to marry him and follow him all the way across the country to the very place she left decades ago, vowing never to return. He lit the joint with a Bic lighter he kept in his pocket, took a big toke off of it, and handed it to me.

I took a drag, but not too deep. I was trying to pace myself, stay in control. Only reason I took a hit off it at all was to keep him from giving me a tongue-lashing. Handing him back the joint, he then passed it on to Susan who, at this point, was sitting so close to Lana she was practically on top of her. They were obviously hitting it off, and in some ways, they were enjoying their own private party. It was as if they'd known one another not just a matter of hours, but weeks, or months, and not just as acquaintances who shared the same P90X class.

At one point, I decided I'd been holding in way too much beer for too long, so I grabbed my crutches and limped my way into the bathroom to relieve myself. By the time I got out, Lana was barking at John, calling him a "dickless wonder." She was so stoned, she laughed when she said it. Even Susan started to laugh, although I could tell she was doing her absolute best to hold back the chuckles. But then, she too was stoned out of her gourd. Susan was no stranger to my pot patch out back (she'd already shredded and bagged the pot I left out on the counter to dry the previous day), but she was not a regular pot smoker, preferring the buzz of alcohol and the occasional pharmaceutical instead.

Lana was relentless.

She kept jabbing her husband, calling him "dickless." And as I hobbled back onto the deck and sat down hard in the chair, I could see his round, hairy face begin to turn red, even in the candlelight. I could see a purple vein popping out on his forehead. The vein throbbed. I could see his hands opening and closing into tight fists, and I could see his Adam's apple bobbing up and down in his throat. As Lana handed me what was left of the joint, I thanked her, and went to pass it right on to John without my taking another hit.

But he ignored me and did something entirely different.

Instead of taking hold of the joint, he pulled out his gun.

CHAPTER 21

HE aimed the piece at both girls. By that, I mean he planted the metallic green laser site on Susan's forehead, then shifted it the few inches to Lana's and back again.

"Hey John," I said, my heart jumping into my throat, "take it easy, man. They're just joking around."

Any semblance of a buzz running through my veins quickly disappeared with the rush of adrenalin.

"You shut the fuck up, Hollywood," he said, his voice low, gravely, mean. "This doesn't concern you." Then, bursting out with laughter. "Well, okay, it's your wife, so yeah, it concerns you."

Lana paused for a moment while she bit down on her bottom lip. But then, just as quickly, her face lit up again. Suddenly it was her turn to bust out laughing.

"See what happens when you're dickless like Dick Tracy here?" she said. "You carry around a spare dick."

Susan didn't think a gun being pointed at her face was any too funny. She wasn't laughing anymore, nor was she about to resume laughing. Her face turned pale white in the candlelight.

That black semi-automatic in his hand, the barrel moving from one woman to the other, John grabbed hold of his beer with his free hand, downed what remained.

"Let's play a different game," he said, slapping down the empty can.

"What kind of game, dickless?" Lana said. She was unrelenting, gun or no gun.

He turned to me, shooting me a quick look with his glazed eyes and disturbing pipe cleaner face. "How about we play your wife kisses my wife? Whaddaya say, Hollywood. You game?"

I shot Susan a look. She caught my glance and didn't have to say a word for me to know what she was thinking. Her eyes said, *Let's just play this stupid game and get him the hell out of our house.*

"Sure thing, John," I said, pulse banging like tympani in my temples. "But maybe you should put the gun down."

"Nonsense," he laughed, thumbing back the hammer. "Lana likes to play with my guns. Isn't that right, Lana?" Then, waving the barrel at the women with the laser sight no longer engaged. "Come on girls, what'll it be? On my count. Five, four, three…"

When he got to one, Lana closed her eyes, lifted her left hand and gently took hold of Susan's lower jaw, aiming her mouth for her hers. When she kissed my wife, she did so as passionately and as truly as she had when she first kissed me the morning before. At first I could only assume that she was as much into girls as she was boys. But then I began to sense this wasn't the first time she'd played a dangerous game with her husband and she knew better than not to be believable in her performance.

He watched them, that evil grin painted on his face, thin lips growing tighter and tighter. When he rubbed his now hard self through his pants with his free hand, I thought I might be sick.

"Now Susan," he whispered from somewhere down deep in his throat, "this is where the fun begins."

Lana pulled away from my wife, locked eyes on her husband.

"We kissed already, John," she said. "Now leave it alone. These are good people."

"We're just getting started, sweetheart," he said. Standing, he aimed the automatic at my wife's chest. If he pulled the trigger at that close range, he'd blow out the entirety of her respiratory system. "Come on Suzy Q, pull off your shirt."

Again, she looked at me. My heart now in my mouth, I was powerless to do anything about it. Maybe I could stab him in the hand with a plastic knife or fork, but even that would take some strength and agility on my part. Strength and agility were something I simply did not have with my mangled foot. Susan knew it too, because without an argument, she stood up, pulled off her top. She did it, not with a look of excitement or lust on her face, but one of defiance, while she glared at John's eyes. Into them, and through them, like white-hot lasers.

She stood there, in her black bra, not at all sure about what was coming next, but waiting to hear it from the mouth of the devil.

"The bra," he said, his Adam's apple bobbing up and down in his throat, waving the pistol in the air as if saying, *And be quick about it.*

Without a word, her brown eyes never veering from his, she reached around her back with both hands, unclasped the bra, set it onto the chair.

Maybe it was the pot or the drinking, or a combination of the two. But sitting at the table, unable to do anything about the creep who was holding a gun on both my wife and his, I felt as though trapped in a dream. This wasn't happening for real. It was happening inside my head, like a vivid nightmare. At the very least, the whole thing was like something I might write for one of my film noir treatments. Things like this just didn't happen in real life. Only in the movies, or in pulp fiction.

"I gotta hand it to you, Hollywood," John said out the corner of his mouth while leaning into me, "you sure know how to pick 'em. Your woman is a primo piece of ass." Then, straightening back up. "Now beautiful, I want you to take my wife's shirt off."

For the first time, Susan seemed rattled, like the game hadn't already gone far enough.

"Do it," he demanded, waving the gun yet again, his shooting finger sliding from the trigger guard to the trigger.

Silently, my wife turned to Lana, began the process of pulling off her shirt.

When she was down to only her white bra, Susan unclasped it, and allowed it to fall away.

John exhaled a sour, rancid breath.

"Sit down, Lana," he said.

Doing as she was told, Lana sat down in the chair immediately beside Susan.

"Now," he said, running his tongue over dry lips, "spread your legs."

Slowly, Lana spread her legs and cocked her hips forward, and slightly upward. While under the circumstances, I should not have been turned on in the least, I found myself aroused and hating myself for it. Maybe the reason behind my excitement had little to do with Lana spreading her legs, but had everything to do with the way she did it. From where I was sitting, she didn't open her thighs because a gun was pointed at her. She did it because she wanted too. Because this was a crucial part of the game. This was how it was played.

This also was how the game was played: Detective John Cattivo pressed the barrel of his service weapon against the back my wife's head.

"You know what I want you to do, Suzey Q, now don't you?"

Her unblinking eyes locked on Lana's face, Susan bit down on her bottom lip. For a brief moment, I thought she might bite right through it. John gave the pistol a slight push against her head. The fire that erupted inside my stomach made me want to kill him on the spot. If I could have, I would have torn his head off and shoved it down his throat, scalp first. But I was helpless and hopeless.

"Do it, Susan," he ordered. "Kiss Lana. Feel her up. Do it now."

Leaning into Lana, my wife kissed her and touched her while John stood over them and watched, his automatic forever aimed for their heads, as if the act they performed had better be good, or the consequences were life or death.

"Lower, Suzey Q," he demanded, his index finger brushing the trigger. "On your knees. Go lower."

Susan knelt down so that her torso was between Lana's legs.

"Now feel for my wife's panties," John said.

Susan reached between Lana's legs, slipped her fingers inside Lana's black panties.

"Push them aside, Suzey Q," he said, his Adams apple bobbing up and down in his throat. "Tease my girl."

Brushing back her hair with her free hand, Susan, pulled the panties aside, revealing Lana's perfectly groomed sex. We all focused on her sex, and Lana was anything but repulsed. Rather, she seemed to enjoy the teasing. But I was not enjoying it. Yet a part of me was loving it. What the hell can I say, because what the hell could I do?

"Come on, Suze baby," John pushed. "Kiss the girl."

Lana leaned forward, wrapped her hands around the back of Susan's head, and began kissing her passionately.

My heart pounded and my head began to fill with adrenalin. The noise in my skull was like a jet plane that had suddenly blown its engines mid-flight, and now the whole thing was taking a nosedive, the wind screaming across the wings, the passengers screaming, crying, wailing.

But my misery was compounded one hundred fold by the fact that I was as hard as a rock, and I despised myself for it. Screw biology, I chanted to myself. Screw the fact that I am an animal as much as John Cattivo. My not having a gun pointed at the two women didn't make me any less savage, any less cowardly. It just meant that I didn't have a gun.

The situation was treacherous. Deadly. Yet, after a full minute had passed, both women were still kissing… kissing passionately, despite the weapon pointed at them. Was it possible that they were enjoying this? This game that really wasn't a game at all? Or perhaps "enjoying" wasn't the right word. Maybe they were simply surviving. Doing what they were told in the interest of saving their skin.

The pregnant robin that lived in the eaves flew out of its nest then, startling me. It flew out into the darkness until it returned a couple of seconds later, perching itself on the deck rail. Her protruding brown belly pulsed with every frantic beat of her heart.

"What have we here?" John said eyeing the bird, while the women separated and the robin chirped, as if screaming at us all to get away from her home. "Bird hunting season."

When he aimed the pistol at the bird and fired, the dark of night flashed brilliant white and the robin evaporated into so much blood, bone, and feathers. The girls shrieked while I grew dizzy and sick. I swallowed something cold and bitter when an apparently satisfied John returned the gun to his hip holster.

"You can all get dressed now," he said, that evil grin still plastered on his face. "Show's over." Then, turning to me. "Was it good for you too, Hollywood? Maybe now you got something to write about."

I watched as both girls stood up, in all their perspiration-glistening semi-nakedness. A glistening made all the more radiant from the candlelight. When Lana whispered something into Susan's ear, my wife nodded, and wiped a tear from her eye with the back of her hand. She then quickly gathered up all her discarded shirt and bra, and walked past John without giving him even a cursory glance. She escaped back into the house, closing the sliding door behind her. I tried to get up to follow her… go to her, but Lana stopped me.

"Don't," she said. "Leave her alone for a while."

"Yeah, she needs to gargle," John said with a gravelly laugh.

I pulled myself up anyway, shoved the crutches under my armpits.

"This night's over," I said, my wide eyes locking onto John's, my bottom lip trembling with an anger so profound it was bleeding from my pores. "You son of a bitch."

"Calm yourself, Hollywood," he said. "We were just having a little adult fun. Besides, judging from that bulge in your pants, you weren't having an entirely crappy time either."

A sheen of red passed by my eyes. "You could have killed my wife. I can have your badge for this."

He took a step forward so that his meaty thighs where pressed up against the table. He squinted his eyes and glared at me.

"You're not thinking of calling the cops are you, Hollywood? Cause I am the cops. Don't forget, I can ruin your life at any time." He once more drew his automatic from its holster, thumbed the clip release, and held it up into the candlelight. "Oh, and sorry about the bird. I know you're like Mister Audubon Society." He laughed, slapped the clip back home, re-holstered the weapon. "Dangerous fucking world out there. For people and birds."

"Come on," Lana said, as she threw her top over her exposed breasts.

"Let's go, John."

The Albany detective began to sing "I fought the law and the law won… I fought the law, and the law won…" He grabbed hold of an apple from the dish, took a big bite out of it, then tossed it like a baseball out into the darkness. Together they stepped off the deck and out of the light. They made their way through my gate and eventually through their gate and into their yard, which, at this point, seemed so close but also a million miles away. When I heard their back sliding glass door open and slam shut behind them, I knew that as soon as the opportunity presented itself, I was going to find a gun and shoot Detective John Cattivo dead.

CHAPTER 22

MOMENTS later, after hobbling my way indoors, I found Susan inside the bedroom.

She was tucked under the summer-weight blanket, lying on her side, already asleep. Or maybe she was just pretending. Without undressing, I leaned the crutches against the wall, laid down on my back, looked up into a darkness that seemed infinite, absolute and so very cold. I listened to the sounds of the summer night. A dog barking incessantly in a distant yard. A train hauling freight cars on the tracks that paralleled the river, its horn blowing loud and lonely. Cicadas buzzing in the trees.

After a time, I could make out the sound of sobs.

I rolled over, rested my hand on Susan's bare arm.

"Don't," she said, her voice low and pained. "There was nothing any of us could do."

I felt my insides drop. "I could have stopped him. I could have put up a fight."

"And got yourself shot in the process."

"He wouldn't have shot me. He's a cop. A bluffing asshole cop who put a

107

gun to my wife's head and made her perform a sexual act with his wife."

"He's crazy. I think he would have shot you and made it look like self-defense. Christ, you saw what he did to that little bird." She wiped her eyes, sniffled.

My mind began to spin out of control. I pictured John, his holding her at gunpoint. I felt like a coward for not peeling myself out of my chair and going after him with my bare hands. So what if I had a bum foot? I should have done something. Anything.

But Susan was right. What good would it have done? I would have only managed to get myself shot. Or maybe there was another reason I didn't do anything about it. Maybe a part of me …a big part of me… was just plain yellow.

My eyes wide open, they remained focused on the back of Susan's head. At her black hair, still somewhat visible in the darkness.

"That man just might be the most evil person I have ever met in my life," I whispered after a time.

"I don't know how Lana can stand living with him," she said. She cried a little more, wiped her eyes again. Then, "We should rescue her from him."

Once more I was reminded about my desire to see him dead. I thought about the gun he pressed against Susan's head. I saw the gun, once more heard the mechanical noise of the hammer being cocked. I saw the pregnant robin disintegrating into the night, felt the concussion of the gunshot. I wondered if any of the neighbors were alarmed by the sound of a gun discharging in the neighborhood. Or perhaps they chalked it up to leftover fireworks?

"I agree with you, Susan," I whispered.

"Good," she said. "Now let's not talk anymore."

"There's something else I need to know first."

"What is it?"

"Yesterday afternoon when you came home from the nursery school… did you see what we…" My voice trailed off, my throat constricting. I just couldn't get myself to say it.

She inhaled deeply, as if requiring more than the usual strength to respond. "Yes, I saw you. You *know* I saw you. You looked directly at me through the plate glass."

Pulse picked up in my temples. "But you weren't angry." It's a question. "It's unbelievable you didn't claw my eyes out."

"I was angry and hurt at first. But then something happened as I watched you… I can't really explain it right now. It's possible I went into immediate denial. I haven't slept with you in a year. I should have expected something like this."

I thought about my obsession with Lana. About the power she had over me. To be honest, I wasn't shocked that I'd been right all along… that Susan had seen Lana and I through the plate glass window. What shocked me was her reaction. It wasn't a normal reaction in any sense of the word. People are people and people get jealous. People kill one another while overcome with jealous rage.

I should have expected something like this…

Actually, no, she should *not* have expected anything like she saw when she peered through the living room window. Didn't matter how long it'd been since we last slept together.

There was no excuse.

Susan's strange reaction to my naked infidelity set off not a red flag, but an alarm inside of me. I thought about Lana's phone. The WhatsApp voice message sent to a woman named Susan. A woman with long brunette hair. *My* Susan. I thought about the lavender-scented perfume on her dressing table. Thought about the silk panties. The alarm inside of me sounded off, and it told me that Lana and Susan had more of a history together than I wanted to believe. And maybe it was because of a secret history she shared with Lana that she wasn't shocked or infuriated when she saw me making love to the blonde devil on the dining room table. She was simply indifferent.

"You don't have to explain it," I said, after a time, not wanting to confront the true nature of her relationship with Lana Cattivo. Not yet, anyway. "But I *am* sorry."

"Sorry for what, Ethan?"

"For straying from our marriage. For stabbing you in the back."

She began to laugh then. Not loud, but softly. "We haven't touched each other all year," she said. "I'd say that at this point, considering what just happened outside on the deck tonight, we've both strayed a little. And with the same woman. So that makes us even. Now go to sleep."

For a long time I laid there listening to my wife's breathing, until I too fell into a dreamless sleep.

CHAPTER 23

WOKE up early the next morning only to find Susan lying on her back beside me, staring up at the ceiling. It was first light, and the unrelenting sun was only beginning to show itself through the thin shades, hot and unpleasant. Like it had put in for a day off weeks ago and was denied by God himself.

Turning silently away from her, I slid out of bed and grabbed hold of my crutches. I shuffled my way into the kitchen and made the coffee while Susan peeled herself away from the bed and showered. When she came back out she was still quiet. Her dark hair was wet and clean and glistening in the rays of sun that poured in through the kitchen windows. She drank some coffee, black, and tried to work up a smile that took terrific effort.

"No P90X?" I said.

"I'm quitting the class," she said. "And I wish not to talk about it further."

Balancing myself on my crutches, my body felt electric with a nervousness I'd never before known. Maybe I'd changed since Lana moved in two months ago, but what I was now witnessing was a profound sea change in my wife, and it was an unnerving experience.

"Don't you want to talk about anything?" I said. "I mean, later on. When you come home?"

She sipped more coffee, pursed her lips.

"Let's not talk about anything anymore," she said. "We talked it all out last night. Right now, I have a kid's summer program to run."

And with that, she set her coffee cup down on the counter, grabbed her car keys, and left for work without a goodbye.

SNAPSHOT

SHE *can't very well afford a hotel room on meager babysitting earnings.*

So she decides that the next best thing is to invite her dates (as she's come to call them) to take walks with her in the thick, wooded areas that line the banks of the Hudson River. The bike path that also parallels the river where once a now abandoned rail-bed existed, is now used by joggers and bicyclists. But at night, the path is deserted and as quiet as a cemetery.

It's also deserted on the warm summer night she walks hand in hand with a boy she went to grammar school with not too many years ago. A boy, now seventeen, named Ted. On the shorter side, Ted sports a thick build, like the champion wrestler he's become. She holds his hand tightly while they make their way through the brush to the riverbank where they can get a view of the lit-up buildings that line the banks on the Troy side of the Hudson. From where they stand, she with her leather bag slung around her shoulder, the water lapping up against the gravel bank, they inhale the gamey fish smell of the river. They also make out the occasional bass that breaks its surface in its hunt for low flying insects.

When the wrestler starts to kiss her and feel her up, she pretends to enjoy it, just like she always does. And in a small way, she does enjoy the touch of his hands on her bare skin and on the patch of soft hair located below her belly button. But then the touching soon becomes clawing. The more he claws and paws at her, the more the enjoyment gives way to revulsion, and revulsion to white-hot anger. At the same time, she feels energized and confident. If that makes any sense. She experiences a real conviction for what she's about to do... for what she's done in the past. Not an ounce of guilt could be mined from her bones. Not after almost four years of enacting her revenge. Not after all those bodies that lie on their backs, headless and soulless.

She no longer bothers with the Mace. Now it's just she and the cleaver.

Pulling herself away from the wrestler, she grabs hold of the blade, which is stored inside her bag.

"Ted," she says, "I want you to meet a friend of mine."

She pulls out the blade.

"Beaver Cleaver meet Ted," she says. "Ted meet Beaver Cleaver."

The wrestler stands paralyzed with confusion, his young eyes locked on the big axe-like blade.

When she swings the blade into his neck, all he manages to do in his defense is work up a near silent gurgle. It sounds almost like the air that suddenly escapes a punctured inner tube. She's just about to finish him off when a pair of bright headlights cut through the night and shine on them through the trees and the scrub brush.

CHAPTER 24

RESUMED my usual spot in front of my typewriter. Stared at the white paper, positioned my fingers on the keys. My mind was spinning with memories of the previous night. My blood still boiling. I replayed them in my brain like a videotape. Lana, shirtless, opening her legs. Susan, leaning into her, kissing her, the barrel of John's gun pressed against the back of her head, the mechanical metal-on-metal noise of his thumbing back the hammer.

Why the hell wasn't I calling the cops right now?

Why the hell wasn't I screaming to having the bastard arrested, his threats be damned?

Maybe because he was the cops, and the cops would never believe my story over his. Or perhaps that's just what I wanted to believe. I needed to be honest here. If I wasn't going to the cops over what happened on my back deck last night, it was because of one thing and one thing only: Lana.

If I went to cops I'd risk losing Lana.

Losing Lana was the last thing I wanted to do.

I'd do anything to be close to her. To smell her, feel her, kiss her all over.

I'd do anything, even if it meant letting her husband get away with murder.

Writing even a word was an impossible fantasy. Knowing that Lana would be outside right this very second made it impossible. My temples pounded and my stomach ached because I only desired one thing.

Lana.

I love you… I lust you… I loathe you with every fiber in my body…

I got up, went into my bedroom, hobbled to the window.

She knew I was watching her. I knew it because instead of laying herself out on her lounge chair, she was standing on the sun-drenched deck, facing me straight on. A full frontal. Her hair was pulled back into a tight ponytail, and she was back to wearing those big square sunglasses. She was also wearing her red kimono. Watching her, I felt my heart pound and my head grow dizzy. How was it possible that this woman possessed so much power over me?

I was spellbound by her… Bewitched.

After a moment or two passed, she did something that took me by surprise but something I should have expected. She raised up her hand and waved at me in a manner that told me she wanted me to come over. Needed me to come over. I couldn't be sure if she actually saw me standing in the bedroom window, but I was certain that, regardless of vision, she knew in her flesh and bones that I was standing there admiring, lusting, bleeding.

Turning on my crutches, I sat down on the bed, put on the jeans and T-shirt that had been tossed there earlier. Lifting myself up, I hobbled to the back sliding doors as fast as my crutches would take me, and exited the house.

The flesh was weak that day.

In just a few moments, I would discover just how weak it was, and how willing I would be to do anything in exchange for Lana's love.

Even kill for it if need be.

CHAPTER 25

AS I entered into her yard through the open gate, I spotted her standing on the edge of the deck. Almost immediately I sensed that something was wrong. Something besides the obvious anyway. Something that went beyond the boundaries of sexual perversion and voyeurism. Like I'd mentioned before, her breasts were uncharacteristically covered up by her kimono, and as she held out a cup of coffee for me… a cup I couldn't possibly take hold of while operating the crutches… she used her free hand to tighten both ends of the robe together in order to hide every trace of bear skin. As if modesty was now as important to her as breathing.

I gestured for her to set the coffee cup on the table, and then I made the step up onto the deck, and sat myself down, leaning the crutches on the table beside me.

"How is Susan?" she said, sitting down across from me.

"She'll live," I said, John's ugly round face flashing in and out of my brain. "That was some game we played last night." Taking a sip of the still hot coffee. "Seems to me you and the husband have played it before."

She stared up and into the hot sun with those thick sunglasses shielding her eyes.

"You have no idea. We've played a lot of games and to be honest, last night was one of the more tame experiences."

"Tame," I said, cynically. "He put a fucking gun to my wife's head." Then, "Why'd you invite me over here?"

"Calm down," she said. "I'm only talking."

"Oh, so that's what this is. You're only talking. I should have known. Did you know that I now suspect that my wife is actually falling in love with you?"

She grinned. "She told you that?"

"No she hasn't come out and said it," I said. "But I have eyes, Lana."

"Why would she fall for me, Ethan? Do you think I'm her type?"

"Is it your habit to send all the neighborhood women perfume and sexy underwear?"

I might have mentioned the WhatsApp message on her phone. But then, I didn't want her to have the satisfaction of my admitting to sneaking a quick look at it behind her back.

She cocked her head, maintained that long stare up at the sun, as if the radiant heat that bathed her face and warmed her blood was never enough.

"I've had girlfriends in the past. Some were in love. Other were in lust. I believe Susan falls into the latter category." She licked her thick lips. "You're not jealous, are you?"

"Are the emotions of an enchanted if not bewitched human being categorical?"

"There you go answering a question with a question again," she said. She inhaled and exhaled. Then, "All things can be explained, until they can't be explained or trying to explain them takes too much out of you…too much pain and sweat and blood."

"And anyway, who'd be willing to explain last night?" I posed with all the sarcasm and acid I could muster. "After all, a proper explanation might scare us to death. It would be one hell of a problem for all of us, now wouldn't it?"

For the first time since I sat down at the table, she pulled her face away from the sun, and locked her black-shielded eyes on me.

"My husband is the problem, Ethan," she said with a blunt coldness that made my spine shiver, like the sun had suddenly been shut off with a light switch. She removed her sunglasses then to reveal a black eye. "But I'm sure you've gathered that by now."

The fine hairs on the back of my neck perked up like the bristles on a frightened cat. There was something in her voice. This wasn't the voice of a frustrated woman or a sad woman at her wits end. It was the frigid, mechanical, calm voice of a woman who was not just now plotting something, but who had been plotting it for a long time. And looking at that shiner, I couldn't blame her one bit.

"The gun thing was a dead giveaway," I said. "Holding my wife at gunpoint while forcing her to perform sexual acts with a woman she hardly knows."

She slipped the sunglasses back on, picked up her coffee, drank some, then set it down again. After a beat, she raised up her hand, pointed to something beyond the fence.

"Look," she said.

I turned.

"You see that tree?" she went on. "The one that's smaller than the others. The one that's not a pine tree."

I noticed it. It was pretty much the only tree that wasn't a pine, and it was partially full of leaves, and there were a few pieces of fruit hanging from the crooked branches. Apples. Small, odd looking apples.

"An apple tree," I said. "What about it?"

"This entire area was once an apple orchard," she said. "But then, I suppose as a resident, you already know that. When I was a kid, I played here. In this very spot. I picked the apples, filled the bushels, helped my family sell them during the fall."

I was a bit shocked to hear what she was saying.

"You grew up right here?" I said. "On Orchard Grove when it was a real apple orchard?"

She nodded. "Orchard Grove was our family farm. Burns Apple Orchard. I was just twelve years old when my stepfather disappeared and the land was sold off, the apple trees cut down, and these houses built."

She was staring at the tree, but I could tell she was seeing something else instead. Something from her past that haunted her. A part of me wanted to ask her what she was seeing, but then another part of me insisted I keep my mouth shut. That whatever was running through her brain was not very pleasant, and perhaps even disturbing.

"Yes," she said, "I grew up on this land. This orchard was my home."

I felt a tightness in my throat and in my chest.

"You've come back home," I said.

"That's one way of putting it," she said. "And that apple tree? It shouldn't be here."

"I don't understand. Why shouldn't it? Maybe they didn't cut them all down."

"They did cut them all. I was here. I watched them destroy all of the trees. I wanted them destroyed. I watched them burn. My mother watched it happen too. She held my hand, and we both watched until every single tree in the orchard was gone."

In my head I saw the tractors, saw the men with their chain saws cutting down the trees. I saw the wood being burned and I saw the charred barren land. I saw what Lana was seeing.

"So why is the tree still here?" I asked.

"Because it was cut down, but not killed. If you really want to kill something… kill it for good… you have to destroy it at its roots. Or else it will grow back. And when it does it will be distorted and ugly and so rotten inside you can't even enjoy its fruit."

I gazed at the ugly, stunted apples. "Those apples are rotten, aren't they?"

"The tree is strangled by the roots of the other trees that have grown around it. The fruit doesn't get enough nutrients from the ground, and it doesn't get enough sun. The apples it produces are bitter and sour."

I shook my head.

She refocused her gaze on me, picked up her coffee, drank some, then set it back down again. "Ethan," she went on, "what would you say if I asked you to help me with something? Something very… well, let's call it delicate and very illegal."

I don't know why the question gave me reason to pause. After last night's less than legal game, it shouldn't have been any more shocking asking me if I preferred apple juice to orange.

"There'd be a great deal of money in it for you, Ethan," she added. "More than a great deal. Perhaps you could use it. Or is that pot garden keeping you flush?"

The corners on her mouth rose up, giving her the look of someone who knew far more about me than I realized.

I stole another sip of coffee.

"I'm listening," I said.

She breathed in slowly, then exhaled even more slowly. She pulled her kimono tighter around her, as if a sharp chill just coursed through her veins.

"I'm not entirely sure how to say this," she said, her eyes once more focused on the sun. "So perhaps I should just come right out and say it."

I looked at her face, her eyes shielded by the sunglasses. Watched her lips move as I listened for the words.

"I want John dead," she said.

The words might have come out as barely more than a whisper, but my ears were ringing, my head pounding, as if she'd gotten up from her chair and screamed in my ear.

"Why are you telling me this?" I said, choking on my words.

"Because I can't do it on my own. I need your help, Ethan. And what's more…"

Her thought trailed off, until I said, "And what's more *what*?"

"And what's more," she repeated, "I know how much you'd like to see him dead too."

She uncrossed her arms, allowed her robe to open up again, just enough so that I could make out the smooth tan flesh in the space between her breasts. It was all I needed to feel my already boiling blood speed rapidly through my veins and capillaries. For my sex to grow hard as a rock. She was right, of course. I did want to see him dead. After what he'd done to Susan last night, and after what he'd done to me by making me watch, I wanted nothing more than to see him dead and gone.

"What exactly did you have in mind, Lana?" I said.

She said, "I'm going to invite you and Susan over for a barbeque tonight to make up for the craziness that went on last night at your house. It will be a way for us to say we're sorry and no hard feelings."

"You don't waste time," I said.

"It must be tonight or never."

"Why? Why tonight?"

"Because John is going to kill me."

Pulse elevated. Throat constricted.

"He's going to kill me and make it look like an accident," she went on.

If it wasn't for my foot, I would have shot up.

"Let's just fucking call the police right now," I said. "He's already hit you in the eye."

Her face went pale.

"You don't understand," she cried. "He *is* the police. They will believe his story, no matter what. Even if they know he's lying. And yes, even if he's already hit me."

"I get it," I said. "That's the way the cops work in Albany. They serve and protect their own."

She nodded, wiped a tear from her face with the back of her hand.

I said, "How do you know he's going to kill you and why? I just assumed he was as much in love with you as I am."

"He knows I committed the worst sin a cop's wife can possibly commit."

"I'm listening, Lana."

"I slept with his partner, Carl. And now he has no choice but to kill me."

News of her sleeping with Carl felt like a punch to the gut, even if I had suspected the truth all along. But I didn't want to give away my emotions.

"He wants to kill you purely out of revenge," I said, trying my best to maintain a straight face.

"No," she said. "To save face."

We sat quiet for a moment, while the cicadas buzzed in the trees and our hearts beat.

She added, "I overheard him on the phone... it must have been one of his minions. Someone he trusts. He asked the guy to come over to do one of his special 'clean up jobs.'" She shuddered, delicately. "How many of those do you think he's ordered?" She leaned forward, her eyes intent on mine. "At some point this afternoon he's going to bring Carl over here so that all three of us can confront one another. It will be the final proof he needs to condemn and convict me, if you want to think of it that way. Then, tonight, before we go to bed, I'm to have an accident. I'm going to fall down the stairs. That's how it's going to look."

"And you're sure this is planned for tonight?" A question for which I already knew the bloody answer.

"Yes. So you see, Ethan, we must do it this evening before he has the chance to get at me first. No choice. We have no choice in the world."

I exhaled. "I see everything clearly now. You want my wife and I to come over so you can buy some time. But tell me something. What if Susan refuses to step foot back over here after what went down last night? What if she never wants to see John again?"

"She'll want to," she said, wiping more tears from her face.

"How can you be so sure I'll help you?" I said, after a beat. "Is John's murder really worth it?"

"You won't have to lay a hand on him," she said. "I have it all figured out. That's the real reason why I need you and Susan to be here tonight. Don't you see, Ethan? John is going to kill himself with a little help from his friends."

SNAPSHOT

SHE'S certain the police did not get a good look at her, because as soon as the white lights broke through the tree cover, she slipped the cleaver into her leather bag, grabbed it by the strap, and put her high school sprinter abilities to the test. She turned and ran as fast as she could into the woods. At best they've captured the fleeting image of someone running away. Someone who's wearing a hoodie and blue jeans. That's as far as the description will go. They won't even be sure if the person they witnessed running away is a man or a woman.

She runs through the brush, the branches slapping her smooth face, stinging it, making blue eyes tear. She scoots down to the gravelly bank in order to heave the bag into the river, which she does. She then runs some more. But in her head, however, she knows that running is futile. That there are too many cops and she will never be able to outrun them all. She needs a hiding place. Needs it now.

Soon she comes upon a concrete culvert that empties into the river. The aroma coming up from the culvert is most unpleasant. Like raw sewage combined with rotting food and toxic chemicals that must come from one of the refineries inside the adjacent Port of Albany.

She stops in her tracks, stands perfectly still.

Up ahead in the distance, she can make out the metal smoke stacks and big iron oil drums inside the port. She sees the flames spouting from out of the stacks of the refineries, sees the bright lights that illuminate the metal trucks and buildings that litter it behind a fence topped with razor wire. Listening carefully, she can make out not only the sounds of trucks, machines, and voices coming from the port, but also the much closer sound of the police as they smash through the brush on foot. They're like human bulldozers. She's convinced then that despite her speed, they've managed to keep up and now they are on her tail.

Locking eyes onto the culvert, she knows she has no choice.

Crouching, she steps inside the culvert opening, drops down to all fours, crawls into the pitch black, foul smelling opening.

"Patience," she whispers to herself. "Chill out, Lana, and it will all be all right."

She crawls into the dark unknown.

CHAPTER 26

SHE poured more coffee for me, this time adding a shot of whiskey. A concoction my long dead grandfather used to refer to as "Coffee Royals" but which she called, "Killer Coffee."

"How appropriate," I said under my breath. A comment that went ignored.

While I sipped the coffee, she began to script, in detail, how she planned on killing her husband. The plot centered around his love of guns. What she had in mind was almost too simple to be believable, but at the same time, possessed a kind of beauty in its uncomplicatedness. Like a rose I guess, its core thorn hidden from view until it pokes you. Draws your blood.

First things first. We would get John drunk at the barbeque. After all, it was a Friday night, and he usually didn't have to play cop on Saturdays. Apparently, his habit on late Friday afternoons was to stop at a downtown watering hole on his way home. In particular, a bar called Thatcher Street Pub way down off North Broadway where the abandoned steel mills were located. According to Lana, the cops owned the joint and paid "a special price for beer and shots" which in her mind translated into free. A bottomless well of alcohol for well-armed men who craved conflict.

"I thought you said he and Carl were coming by for a final showdown?"

"They are. But they'll come here first, before the drinking begins. That will provide the fuel for his alibi, everyone will know he'll need to get good and loaded this afternoon."

"Nothing like a little heartbreak for working up a mean, mean thirst," I said.

She sat back in her chair and said, "By the time he'll arrive back from two hours of nonstop drinking, he'll already be pretty lit up."

"So what, precisely, do you expect of me?" I asked.

"When he arrives, I want you to insist there's no hard feelings over last night. You understand some serious swinging when you see it. If you acted upset at all, it's just because you're not used to that kind of swinger's game. The mixing of the dangerous with the erotic." She inhaled and exhaled once more, as if all this were taking a great effort to explain. And maybe it was. "Then, when that's over, I want you to praise him for what a great cop he must be. He loves to be buttered up. What kind of pig doesn't? Finally, once that's accomplished, you will ask him if you can get a look at his prized gun collection."

"Gun collection," I said, like a question.

"A gunroom inside a converted bedroom. He has fifty or one hundred or I don't know how the hell many pistols and rifles, all under glass on display." She smiled. "It's what you do when your dick is too small. How you compensate, I guess."

"You made that apparent last evening," I said. Then, "There's something I want you to know." She looked me in the eyes. "I'm in love with you or maybe what I'm going through is some sort of intense, over the top hunger. But I will tell you this: I will not kill for you under any circumstance." I took a second to catch my breath. "But the man put a gun to Susan's head. A loaded… fucking… gun. He made her do things she might otherwise not do. I might not kill John for you, but I would kill him for that."

"Like I told you," she said. "The way I've worked it out, he will kill himself. You just have to help him along a little bit."

"I don't get it," I said.

She got up.

"Follow me," she said.

I tailed her into the house, where she led me to a bedroom that was located a few feet beyond the front vestibule. The square room had been painted black, and the windowless wall to my right was covered in floor-to-ceiling glass cases. When Lana flicked on the light switches, the cases lit up with a soft backlighting. The collection was impressive even for a man like me who hardly ever held a real gun in his life, much less owned one. I did however possess some knowledge of both pistols and rifles since I often found myself writing about them in my scripts. So it was no accident that I immediately recognized the collection of Colt .45s.

Far as I could tell, the cases housed Colt automatics from every era they were manufactured, right down to its birthday in 1911. Besides the automatics, there were some Old West Colt revolvers (also .45 caliber if my memory was correct), and even a couple of flintlock pistols that must have dated back to the early nineteenth century. Positioned vertically on their stocks to the far left of the second case were several machineguns and automatic weapons. There was a Browning Automatic Rifle, a Thompson submachine gun with a round magazine like the kind FBI "G-men" used for killing rumrunners like Al Capone's gang back in the 1920s and 30s, and an AK47 with duct-taped, piggybacked banana clips that surly would have made a terrorist hard as a rock. The collection was finished off by a mini-M16 and an AR15.

I turned to Lana, asked her what I was supposed to do once I managed get her husband inside the room.

"Persuade him to take out one of the guns," she said.

"Any gun in particular?"

"I'm glad you asked that." She made her way across the short expanse of room to a wood desk positioned in front of the far wall that also contained a picture window. To the left of the desk on the wall opposite the cases were a pair of sliding closet doors. Bending down, she felt underneath the top desk drawer with her fingertips, until she came back out with a key. Making her way back around the desk, she approached the case with key secured in her fingertips.

"Naturally he's the only one who has a key to his precious firearms," she said. "But what he doesn't know won't kill him."

"Until now," I said.

She nodded and unlocked the case that contained the Colt semi-automatics. Reaching inside she pulled out the first in the series of Colt .45 Model 1911s off the wall, and released the magazine with her thumb. She held the magazine up before me, like Eve offering up the forbidden fruit to Adam.

"It's empty," she said. "Tonight it won't be. There will be a single round inside it." She shuffled back to the closet, reached up on the shelf, pulled down a green and yellow box that said Remington Pistol and Revolver Cartridges on it. .45 caliber. She opened the box, revealing the neatly packed ammo. "Don't be afraid," she said. "Help yourself."

I reached out, took hold of the one of the cartridges, rolled it around between my fingers. It was surprisingly heavy and solid for a single bullet. After a time, I put it back in its slot in the box, and she returned the package to the closet.

"So I'm going to somehow load the gun later and shoot him?" I said. "That's your plan?" I shifted the crutches just a little so that the rubber pads didn't continue to irritate the skin that surrounded my armpits on what was turning out to be yet another hot summer's day.

"You don't understand," she said. "I want you to ask him to demonstrate something. For one of your upcoming movies."

"Demonstrate what?"

"A suicide."

Those two words slapped me upside the head. But at the same time, I was beginning to see how her scheme might actually work. I was a scriptwriter after all. Naturally I'd be inquisitive and curious about how things work in Copland. Not only with guns, but also with cops, their dangerous lives, their successes, losses, depressions, and yes, their suicides.

"You want me to ask him how cops go about eating their piece," I said, a wave of optimism suddenly filling my lungs like cool, fresh air. "And because he no doubt has a friend or two who has actually succeeded at performing the ultimate desperate deed, he'll be all too willing to demonstrate."

"He'll cock back the housing just to make sure there's no round in the chamber. But what he'll be doing instead is cocking a round *into* the chamber.

And trust me, I've seen him eat his piece on a dozen occasions before with an unloaded gun. Usually at a party. Of course, none of the horrified onlookers are supposed to know that it's unloaded. You could say John goes for the jugular when it comes to shock value."

I tried to picture him pumping the slide. I knew that if he were staring at the slide, he might actually see the round enter into the chamber through the ejection port. But I knew that if I could somehow keep his eyes diverted, or better yet, if I were to cock the automatic for him, he would never have a clue. The plan was simple but brilliant, as all plans are when they go off without hitch. It made sense to me. And if, in the end, he actually noticed the round inside the chamber or if it popped out, he would chalk that up to his own carelessness. He would live to die another time. But then where would that leave Lana? Dead, at the bottom of the basement steps?

"The plan's not half bad," I said. "But like Adam said to Eve after she got him to bite into the forbidden fruit, *What's in it for me?*"

Loosening her shoulders, she allowed the kimono to fall to the floor, exposing her naked body.

"How's this for starters?" she said, kissing me on the mouth.

CHAPTER 27

BUT I couldn't get myself to do it.

My nerves were frayed and as much as I desired Lana, I couldn't help but see that gun pressed up against Susan's skull. I also couldn't get myself to cheat any longer. Maybe Susan was also falling for Lana, but until we came to some sort of understanding on how exactly we would handle our separate feelings for our new neighbor, I didn't want to stab Susan in the back any longer. Now, above all else, was the matter of John's suicide. If I didn't work with Lana in making it go off without a hitch, there was a good chance the son of a bitch would kill her.

Christ, I need a drink...

Sensing my anxiety... my conflicted emotions... Lana slipped back into her robe and began to talk about what I stood to earn should I actually succeed in getting John to kill himself. She spouted off about several life insurance policies, including one biggie from John's Law Enforcement Union 82 annuity that would pay out in the high six figures, in the event of accidental fatal gunshot wound. All totaled we were looking at more than a million dollars, all of which Lana seemed all too willing to share.

"But the best part about having my husband dead and buried," she said with a smile, "is having me all to yourself. When he's gone, it will just be you, me, and, if you prefer, Susan. We'll be a threesome. Committed and in love."

"I still haven't told you that I'd do it yet," I said. "I need some time to think it over. So would Susan."

"Don't take too long," she said. "By this time tomorrow, I could be dead. And once he finds out for certain about us… you *and* me… he will kill you too."

I nodded while my throat constricted and my mouth went dry. She was right. If John was going to kill Lana, then it was also possible he'd kill me, and his partner Carl. Used to be my world consisted of my scripts and stable life on Orchard Grove. Now my world was spinning out of control.

"Do you love me, Ethan? Or are you convinced this obsession is purely physical?"

"That's the ultimate question, isn't it?"

I felt my insides tighten. Like a schoolboy holding the hand of a girl he'd been loving from a distance for a long, long time.

"Maybe it's true," I said. "Maybe I do love you for real."

"Then let's do this thing," she said. "Let's rid this world of John Cattivo before he kills us first."

As I followed her out of the gunroom, down the hall, and back into the kitchen I started to think how strange and utterly bizarre life could be. Just a few days ago I was struggling with the pain that came from a foot that had been surgically reconstructed with four screws and a six inch steel pin that stuck out of the index toe like the sword on a billfish. I was drinking too much, smoking the green weed that came from my backyard pot patch, and staring at the blank page on my typewriter. Now I was contemplating a plot to coerce a man into committing suicide. Doing it along with a woman who'd managed somehow to bewitch not only myself but, quite possibly, my wife. And the most bizarre thing of all? A big part of me was looking forward to seeing her husband blow his brains out.

"You sure that gunroom isn't bugged?" I said.

"I've thought of that, believe me," she said. "But we're in the clear. John believes that I would never dare enter into his private sanctum."

"Until now," I said. "I guess we've officially defiled the place merely with our presence."

But then I recalled Lana's and John's argument outside on the back deck two morning's ago when he accused her of once more playing with the next door neighbor while the cat was away.

"Have you had a lot of boyfriends, Lana?" I asked. "Extramarital boyfriends? Girlfriends?"

"I do what I want, when I want," she said, heading for the open door.

"Why have you stayed with him this long?"

"Like I said. I have no career of my own, no money, no family. I have only John and he's a cop. The police network is vast. He could make things very miserable for me if I were to pack a bag right now and slip out the back, Jack. You could say I'm trapped."

"But should he accidentally die," I said, "you'd have a bright future."

"Correction," she said. "*We'll* have a bright future."

"What about Carl? He in love with you too?"

She bit down on her bottom lip.

"I despise that man," she said. "Yes, if you need to know. Listen, it was a mistake sleeping with him, even if it did only happen once. Just once. And once was enough. Now he will not leave me alone."

I pictured the big, goateed man, felt his cold, soft handshake, his even colder stare.

"I know he's coming here this afternoon. But what if he gets belligerent and happens to show up later tonight? What if he decides to join us for dinner, regardless of what John feels about him?"

"He won't. He has a wife and a little baby girl at home. The protectors of Albany place family first. Even before illicit lays like myself."

She took a step, as if about to head back outside.

"Wait," I said. "If we do this tonight. If we pull it off, what's to stop you from sleeping with all the people you want to sleep with? What's to stop you from cutting me out altogether?"

She grinned and stared into me with blue eyes that stabbed through me like a blade through rotten fruit. But in this case, flesh and blood.

133

"There isn't anything to stop me," she said through a sly smirk. "Chance you gotta take. Does that bother you?"

A rock settled itself inside my sternum. I felt my heart struggling to pump blood far faster than it needed to be pumped, like my brain had nothing to do with controlling my functions anymore, having given over to a greater power. Surrounding me on all sides was the home of a cop. A gunroom filled with guns of all shapes and sizes and killing capacities. On the other side, a photographic essay of the cop's career thus far. Standing directly before me, the young blonde trophy wife who wanted the cop dead.

I had to ask myself, Why was I helpless in the face of Lana's evil? Why did I still want her more than anything in the world? Why was I so willing to do almost anything for her if only it meant I could have her all to myself? If only I'd had some bullets to go with the guns, I might have shot her on the spot and ended the source of my obsession right there and then. That's how much I hated her at that very moment. Or maybe it's more true to say that I hated myself for becoming her slave.

The strength in her was enormous as it was deeply rooted, like that apple tree outback that had survived its own murder, only to grow back distorted and poisoned. That strength was matched only by my weakness. We are prisoners to our most basic desires to varying degrees. But I was a prisoner more than most. Perhaps John's partner Carl was as well. My guess is that John became a slave a long time ago, and over the years his soul became sick and crippled, changing him forever. I could only wonder how many slaves there had been along the way. I wondered how many of them had survived the experience, and how many of them now resided six feet under, smiles on their stiff, cold, rotting faces, forever happy to be rid of the shackles called Lana.

"You coming… Killer?" she said, making her way through the kitchen, into the living room, and down the two steps to the sliding glass doors.

Killer… that's me…

"Yes," I said, gripping my crutch handles. "The killer is right behind you."

CHAPTER 28

I **LEFT** Lana standing on the back deck, sunglasses covering her eyes, arms wrapped around her chest. I hobbled back to my house where I immediately poured myself a late morning shot of Jack Daniels. Sitting myself down before my typewriter, I stared at my pages of notes. But all I could see was Lana. And when I saw Lana I began to see John, and how he would look with a bullet having barreled through his brains. Saw the blood even before it began to spray out of his skull along with his brains.

What the hell was I about to do?

Reaching out with both hands, I typed those very words.

> What the hell am I about to do?
> What the hell am I about to do?
> What the hell am I about to do?

The sudden bang and motorized noise of the ceiling-mounted chain pulling open the overhead garage door nearly shot me out of my chair and through the roof. Susan was home early. When she came through the door,

I immediately turned to see that her tight face bore the expression of a determined woman. She never spoke a word when she took hold of my hand and assisted me with standing up. Then, pulling down her jeans and panties, she bent herself over the table in the space between my typewriter and the bowl of apples. In the same exact place where I had Lana two days before.

"Be with me," she said, her voice deep and throaty, filled with a starving desire. "I want to feel like her. I want to be her."

It didn't matter that I'd been with Lana only an hour before. Less than an hour before. That her lavender scent tainted my skin. My wife excited me almost as much as Lana did.

I don't know what prompted me to say the things I was about to say. But I only know that I felt an overwhelming need to say them.

"I want you to know something. Something… about… Lana."

"Tell me," she begged. "Tell… me… now."

"I was with her," I whispered. "This morning."

She made a little crying sound, followed by another moan. "Did you fuck her?"

"No. I did not. But I wanted to. I wanted to fuck you both, together, in the same bed."

She shouted out then, climaxing violently. I lost my balance and nearly dropped down onto my right side. If I hadn't managed to reach out for the table, I would have gone over and damaged yet another piece of my body.

Susan breathed in and out, then ran her hands through her hair. She turned, slowly pulled up her jeans. When she leaned into me and kissed me on the mouth, I felt like she wasn't my wife, but an imposter. But when she raised up her hand, slapped me across the face, I knew that the imposter had exited the building, and the real Susan had returned.

"I love you," she said. "And I hate you so much right now, because I know that you love her. And the worst part is that I can't blame you."

She stepped away from the table, crossed over the dining room, through the kitchen and into our bedroom, slamming the door behind her.

CHAPTER 29

MAYBE my face still stung from Susan's slap, but my foot was throbbing. I knew that if I didn't start taking better care of it, I would lose the index toe entirely. Stealing a quick glance at the white sock that covered it I could see that it was bleeding again, the tip of the sock stained with rich red blood.

Getting myself dressed, I poured another shot of whiskey and drank it down. It was going on high noon, and in only a few hours we would be heading back over to the Cattivo's for a barbeque in which it was quite possible I'd play an instrumental role in John's accidental death. The only thing that stood in the way of the plan now was letting Susan in on it. It was something I had to do, whether I liked it or not.

Feeling the effects of the whiskey kicking in, calming and sedating me, I hobbled across the kitchen floor to the bedroom door, gently rapped my knuckles against the solid wood panel.

No answer.

Placing my hand on the opener, I turned it counter-clockwise and pushed the door open. That's when I saw that Susan was lying on the bed face down in her pillow. I made my way over to her, set myself down beside her on the mattress. I knew I had to tell her about my conversation with Lana, about what she'd asked me to do. But how the hell do you go about explaining something like that to a woman who is already deeply confused and brokenhearted? Where exactly, do you begin?

Reaching out, I gently set my hand on her shoulder, and began to massage it.

She rolled over, looked up at me. Her eyes were red and swelled. We were quiet while I focused on the slider window that provided the view onto the wood deck where Lana was, no doubt, sunning herself right at this very moment. I so badly wanted to make my way to the window and look at her. But I used every ounce of strength left in my body to resist the temptation.

"Lana has asked for a favor," I said after a time.

Her melancholy eyes suddenly grew wide, not like she was surprised over Lana asking me for a favor, but more like she already knew what the favor entailed. Almost like she'd been standing outside the door of the Cattivo gunroom when the question was posed.

"You have my attention," she said softly. "What kind of favor, Ethan?"

I told her. Straight up. No rocks. No whiskey chaser. Told her about the accidental suicide plan and the reward of insurance money. About John's plan to kill Lana. About her black eye. About having her all to ourselves.

She did something that surprised me then. Instead of sitting up straight and announcing to me in no uncertain terms that we needed to go directly to the police… the very police with whom John belonged… she did something completely different. She laughed. Not loud, or silly, but gently and thoughtfully. Like I'd just told her a joke that was neither brilliant nor memorable, but that nonetheless made her think and grin for a few seconds.

"Did you give Lana your answer?" she said.

Her question or questions, came as yet another surprise.

"Do you really want to know?" I said.

"Tell you what. You keep your answer to yourself."

"I don't understand."

"John Cattivo is one of the most horrible men I've met in my life. I also believe he somehow enslaves her. Or why else would she be with him?"

Funny her use of the word enslaved, especially when I saw their relationship as having worked the other way around. Lana having enslaved John a long time ago, turning him into the monster that he is today. Still, she is dependent upon him, and under that circumstance, she is most definitely a slave.

"Money," I said after a beat. "Lana claims to have nothing of her own. John is all she has. And now, she enslaves *us*, Suze. You *and* me."

"Money," she repeated. "And we're irreparably broke. This isn't about love or lust or desire anymore, and it's not about ridding the world of a man better off dead. It's about money. But what you have to ask yourself is this, Ethan. Are you willing to commit murder in the first for money? Or are you willing to commit murder for the woman? Because either way, you're going to rot in hell."

I looked at my wife lying on the bed beside me while my back was pressed up against the headboard, my right foot laid out on the mattress, the white sock stained with dried blood. Her brown eyes were gazing upon me and into me. I pictured the stunning blonde woman sitting out on the back deck just a few feet away. I wanted her right now. I wanted Susan too. Wanted them both, again, and again. Wanted them together.

"The devil won't know a goddamned thing," I said. "That is, unless you tell him first. You wouldn't do that to me, would you Susan?"

She didn't get the chance to answer me. Because through the slider window came the heavy engine noise of an SUV pulling up in the Cattivo driveway.

Detective Cattivo was home again, and if what Lana said was correct, he brought Carl Pressman with him.

CHAPTER 30

STOOD up, shoved the crutches under my arms, hopped on over to the window. As suspected, Lana was sitting out on the deck, sunning her body, only a pair of black bikini panties for clothing. After a few seconds, John came storming out the sliding glass doors. As anticipated, he was accompanied by his partner, Carl. John was wearing a blue blazer, but the front tails on his gray button down were no longer tucked in while his beer gut protruded over his belt buckle. From where I stood in front of the slider, he looked like he'd been wrestling around with someone or something, and enjoying it.

The taller, darker Carl was also wearing a lightweight blue blazer, but his shirt was neatly tucked in, his goatee impeccably trimmed, the aviator sunglasses masking his eyes.

Lana sat up, grabbed her robe from off the chaise beside her, and put it on. Did it with no special sense of urgency, which convinced me first that both men had seen her naked plenty of times before, and second, that she moved slowly on purpose, just to further piss off her husband.

"What's happening?" Susan said from the bed.

I raised up my hand, as if to shush her.

I listened while a few indiscernible words were exchanged between John and Lana. By now, Susan had gotten up and come around the bed, taken her place beside me at the window. We should have been more careful with our eavesdropping. But when John turned, focused his eyes directly at us, as if he could see our faces through the glass, I instinctively pulled back and so did Susan.

"Do you think he caught us in the act?" Susan said.

"I think we're standing far enough away from the window," I said. "The glare from the sun should be enough to shield us."

She stood with her back pressed up against the wall. She was breathing heavily, and very afraid. "But they know we're looking at them. Lana can feel it."

"I know what you mean about Lana," I said. "About what she can intuit and what she can't."

This time when I looked out the window, I used only my right eye, and from a farther distance from the glass.

"What's happening?" Lana said.

I saw Lana get up from the chaise lounge. But John reached out, pushed her back down.

"The son of bitch just shoved her," I said. She was wearing her sunglasses, but I could see her black eye plain enough inside my head. I could feel her pain.

"Oh Christ," Susan said. She pulled away from the wall and assumed a similar position to myself. One in which she was more or less peeking with only one eye and from a greater distance away from the window.

Together we saw John pull out his automatic and point it at Lana.

"My own goddamned partner," he barked.

Even from where I was still standing, I could see Lana's face turn pale.

"Stop it, John," Carl said.

But Cattivo swung the pistol around, aimed at his partner's face.

"You shut up," he said. Then, smiling, he added, "You know, Carl. I don't blame you. You fell under her spell like everyone else does. When you fuck my wife's mouth, you're just doing what comes naturally. Doing what dozens have done before you."

Carl's hands were raised up in surrender. But I wondered just who he was surrendering to.

"I won't see her ever again," he said. "I promise, John."

"Sure you do, Carl. They always make promises they can't keep."

He shifted the pistol back to his wife.

"This thing ends today, Lana," he said. "You got it? My partner is entirely off limits. You got that?"

Lana issued him a stare, her blue eyes unblinking. She nodded.

As John returned his service weapon to its hip holster, he once more turned and stared directly at our window, offering up a wide, strangely satisfied, if not evil grin, as if he knew full well I was watching. Then he disappeared back inside the house, with Carl on his tail. Less than a minute later, we heard the SUV starting up, and backing out of the drive.

Lana crossed her arms over her chest and stared down at her bare feet, the crying heart tattoo plainly visible. I couldn't be sure, but I swear she had to be crying. For certain I knew she was crying when she wiped her cheeks with the backs of her hands and slowly, achingly, stood up.

Susan and I turned toward each other at the same time, locked eyes.

"I'm going to buy some wine," she said. "Some red, bloody fruit of the vine to bring as a gift tonight to the Cattivos."

"Then you agree to Lana's plan?"

"I'm agreeing to seeing that horrible piece of scum go to hell, even if it means we follow him there."

CHAPTER 31

WE didn't discuss what would or wouldn't happen at the Cattivos house anymore that afternoon. Resolved to what we, or I, had to do to save Lana's life and rid the world of John's, we simply went about our business with a strange new sense of optimism. So optimistic in fact, that I sat in front of my typewriter and began to write something other than notes.

FADE IN: I typed.

I began a script about a writer who lives in downtown Manhattan and who falls hopelessly in love with a married woman when she and her banker husband move into the vacant apartment next door. He's not sure why he should fall so desperately in love with this woman whom he knows nothing about. Only that he does.

The wrinkle comes about when the woman asks him to help kill her husband. The husband is worth a lot of money dead, and if it was made to look like an accident, they both share in the insurance money and become millionaires overnight.

I guess it was the same plot as the 1940s film classic, *Double Indemnity*. But I didn't care. It was a timeless story that resembled real life, and the studios, especially big Hollywood studios, were suckers for new twists on old classic plots. Even if in the end, I had no choice but to shelve the project or else implicate my own participation in a murder-for-money-and-lust scheme, it felt good to be writing scripts again. To hear the clatter of the typewriter, to be filling the blank page with directions and dialogue for first time since Lana moved in next door, and wrapped a ball and chain around my soul.

BY the time Susan returned from the liquor store with three bottles of red wine, I'd already written five pages. It was going on five o'clock and if what Lana told me was true, John would be arriving home drunk from his Friday afternoon out with his fellow officers within the hour. Heading into the bedroom, Susan changed out of her jeans and into a short denim skirt and a tight black T-shirt accented with a silver necklace that supported a metal cross. Her dark hair was long and brushed out, and I wanted to swim in it. Wanted to swim in it along with Lana.

Taking her into my arms, I kissed my wife on the mouth. I was dreading what I was about to do to John, but at the same time, feeling somehow optimistic about the future. About the three of us together. I felt like a man who was about to enter into a decisive battle, but somehow knew of the outcome before anyone else did. And the outcome was wonderful.

"Do you think it's possible for three people to fall in love with one another?" I said.

"Life is strange," she said. "That's as far as I go with this."

She grabbed up the wine bottles and made for the back sliding glass doors.

CHAPTER 32

LANA was already waiting for us on the deck. Despite the ordeal she was put through earlier with her husband, his partner, and a gun pointed at her face, she looked fresh and lovely in a short, white, summer-weight skirt that stopped just short of mid-thigh. Instead of wearing her leather sandals, she chose to go barefoot, her toes having been manicured and painted in lipstick-red nail polish. A fresh application of makeup covered up her shiner, and the blood tears that fell from the crying heart tattoo on her ankle seemed to pulsate with her every step, as if they were fully anticipating precisely how this night was going to end.

"Come in," she said, wrapping her arms around Susan, kissing her gently on the mouth. "John's not home yet."

She took the wine bottles from Susan and set them out on the outdoor table beside a wood cutting board that contained a hunk of blue cheese and a green apple that had already been sliced up into several wedges with the paring knife that also rested on the board. Lana did not say a word about our plan to kill her husband, but instead she insisted that I open up one of the bottles and pour three big glasses, which I did.

"To us," she said, her smile sly and somewhat energetic, as she raised her glass with one hand and fingered an apple wedge with the other. "To a brighter future." She sipped the wine, then bit down on the slice of apple.

Raising our glasses to our lips, Susan and I drank. The wine was warm, rich, sweet and bitter at the same time. I swear, as the liquid descended into my body, I felt something more than just liquid enter into me then. It felt warm but also cold, and it seemed to lodge itself inside my ribcage beside my heart where the soul resides. All that needed to happen then was a lightning bolt to strike the apple tree out back, and the voice of Satan rising up from out of the depths screaming, "You're mine now!" But of course, it was a nice peaceful evening on Orchard Grove, with a welcome breeze soothing us from out of the north.

The strange thing was that I hadn't yet let on to Lana that Susan knew about our plan. But somehow Lana already knew the truth. I could read it on her face like the title page on a script. Maybe the last thing Susan wanted was to openly speak about assisting in a murder, but as soon as her eyes met Lana's I'm sure she had nothing else in mind other than getting rid of John before he got rid of her first and did so under the guise of a legal circumstance... a tragic, but oh so common, accident. If it could only be accomplished so that it looked like an accident, all the better.

We stood on the back deck drinking wine, eating cheese and apple wedges as the late afternoon sun assumed its summertime orange afterglow. Susan and Lana seemed as happy as two girlfriends who'd just spent the day shopping. How is it that they were so calm? So confident? At the same time, my heart was pounding and I could feel cold droplets of sweat pouring down my backbone.

Holy Christ, I was about to become a murderer... Didn't matter that the guy who was going to die had it coming...

Something else made the situation surreal: The sexual tension between the three of us was so thick and palpable you could cut it with the paring knife that rested on the cutting board. But it was replaced by sudden alertness and a kind of call-to-action when we heard the SUV pulling up in the driveway, its tires squealing on the macadam when it came to an abrupt stop.

"And that, my lovelies, will be the resident evil of the Cattivo household,"

Lana said, her face growing noticeably tight. She finished off her wine, set the glass down onto the table.

Turning to Susan, we locked eyes. She didn't have to say word for me to know what she was thinking. *Do what you must do, and I will support you one hundred percent because I love you and because the man who is about to die aimed a loaded gun to my head and plans on killing Lana.*

Coming from inside the house, a door opening and slamming shut. Heavy footsteps followed, and after that, the sliding glass doors were thrown open. John walked out, his face red, wide-eyed and as agitated as an angry pit bull. His 9mm was holstered to his hip.

"Well if it isn't my friends, Hollywood and Suzy Q," he barked. "So who wants to get naked first?"

CHAPTER 33

ONE thing quickly became evident: drunk as a skunk or not, John could be tamed. At least, for a brief time anyway. And, not surprisingly, the tamer of the beast was Lana. She immediately took him by the arm, led him back inside the house where she proceeded to speak with him. I can't be certain the words exchanged between them, or if John even said anything at all. But all I know is that when he returned to the deck, he'd washed his face, straightened out his shirt, and seemed far less aggressive and insulting in manner. He'd even removed his sidearm which took me completely by surprise since I could only assume it was biologically attached. In a word, he seemed suddenly to be acting on his best behavior. Naturally, his sudden attitude adjustment, temporary or not, made the task I was about to perform all the more difficult to contemplate.

He popped the top on a tall-necked beer and took a seat at the table while Lana and Susan did the grilling. I was thankful that we didn't attempt to shake hands or come too close to one another. After all, the palms of my hands were sweating, and my heart was beating so loudly I couldn't believe no one else heard it. I needed to get this over with. Do it now.

While the steaks roasted, I made my move.

"You know, John," I said. "I very much admire you."

He drank some beer and issued me a slanty-eyed look like, *You've got to be kidding me.*

"Must be because of the wife," he said.

I laughed, trying my damnedest to be convincing.

"Oh, you got me there, John," I said, masking the fear in my voice. "But I was talking more along the lines of your occupation. You know, I write about cops in my scripts."

He shook his head, rolled his eyes. "TV and movie guys like you always get it wrong, Hollywood. Like I said before, you never get your facts straight."

Lana snuck a look at me over her shoulder from where she was standing at the grill with Susan. The look told me I was doing great, baiting John perfectly.

"Facts," I repeated. "How do you mean, John?"

"I mean you guys have no idea about police standard operating procedure. You always get it wrong. You arrest guys without reading them their Miranda's. You put a homicide dick in charge of a drug bust. You conduct high-speed chases in quaint suburban puckered ass neighborhoods like Orchard Grove. And then the next thing you know you're winning some prestigious award like an Oscar or sticking your hands in wet concrete outside the TLC Chinese Theater. It just doesn't go down like that in real life, Hollywood."

He drank down the rest of his beer, set the empty onto the table. He got up, retrieved another one, sat back down.

"Well, believe me when I say I admire what you do, John," I said. "Putting your life on the line day in and day out. It not only takes firepower. It takes guts. Real guts."

"Gee, thanks, Hollywood," he said, his words slurring some. "How very white and neighborly of you to say so. Remind me to make your wife do things to my wife at gunpoint more often. Brings out the real pussy in you."

The old John was back and I was somehow happy for it. He laughed out loud like he'd just issued the most hysterical quip of his life. It was something a big bully would bark at the littlest guy on the playground. I was glad he said it though. Because that's when the fear and anxiety exited my body like an exorcised demon, leaving only the desire to see him dead.

"It's okay, John," I said. "I know you like to play rough. That's understandable. No hard feelings."

"No hard feelings?" he said. "Like for realz?"

"For realz," I said.

"Bullshit," he said. "But then, I'd do it again in an instant. Maybe even tonight."

He tossed Susan and Lana a look like he was about to sink his fangs into the both of them. As for me, I just wanted him dead already.

The girls stood by the grill, drinking glass after glass of red wine, laughing and flirting with one another as if they were the oldest friends on earth. What in God's name was happening here? My brain was spinning with worry, anger, and the desperation I still felt for both women, especially Lana. For a woman who had only hours to live, that is I didn't pull through with our plan to beat John to the death punch, she seemed relieved and worry free.

I stole a look at Lana and Susan where they stood before the cooker grilling the red meat. Rubbing one another's backs, planting little kisses on one another's lips. I felt such an extreme need for both women that I knew I couldn't possibly live without them. Maybe I was scared to death of what I was about to do to John, but I wanted to be with them right now, on the deck. I had to have their bodies all to myself. The sooner I could accomplish that, the better. My need for them was outweighed only my by hatred for John. Maybe the devil or one of his angels had somehow taken up residence inside of me, or maybe he hadn't. In the final analysis, I knew the results were the same. I needed to remove John from the equation. Do it fast.

"So where were we, John?" I said, bringing the beer to my lips, drinking.

"We were discussing how you film writers screw up everything." He raised both his hands, made pretend quotation marks with his fingers when he said "film writers."

"Oh yes," I said. "I'll tell you what I could use some help with."

"Oh you will, will you, Hollywood?" he said, lifting up his hand, bitch-slapping the air with it, as if it were my face.

"I need to know about guns," I said. "My knowledge comes only from books and the Internet. Now if I were to have access to some real guns, and an expert like yourself to tell me all about them, that might make a real difference in my work."

Lana turned so quick I could practically feel the breeze blowing off her.

"Why don't you take Ethan inside, darling, show him your collection?" she said, a broad smile plastered on her face. A smile that looked and felt as natural as the waning sun.

He drank some beer, wiped his mouth with the back of his hand while rolling his eyes.

"I don't show many people my collection," he said. "Hollywood types especially."

"Come on, honey," Lana pressed. "Dinner won't be ready for a half hour, and Susan and I would love some girl-on-girl time." She took hold of Susan's hand. Meanwhile my wife moved in closer to her, pressing herself against Lana's side.

"Girls will be girls," John said, as he stood back up, a bit unsteady. Then, his eyes shifting from me to the wood deck. "What is that stuff?" he said. "That blood?"

I stood up, adjusted my crutches. Looking down at my foot I could see that the blood on the sock was fresh.

"My apologies," I said. "Can't seem to stem the flow."

He shook his head.

"Well, don't bleed on anything in my house," he said. "Blood's a bitch to get out. Take it from a cop." Then, opening the screen door. "Follow me and don't forget to bring your crutches, Tiny Tim."

"Right behind you, Detective Cattivo," I said in my best imitation Boy Scout.

CHAPTER 34

HIS gunroom seemed a million miles away from the spot in which Lana and I stood this morning. It even smelled fresh, like it had just been Febrezed. I made sure to feign an expression of absolute awe as soon as I stood stone stiff inside the open door frame, as if this were the very first time I'd been exposed to his collection of firearms.

"You see these weapons, Hollywood?" John said, waving his hand at the many pistols, automatics, and machineguns on display in the light-up cases. "I love them more than my wife."

"You really mean that?"

"With all my frozen heart. Truth is, I'm not sure what it is exactly that I carry for Lana. It's not love, I can tell you that. It's more like a need, or a thirst I just can't quench no matter how many trips I take to the well." He pursed his lips, shook his hand, like he'd been struggling with the issue for years. "It's the same way a lot of people end up feeling about her."

Jesus H, I thought. Was this son of bitch actually opening up to me? Bearing his soul now that we were alone in his special room filled with one hundred different ways to die by gunshot? I looked at his round face, into his bloodshot eyes, and I nodded. Because in a small way he was taking the words right out of my own mouth. Susan's too. But that didn't make him a good person. It made him even weaker. A weak man who physically abused his wife.

"I see the way you look at her, big shot," he said. "I see the way your wife looks at her too. Saw the way she felt about swapping spit with her, and believe me, that gun I was pointing at her was only a prop, a sex toy, and an unnecessary one at that. You know it and I know it."

My pulse picked up. It's no surprise he was on to me... to *us*. But this was the first time he'd decided to get it all out in the open.

"Let me guess," he went on, his face turning pale, "you've already fucked her."

My spine felt injected with ice water. I was standing in the doorway of a room filled with guns and he was accusing me of having sex with his wife, and he was right. But then, like a switch had gone off in his brain, he burst out laughing, slapping me on the shoulder so hard I thought the crutch might pop out from under me.

Lifting my hand, I wiped the beaded sweat from my brow.

"Don't piss yourself, Hollywood," he said, as he pulled a key from his pants pocket. "If I had a dime for everybody, man and female, who's nailed my wife since I made the mistake of marrying her, I wouldn't be living on Orchard Grove, trust me. I'd me living on a mansion on the beach in the Caribbean." He exhaled. "But I've learned to get used to it, enjoy it even. Sometimes I get a kick out of watching her bed down with other people. But not you, Hollywood. So don't get any ideas."

His partner Carl came immediately to mind. My guess is he would *not* have enjoyed watching him get it on with Lana anymore than he'd enjoy watching me. Not if he was planning on killing her for it. My guess is he loved Lana as much as he hated her, and the conflicting emotions were driving him insane. Driving him to murder. But then what the hell was I doing? Why was I so willing to be a part of a plot to commit murder for a woman who obviously had real issues when it came to fidelity? Maybe I was just as insane as John.

Maybe I should have stopped what I was doing right there and then. Cancelled the plan I conjured with Lana. If I were a sane man, I should have quickly added it all up in my brain and called our plan (let's be clear about this: *Our* collective plan) to assassinate John quits right there and then. I should have walked, or crutched, my way out of the house altogether, grabbed Susan by the arm and demanded that we head home and never speak with the Cattivo's again. If I weren't a crazy man at that point, I would have closed up the house, and got us the hell away from Orchard Grove as fast as possible.

But I didn't move from that gunroom doorway, precisely because I could not physically get myself to do it. It was the obsession inside me, controlling me, speaking for me. I was over the top crazy. Not common sense, not my sense of right and wrong, not my ever-wavering belief in heaven for good people and hell for bad, could dissuade me from taking control of John's fate. Of playing God with his life and death. Of killing him at the roots once and forever. I wanted to do what Lana wanted me to do, and I wanted revenge for his pressing a loaded automatic against Susan's head, and I wanted to kill him right this second, even if hell fire awaited me when they laid my coffin in the cold, cold ground.

My heart pounded. My mouth went dry. My brain buzzed and my temples pounded. My Judas moment had arrived. It was now or never.

"Excuse me, John," I said, pointing to the agreed upon pistol, "that's a Colt .45 Model 1911, if I'm not mistaken. It's the exact make and model that the main character in my new script… a hell of a good detective like you… carries with him into the mean streets of Albany. I've never touched one in real life and if it's okay with you, I'd like to finally enjoy the opportunity."

He turned to me. "You get paid a God-forsaken amount of money for writing stupid stuff that includes idiots with guns and you've never actually handled a firearm up close and personal? Doesn't seem right. But then, I'm not the least bit surprised, Hollywood."

"Hey," I said, "you know what they say, John. Some shit you just can't make up."

"No truer words," he said, unlocking the case, pulling the Colt .45 off the wall. "Here you go. Don't hurt yourself."

Won't be me who gets hurt…

He reached over to where I was propped up by my crutches in the open doorway, handing me the weapon. I felt its solid weight and its power. Raising it up, I planted a bead on the big oak tree that stood directly outside the slider window behind his wood desk. I closed the lid on my left eye, bit down on my bottom lip, like some excitable boy who'd stumbled upon his dad's gun and now was about to shoot a squirrel off one of the green leafy branches.

But then I slowly retracted my shooting hand and began to do something else. Inverting the barrel, I opened my mouth and brought the barrel to within inches of it.

"What the hell are you doing?" he said, snatching the gun out of my hand.

"Oh, my bad," I said, not without a faux giggle. "You see, John, in the screenplay I'm working on now, my police detective finally dies from a self-inflicted gunshot wound to the roof of his mouth. I believe officers of the law refer to the sad action as, 'Eating your piece.'"

He gripped the Colt, its barrel aimed safely at the floor.

"That's right," he said, not without a profound exhale. "And it's the only honorable way for a good cop to go out if suicide becomes the only option."

My face began to beam. I looked one way and then the other, as if I were making sure I wasn't being watched or overheard.

"John," I said, "would you mind doing me a favor? Would you demonstrate for me how exactly one goes about eating one's piece?"

"You serious?" He looked at me with a crooked grin, eyelids at half-mast.

"Dead serious," I pressed. "I have a script to finish and I positively need to get it right or my producer is going to drop me on my ass. And I soooo need this gig, bad. Need the dough-rei-mi."

"Pot patch casheshe isn't cutting it, huh?"

I shook my head, sadly. "You're like Mister Supercop, John. You know so much and I know so little. I want to observe an expert in action, even if he's only acting the part." My face lit up. "And hey, if my new script gets produced out in Hollywood, I'll have you hired on as an expert consultant. They pay ten large per week for that shit."

His eyes went wide. "Think you could get me a part? Like for real? Beside Bruce Willis maybe. Or Stallone. He's a bad ass mofo."

I nodded, emphatically, crossed my hand over my heart. "With your good looks and solid steel frame, I know I could."

He cocked his head and smiled tightly, proudly, hopefully, his gray-white teeth grinding together at the promise of the Hollywood screen. I barely knew him, but I'd never seen him so happy. So encouraged. So looking forward to the future.

"Looks like it's time you saw the expert in action," he said. "Even if I do think you're kind of a pussy, Hollywood."

"I believe it is and I'm not really all that much of a pussy." Then, "Quickly, John, before the girls come in and ruin our fun." Bringing my hands together, making like a camera with my thumbs extended horizontally, fingers standing vertically at attention. "Action!" I said.

"First of all," he said, "you want to be sitting down for this, so that you're perfectly steady, and comfortable."

He settled himself into the swivel chair behind his desk, making a show of relaxing his shoulders, like he was already an expert at preparing himself for suicide. It dawned on me then that it was possible he'd not only contemplated the act, but that he'd even gone so far as to attempt it on more than one occasion. Without actually pulling the trigger, that is. I recalled Lana telling me that he'd demonstrated the act previously on numerous occasions before his friends, omitting the little part about the gun *not* being loaded.

"Once you're comfortable," he continued, the teacher to the student or, in this case, the actor to the camera, "you pick up the piece with your right hand, if you're right handed, which in my case, I am." He grabbed hold of the Colt, the barrel held at a sixty-five degree angle to the floor. "Then you cock a round into the chamber, like this."

It hit me then that there was the possibility of his catching the round entering into the chamber either by sight or by sound or both. Sure he was plastered, but I decided to distract him anyway, just to be sure. As he pulled back on the slide, cocking the gun, I dropped a crutch so that it fell from the doorway into the room. His eyes automatically shifted to me and the fallen crutch as the noise from the mechanical metal-workings on the Colt .45 filled the small room. It sounded almost pleasant. Solid, well-oiled craftsmanship in action even on a weapon that was more than one hundred years old. I had to wonder then, while I awkwardly bent over to pick up my crutch and return it to under my arm, if Lana had fulfilled her end of the bargain. I had to believe that the sound of a single .45 caliber round entering the chamber did not register with him since he was already convinced the barrel was empty. Call it a matter of mind over bullets.

I approached the desk, positioning myself only about a foot away from his profile. Then, making like a camera once more, I whispered, "Close up."

"Now that we're locked and loaded, in theory," he said, "you turn the gun around so that the barrel is facing you, the grip flipped over." He did that too, turning the Colt upside down, so that his thumb rested on the trigger, and the inverted grip was held steady between his fingers. "You then open your mouth wide, allow the barrel to assume the position up against the soft roof of your mouth, just like this." He opened his mouth wide, pressed the barrel against the upper palate. "And finally," he said, his voice distorted and choked by the gun barrel, "you do the deed."

But that's when he slowly pulled the barrel away from his mouth as he focused on something on the floor only inches away from the gun cabinets on the opposite side of the room. It was smear of blood. My blood. My blood from this morning. Neither of us noticed it until now.

"Is that blood on the floor?" he said. Then, looking up at me, the pistol barrel still only inches from his face. "You've been standing by the door this whole time. How did you get blood all the way over there while you were standing there? That is, unless you were here already. Maybe today, while I was at work."

Pulse throbbed, my breathing coming in short breaths, brow soaked in sweat.

"You *have* been fucking my wife, Hollywood. This whole time, you've been fucking her."

Releasing the crutches, I took hold of the inverted pistol grip with one hand, and grabbed a fist full of his hair with the other, and I rammed the metal barrel into his mouth. He reached up, grabbed hold of my neck as I shoved my index finger into the trigger guard and pressed down on his thumb.

157

PART II
FADE OUT

CHAPTER 35

THE explosion took the back third of his head off, the meat, bone, and blood slapping up against the window glass directly behind him, while scarlet arterial blood gushed out both nostrils, pulsating with the final beats of his taken-entirely-by-surprise heart. His dark eyes went wide, as if he were thinking, *How stupid can any one man be?* His stocky body relaxed after only a few seconds while his cancerous soul exited his body, and no doubt, made a beeline straight for hell.

Coming from the opposite end of the house, a scream.

Lana.

"For the love of Christ!" she shrieked. "Was that a gunshot?!"

I released my hold on the pistol and his hair, gathered up my crutches, shoving them under my armpits, my entire body trembling but also feeling as though it were levitating. For a brief second I considered wiping my prints from the gun barrel but it was now covered in John's blood. What good would my wiping anything away do?

"Lana!" I barked, pressing my fingers against the soreness in my neck. "Call 9-1-1. Your husband's had a bad accident!"

CHAPTER 36

WASN'T sure why Lana decided to play it like she didn't know what was coming. Like she hadn't played a pivotal role in making it all happen. Like she hadn't asked me to do it!

Maybe she acted innocent of the whole bloody affair because she didn't want to implicate Susan in any of this. It's possible she wanted Susan, who possessed full knowledge of the plan, to somehow remain entirely free of guilt. As if simple denial had the potential to erase any shred of truth. As if it could be equated with plausible denial. Whatever the case, as I heard the two women making their way from the back end of the house to the gunroom, I decided that the best idea was to play along.

Entering into the room, Lana caught sight of John's now smashed pumpkin of a head, and dropped to her knees on the carpeted floor.

"Oh dear God," she cried, the tears bursting from her blue eyes. "My God, John, how could you do this to me? To us?"

My wife stood behind the grieving woman. Her face had turned pale at the gruesome sight of John, and she seemed to lose her balance so that she was forced to grab hold of the solid wood doorframe to hold herself up.

Then, making an abrupt about-face, she took the corner into the adjoining bathroom where she began to vomit into the toilet.

I too began to feel sick to my stomach, like my guts had spilled out of me. Not at the sight of the blood and brain that covered the window behind John's now blown away head, but at the reality of what I'd just done. I'd not only assisted in plotting a man's death, I pulled the damn trigger. I knew full well that if, in the end, it turned out the police smelled foul play, I would face lethal injection. So would Lana. It was even possible that Susan would receive twenty or thirty years for having been privy to the plot and in turn, doing nothing about it. Sure, John put a gun to Susan's head. Sure he was going to kill Lana, and perhaps even Carl and me. But he was also a cop. And cops took care of their own. There would be no mercy for a team of cop killers. Still, inviting the police to the scene of the suicide was the next item on the grisly to-do list.

I made a cursory inventory of my body.

Was I covered in any spatter? None that I could see, almost the entirety of his brains, blood, and bone, shooting away from me out the back of his head. Once more, I caught sight of the blood smear on the floor. My blood. It could be easily explained. The surgical wounds on my foot have been bleeding, and when John invited me into his gunroom, I couldn't help but shed blood on the floor. Simple as that.

"Lana," I said, the word scraping itself from off the back of my throat, "we have to call the Albany Police Department."

She continued to sob while down on her knees, her body rocking back and forth like a penitent woman at the Wailing Wall.

"Lana," I repeated, louder this time. "We must call the police."

But she just kept right on crying like all this death and destruction had come as a tragic surprise. Susan came back in. I turned to her.

"I don't know what's come over her," I whispered. "This is what she fucking *wanted*."

My wife looked at me with hard eyes, and a coldness that cut right through me like razor sharp steel.

"Maybe it's what *you* wanted," she said.

CHAPTER 37

HOBBLING along the hallway I entered into the kitchen, opened the refrigerator door, grabbed a beer, popped the top and drank it down on the spot. Wiping away foam from my mouth with the back of my hand, I noticed Susan's cell phone set out on the counter. Acting on instinct, I grabbed it, quickly punching in the security code, which was her birthday. When the main screen appeared I went to Texts. There was a text from Lana.

No, that's wrong…

There were dozens of texts from Lana dating all the way back to early June when the Cattivo's first moved in. My brain on fire, I scrolled through some of the messages, speed reading them as I went. "I'm falling for you," Susan said in one. "Go with your feelings," Lana responded. In another text, Lana said, "I'm going to kill my husband." Susan responded with, "My husband can do it for you."

I put the phone down, not because I thought I heard Susan coming my way, but because I didn't want to see anymore. My head was spinning, my heart lodged in my throat. It was as if the earth had shifted on its rotation around the sun somehow, and gravity was no longer working for me.

What the hell was happening?

Susan had been lying to me after all, that's what was happening. So had Lana. The two have known one another far longer than they've let on. It's possible they weren't just acquaintances who occasionally carpooled to the downtown P90X class or waved to one another across the front lawns. I couldn't be sure, but judging from some of their texts, their relationship was physical. Had they set me up to kill John? Is that what this had been all about? I'd have to read all the texts to be sure.

Christ, if only I'd snuck a look at Susan's emails four or five hours ago, John would still be alive and I would be packing my bags, getting the hell out of Orchard Grove for good...

Before I snuck a look at any more texts, I needed to do something else first. The police had to be notified now. With every minute that passed, John grew colder and colder. If we waited too long, the APD forensics team would become suspicious. Right now, it still looked like an accident and that's the way I had to keep on playing it, especially now that the true nature of Lana's and Susan's relationship was slowly being revealed to me. If Lana wanted to continue to play things straight throughout the ordeal... if playing the innocent and shocked wife of a suicide was her modus operandi... then so be it. In truth, it could only help our cause. *My* cause, which was to be free of this mess.

The cordless phone was also sitting out on the counter, not far from Susan's cell phone, near the sink. I went to it and, releasing my crutch so that it leaned against the counter, I picked it up. Inhaling a calming breath, I dialed 911, pressed the phone against my ear and waited for an operator to come on the line.

"Please state the nature of your emergency," ordered the dispatcher.

"I'd like to report a suicide," I said.

"Is the victim alive and/or in need of medical assistance?"

"The victim is fucking dead."

"I see," she said. "Please stay on the line and refrain from any further foul language."

I didn't exhale until she placed me on hold.

CHAPTER 38

It took the cops, a team of EMTS, and the fire department only a few minutes to get to Orchard Grove. During that time, Lana never moved an inch from down on her knees on the gunroom floor. Susan stood out in the hall, her arms crossed tightly over her chest, her face tight as a tick, every single pore and wrinkle filled with anxiety. She wasn't speaking and neither was I, even if I did want to scream at her. She wasn't looking at me either, avoiding eye contact altogether, as though to lock eyes would be an admission of guilt, both in her complicity in the plot to kill John, and in her withholding the truth about her relationship with Lana. In the time it had taken that bullet to pass through John's brains until now, she had transformed herself into a person whom I did not recognize.

While the blue-uniformed EMTs looked over the body, checking for vitals that were obviously no longer vital, another crew of uniformed cops scoured the house. What exactly they were looking for, I had no idea. But these were the men and women who had worked with John, however briefly, and maybe it was standard operating procedure for them to make a thorough examination of the home that belonged to one of their own brothers in arms.

They also made sure to take care of Lana, escorting her from the gunroom to the kitchen where they tried to coerce a statement from her, however gently. Susan never left her side, making her tea, holding her hand, wiping her tears as they fell from her blue eyes down her smooth cheeks. It was all very dramatic and convincing. Had I been one of the cops placed in charge of questioning her, I would have said she was truly upset, truly grieving, truly shocked. But I wasn't a cop.

I was a killer.

Then Carl showed up.

The big plain clothes detective just barged through the front door, barreled his way through the cops and emergency professionals standing in the vestibule, and entered into the gunroom where his partner still sat in the swivel chair behind his desk. Carl was dressed in the same blue blazer and tie he was wearing that afternoon when he, John, and Lana got together for their little come-to-Jesus regarding his feelings for his partner's wife. For sure I smelled alcohol on his breath as he brushed past me without so much as glancing my way.

Following him into the room, I stared at what was left of his dead partner's head. He made a point to examine the blood-stained gun that was still gripped upside down in John's right hand, as though not entirely convinced his partner managed to perform the ultimate final act of self-destruction on his own. By then Lana had come back into the room, her eyes still filled with tears, a pink tissue crushed in her hand. The tension between the two was almost too much to bear, even for me.

After a beat he turned to her, staring her down with big brown eyes that were no longer hidden by aviator sunglasses. She returned his gaze and sniffled.

"He was always so careful," she said. "Even when he was messing around… he was careful, you know?"

"It was an accident," I said, picturing myself grabbing John's hair, shoving the piece in his mouth, pulling the trigger. I swallowed something that felt and tasted like a brick. "He was showing me his collection. He insisted on demonstrating how a cop eats his piece. He obviously didn't know the gun was loaded."

Carl turned quick, shot me a look, then reached out with his hand, placed it on Lana's shoulder.

"Don't stay in here anymore," he said.

Wiping her eyes with the tissue, Lana walked out, as ordered.

Then, turning back to the couple of forensics cops who were also standing in the room on either side of the body, their hands covered in blue latex gloves, Carl said, "Tag him and bag him, for Christ sake's. Then get him the hell out of here already."

He took a step toward me, eyed me once more.

"I'll be in touch," he said, and the way he said it, made my blood turn to ice.

Brushing past me for a second time, he left the house through the front door.

SNAPSHOT

It takes an enormous amount of energy and concentration to keep from gagging. Her stomach muscles are convulsing, her chest heaving as she watches two separate beams of bright white Maglite dancing on the gravelly riverbank. When she begins to make out voices along with the stomping of boot heels, she knows that two police officers are standing only a few feet away from her.

"Whaddaya think, Detective Miller?" says the first cop.

"What do I think?" says, Miller. "I think two things are possible here, Brad. Either we've scared away the perp. Or, we scared away somebody who just happened to come upon that mutilated body back there. That's what I think."

"And he or she ran away because he or she don't want to be accused of no homicide, ain't I right?"

"Only reason people hang out in these woods at night is to shoot up. No junkie in my book is taking a chance on getting snagged for murder one. 'Sides, Brad, whole thing doesn't fit the profile. The North Albany Mauler knows what he's doing. He's methodical and precise in the method and manner by which he kills. No way he'd be caught out in the open like that. Having studied this case for three years, I suspect our killer…our Mauler…is white, single, fairly well off, *and gay."*

"That the shit they teach you in college, Miller? I remember when cops didn't go to no college, me included."

"Times're changing. It's the 1980s. Computers can help us narrow down the playing field. Soon everyone will have a computer in their house, access to more information than is stored in the Library of Congress, right at their fingertips."

"Sounds like science fiction. But then, I guess everybody's got cable TV now. Fifty freakin' channels and a Home Box Office station that shows movies. It's like the Jetson's."

"High technology is advancing right now... right this very second... as we jerk off on this riverbank doing absolutely nothing."

"Okay then, young Detective Miller, your call. What the fuck do we do now?"

"Let's get back, Brad. I wanna take a closer look at that poor young man who's sliced from ear to ear."

"But what about down there in that concrete hole in the ground? Shouldn't we check that out?"

"The culvert? Good idea. But be quick."

She panics. She has no choice but to try and make herself invisible. But how exactly? The tubular culvert is partially filled with fluid. Rancid, toxic fluid that contains God knows what. Instant cancer is what she's breathing. And now she's got to soak in it? She hears footsteps outside the tube. No choice. Lays herself out, face-first down into the filthy water, hopes for the best.

CHAPTER 39

A **FEW** minutes later a man dressed in plain clothes entered through the front door. When one of the uniformed officers identified me as the man who'd been with Detective Cattivo in the gunroom when he shot himself, Plain Clothes approached me.

"I'm Senior Homicide Detective Nick Miller," he said, holding out his right hand. "The deceased worked with me at the APD. You're the writer? The movie guy? I understand you were with him when the, ahhhh, accident occurred."

Why isn't Carl in charge of the investigation? Maybe Carl, as John's partner, is too close to the victim. Maybe the situation is too emotional for him. Maybe his judgment would be called into question, especially if he was sleeping with the deceased's wife…

I took Miller's hand, shook it. The hand was cold but strong.

"Yes," I said. "I was there. In the room. Unfortunately. He insisted on demonstrating."

"Demonstrating a suicide?"

"Eating his piece. He was insistent, Detective. It was his idea, his gun, his bullet. Hell could I do?"

He took back his hand, shoved both hands into the pockets on his professionally cleaned and pressed khaki trousers. Looking down, his eye caught something.

"You've got some blood on your wrist," he said. "Lots of blood inside a brain. It tends to spatter. Ever see the Zapruder Film… JFK's murder?"

I swallowed something cold and bitter, released my crutch, raised up my hand. On the wrist, several specs of blood. How in God's name was he able to see it? I guess he was trained to notice such things. Trained to spot even minute traces of blood.

He got the attention of one of the forensics people working inside the gunroom. A woman. He asked her to step out and take a picture of my wrist, which she did. He then gave her my name, which she jotted down in a notebook before making her way back into the room.

"Look," he went on, looking downwards, taking notice of my foot, "I'm going to take a decent look at the deceased before they ship him out. You can either come along or wait right here for me."

"Which would you prefer?" I said, my mouth still dry and pasty from frayed nerves.

"You gotta ask?" he said.

I followed him into the gunroom.

Miller was a tall guy. Thin and wiry, like a life-long competitive runner. Maybe even a marathoner. I pegged him for his mid-fifties. Getting on in cop years anyway. He had all his hair, but it was cut Marine Corps short, and what I took to once be sandy blond had by now morphed into an almost snow white gray. His face was narrow, if not concave at the cheeks, and shaved close. But then, I'm not too sure the fair-skinned Miller could grow a beard if he wanted to.

His baby blue summer-weight button-down was ironed and immaculate, as was his yellow necktie, which was knotted perfectly under his strong chin. His blazer was also lightweight and only when I looked for it, could I find his sidearm, which was nicely concealed by fabric that more than likely had been specially tailored to accommodate the piece.

I only point all this out because he struck me as the polar opposite of John Cattivo who, in life, was as obvious about his distaste for neatness as he was his love of guns and love/hatred for himself and his wife.

The same two forensics officers were still working on John. The young woman who'd taken a photo of my wrist was still snapping away at John's head. When Miller walked in, she shot him a look and issued him a pleasant smile, as if they were two coworkers mingling around the water cooler. Funny how commonplace violent death is to some people who are in the business.

Miller didn't start right in on examining his coworker. In fact, he didn't give John's shattered head a second look, as if the carnage that painted the wall and window behind him were just another aspect of the interior decorating, and a mundane aspect at that.

Instead he took some time to admire the impressive Cattivo firearms collection.

"I'm aware Cattivo was a gun nut," he said contemplatively. "But I wasn't aware to what extent. Christ, there's gotta be three-hundred grand hanging on these walls." Then, turning to face the dead detective. "And a whole lot of *Oops* spread out over that wall." He smiled. "At least, *Oops* is your story. Isn't that right, Mr. Forrester?"

I felt the ice water once more fill up my spine. I didn't like the way Miller said that. But then, I guess that was his job. To make me uncomfortable. To make me slip up if indeed, there was a good reason for me to slip up.

He took one more good look at the guns, eyeing them up and down. "I suppose the Missus will sell off the collection now. Make herself enough money to buy up some property down in Florida." He shifted his focus to me. "I'm told she enjoys her sunbathing." He followed up with a wink of his eye. "Surprised I've never heard of anyone at the APD fielding a complaint from one of the neighbors."

"She's pretty well hidden back there," I said, knowing immediately that I should not have.

"Really," he said, shooting me a gaze. "You speak as an experienced watcher."

"Not really," I said. "I'm the next door neighbor. I'm home all day when most of the neighborhood is at work or school."

"That so?" he said, turning slowly back to the guns.

After a time, he peeled himself from the gun case, dismissed the two forensic cops. Then, when we were alone, he walked around the desk, took his first good look at John. He took his time examining the corpse, at one point, positioning himself so that he faced the desk the same way Cattivo faced the desk when he put the barrel of the Colt .45 in his mouth moments before spotting the blood stain on the floor. After a contemplative few beats, he shoved both hands back into his trouser pockets, and came back around the desk.

"Say, I've got one for you," he said. "What do you call a man with a shovel impaled in his head?" He turned toward John's busted up head, then back to me.

"I don't know," I said.

"Doug," he said, with a grin. "Get it?"

"Yeah," I said. "Ha. I get it." But I didn't feel much like joking. "Can we be done with this now? I'm starting to feel sick. And to be honest, I could use a drink."

He lifted up his hand as if to tell me to hold on, take some time out to smell the roses.

"And what do you call a man who *doesn't* have a shovel impaled in his brains?"

Fuck, when is this gonna end?

I shook my head.

"Doug*las*," he said like Doug-*less*, while bursting out in laughter. "That one always busts me up."

"Must be John's head-shot made you think of it," I said.

He nodded, bit down on his lip. "Sorry to appear flippant in the face of such serious circumstances, Mr. Forrester," he said. "But I'm sure as a script writer, you understand the need for comic relief now and again."

"Oh most definitely," I said.

"So then," he said, pulling a notepad and pen from the interior pocket on his blazer, "I'd like for you to recount exactly what happened here this evening."

"I already did that for the officers," I swallowed.

He smiled politely, issued me another wink.

"Now you get to do it for me," he said. "If you don't mind."

I felt myself hesitating while I locked eyes on John's face and head. His eyes had since been closed by the forensics people, but I still felt them staring me down. The stare said, *"I'm gonna get you for this, Hollywood!"*

Miller must have sensed my apprehension. My discomfort. My ever-growing paranoia…

"We can go somewhere else if you'd feel more comfortable," he suggested.

"You mind?" I said.

He waved for the forensics cops to come back in, adding, "We're gonna take a walk, guys. Bag Detective Cattivo and get him a date for a slice and dice at the Albany Med morgue. Looks like you're all done here."

"Roger that, Detective Miller," said the ponytailed woman with the digital camera. "So it's a suicide then?"

"Until I say it ain't, Laura," Miller said.

"Beer later?" she said.

"Most certainly," he said.

I had trouble picturing Detective Miller having a private life, as though he were a police robot that someone unplugged at the end of the day. He was about to walk out of the room when he spotted something by the gun cases. He stepped over to the case, bent down at the knees, and stared at the same bloodstain that John discovered.

"That's mine," I said, immediately wishing I hadn't spoken up at all.

"What?" he said, looking up at me.

"That's my blood," I said. "My foot."

"So you were standing right here when he shot himself?"

Pulse picking up. Brain buzzing.

"Yes," I lied. "I suppose I was."

He nodded, stared at the stain once more.

"Looks kind of like old blood," he said. "Not blood that would have stained the floor just a few minutes ago. But then, hey, I could be wrong." He stood. "Get a sample of this, will you Laura? Try and get somebody to tell you how old it is."

I wanted to scream. But what the hell could I do?

He approached me, his face beaming with a smile as he squeezed out the door, careful not to knock into one of my crutches.

"Let's go get some air outside," he said.

"There's a deck out back."

"The deck for sun worshipping," he said. "Tell you what, I'll even let you enjoy a cold beer while we chat."

CHAPTER 40

CRUTCHING across the kitchen floor, I gazed upon Lana and Susan who were seated at the round kitchen table. Lana had a blanket wrapped around her shoulders as if the winter had arrived early. She also appeared to be shivering. Although I tried to capture her attention by clearing a dead frog from my throat, she wouldn't look up at me or do anything to acknowledge my presence. All she could manage, or so it seemed, was to keep her face down, her blue eyes peering into her cup of tea like it had the power to transport her a million miles away from Orchard Grove.

However, for the first time since John's killing, Susan made a point of peering directly at me, issuing me a stare that was both blank and stone cold silent.

"How is she?" I asked.

"How would you be, Ethan?" she groused, while wrapping her right arm around Lana, hugging her tightly.

Behind me stood Detective Miller, who was witnessing the exchange. I wondered if he could sense the pounding of my heart. Once more, I had to ask myself, *What the hell is happening here?* My stomach was tied up in a knot. I knew we had to make things look realistic in front of the cops. Like whatever happened to John was truly an accident. But this was taking things too far. By ignoring me or snapping at me, the women were making it look like I actually shoved the barrel of the .45 into Cattivo's mouth and pulled the trigger. But then, that's exactly what happened. What I mean is, they had no way of seeing me shove the gun barrel into his mouth. And even if they did, it's what Lana wanted. It's what she needed if she was going to live. If I was going to keep on living.

Miller pulled ahead of me, descended to the two steps into the playroom, opened the sliding door.

"Mr. Forrester," he said, "time is getting tight."

"Coming," I said, hobbling down into the family room, and out the open door, the many framed faces of John that hung on the wall staring me down the entire way.

INSTEAD of standing or sitting, he leaned his left thigh over the edge of the table while planting his right foot flat on the wood deck. That way he was neither standing nor sitting. He also crossed his arms over his chest, that little notebook still gripped in one hand, the pen in the other. If he were one of the characters in my scripts, I would have described him as tough, neat, confident, experienced.

I took the chair beside him, leaning my crutches against the tabletop. I didn't realize it at first, but my hands were trembling. When I looked up at Miller, he was staring at my hands.

"Your first dead body, huh?" he said.

"Yes," I said, knowing full well that the killer inside me was responsible for that dead body, and for the trembling hands.

"You know, this place… Orchard Grove… wasn't always a sleepy peaceful suburban neighborhood."

"How so?"

"Back in the early Eighties, more than a dozen men and boys disappeared or were found dead, including the original owner of the apple orchard that once occupied this very spot."

"You mean, like a serial killer?"

"Who was never found. We called him the North Albany Mauler. It's a case that didn't go cold, but that froze solid. One of the first cases I worked right out of college for the APD. My absolute first as a young detective. And one of the only cases, it turns out, that I wasn't able to solve."

"Things like that must come back to haunt your dreams," I said. "A serial killer in little old Albany."

"Crazy isn't it?" he said. "But let me tell you something. The first body I came across… the Mauler's first victim… not only made my hands tremble just like yours, but I found myself tossing my cookies for a period of about forty-eight hours. It wasn't the sight of a decapitated body that got to me, so much as the smell of him. I could almost taste the death. It was a taste that would not go away for a long time. I guess I still taste it. Only difference between then and now, is that I'm used to it."

We pondered that for a minute while I wished for a stiff drink.

"Now," he said, after a time. "Start from the beginning. From the time you arrived here tonight."

I did as he told me. Recounted the evening's events from the moment we arrived at the Cattivo house, to the moment he arrived back home drunk, to my questioning him about his willingness to teach me about guns and how they work, to his agreeing to show me his collection. Then I got to the part about his demonstrating a cop suicide by eating his piece. Something I needed for a crucial scene in the script I was presently writing.

Miller smiled, but it wasn't out of happiness. More like an inquisitive smirk.

"Why ask him to go through the motions of demonstrating something like that when you're certainly smart enough to imagine how it's done? You make your living from writing scripts, am I right?"

I nodded. "Research from the Internet is one thing. To see something live, up close, and personal is another thing altogether."

There was a pause filled by the sound of a pair of squirrels rustling in the apple tree beyond the fence.

He said, "You sure got the up close and personal treatment, all right. That blood on your arm is the proof."

I resisted the urge to look at my wrist.

He said, "I suppose Cattivo must have derived some sort of perverse kick out of displaying his own murder for your benefit. How drunk was he?"

"Staggering," I said. Then, "Listen, Detective Miller, obviously I wouldn't have asked him to stick the barrel of a gun in his mouth if I knew it was loaded. But yes, he seemed hell bent on showing me how it was done. Almost like he wanted to do it for real. Like he had a death wish." I was pouring it on, for obvious reasons.

Biting down on his thin bottom lip, the detective cocked his head, shrugged his shoulders.

"Or so we can only assume at this point," he said. "Because even from where I'm standing, I could see that his two top teeth were broken off at the mid-point. Holy Christ in a breadbasket, he must have really wanted to show you how it was done." Then, leaning into me, like he needed to communicate something under his breath. "I'm gonna be frank with you, Mr. Forrester. Not a lot of people on the force were too crazy about ole' John. He was kind of an asshole, if you know what I mean. Not even his partner liked him."

I felt a jolt in my stomach. Lana's warning came to mind. If we didn't figure out a way to make John dead first, he would kill her for sleeping with Carl. For breaking the cop cardinal rule.

"His partner was just here," I said. "Maybe you saw him coming out on your way into the house?"

He shook his head.

"Carl Pressman," he said. "He say anything to you about the situation? Anything at all?"

"Not a whole lot," I said, all the time wondering if Miller knew about his affair with Lana. "He just gave me a look like I personally just blew his partner's brains out, then he mumbled something about his being in touch soon."

"He seem visibly upset?"

"Angry, I guess," I said. "But he didn't seem to be shedding any tears for his partner."

I might have told Miller about the confrontation John, Lana, and Carl had out on the deck earlier this afternoon, but I decided to let it go for now. It would only further implicate me as a voyeur.

He bowed his head, said, "Like I told you, John wasn't too well liked." He finished with a wink of his eye, like he and I now shared a secret, and having shared that secret, we now possessed a common bond. Cop to script writer, script writer to cop.

Miller didn't stop there.

"Word up on the street," he added, "is that John wasn't very nice to the old lady. You know, he'd wave around that APD hand cannon of his like it was a toy. Fact is, he was reprimanded more than a couple of times at the Poughkeepsie PD for mishandling his service weapon. My guess is Carl was making a check on the scene of his old partner's unfortunate demise just to make certain Lana hadn't actually been the one to pull the trigger herself. Something she'd probably fantasized about in the past."

"Guess I never figured that," I said, now feeling somewhat encouraged by his logic. "He ever shoot anyone with his service weapon? By accident?"

Flashing through my brain, Cattivo holding his automatic on my wife and his, just last night out on my back deck.

"Good question, Mr. Forrester. Say, you don't mind my calling you, Ethan, do you? Too many syllables to get through with Mister Forrester."

"Not at all."

"Well, Ethan, in answer to your query, as far as I know, Cattivo never shot anyone he didn't mean to shoot. But he has shot and killed several perps who threatened his life with firearms of their own. Mostly inner-city situations. In Los Angeles and Poughkeepsie."

"Go figure."

"Yes, go figure. Detective Cattivo was pretty good at getting himself in trouble with his gun. Did you know some cops can go their entire career without ever having to draw their firearm in the line of duty even once?"

"I wasn't aware of that."

"It would make for a pretty boring crime flick I would imagine, should you decide to write about a cop like that. Now wouldn't it?"

"Sure. But if John was so much trouble, why hire him on?"

"It's Albany, Ethan. We have enough trouble filling the force with top cops as it is. And despite his trigger-happy ways, John was a very good cop. An experienced cop. Hard to come by."

"Now it'll be even harder," I said, knowing I shouldn't have.

He fell quiet for a moment. If he were a smoker, this would have been the perfect time to pull out his pack, shake one loose, light it with a silver-plated Zippo. Instead he slapped a mosquito off the back of his neck with his little notebook. Bringing the notebook around front, he flicked the remains of the insect off the cover.

"I'll tell you something else, Ethan," he said, after a beat. "In confidence, of course."

Raising my hand, I made the sign-of-the-cross.

He said, "From what I also understand, Mrs. Cattivo hasn't been all that faithful to her husband." He followed with another wink of the same eye.

Pulse elevating. "You don't say."

"I do, and I'm sorry to bring it up at a time like this when his body isn't even cold yet. But apparently, Lana's what we describe at the APD as a player. Do you know what a player is, Ethan?"

"Of course I do," I said. "I lived in LA for a while."

If our dialogue was something from out of a 1950s black and white film noir, I would have added "copper" to the end of my sentence.

"Hey, that's pretty funny," he said though a faux laugh. Then, leaning into me once more. "The reason they had to pull up stakes downstate is over her numerous affairs, I'm told. One of them having occurred with John's own partner at the time."

My stomach muscles bunched up and my mouth went dry. Did he know about Lana and Pressman? Was he playing with my head to see if I'd back down and confess something? I should have taken him up on that offer of a beer while we chatted.

"What's any of this got to do with what happened tonight?"

Cocking his head over his shoulder, he said, "Not a whole lot, from a direct perspective. But indirectly, her actions could bear some significant weight. That is, he still loved her."

"I see."

For a time, we listened to the squirrels chasing tail on the trees in the heart of darkness.

"Mind if I ask you a personal question, Ethan?"

"You're going to ask me whether I give you permission or not."

He snickered again. "You know, you writers. You really are sharp, I tell you. Anyway, here goes. Do you have any reason to believe that Lana was cheating on John?"

My stomach went from feeling tight to feeling like it had just been pounded with a sledgehammer. Blood filled my face. I was sure it had because I could feel the heat in the skin and flesh. I was certain that I was blushing and that it must have shown beneath the scruffy five-day growth in the yellow, deck-mounted LED lanterns. A mosquito stuck its pincer into my forearm. When I slapped it, the blood it stored in its belly spattered and stained my skin.

"Cat got your tongue, Ethan?"

I cleared my throat, scratched the itchy bump on my forearm. In my head, I saw myself fucking Lana on my dining room table, Susan watching from outside the living room picture window.

"No," I lied. "I have no reason to believe she was cheating on him."

His face went stone stiff. It showed no sign of happiness, sadness, anger, melancholy, or anything at all resembling human emotion even if it was constructed of human flesh and blood. He slid his leg off the table, unfolded his arms, stood up straight and tall. In the semi-darkness of the deck, he reminded me of *Dirty Harry*.

"That's all for now, Mr. Forrester," he said, returning the notepad and pen back to his pocket. He hadn't written anything in it. "I'll be in touch."

"That's what Carl said."

He gave me a look. "Excuse me?"

"That's what Carl said... I'll be in touch."

"Oh," he said. "Must be a cop thing."

He went for the sliding glass door, but stopped just short of it. He turned.

"Oh and do me a favor, Mr. Forrester," he said. "Please don't leave town for anything until I give you the green light. Okay?"

"Am I suspected of something?"

"Why do you ask?"

His question took me by surprise. I had nothing for him. Nothing to say in response or, in this case, my defense. He made a pistol with his left hand, aimed the extended index finger at me.

"One more thing," he said. "Your wife, Susan. She and Lana... have they been friends for a while? Did they know one another prior to Lana moving into Orchard Grove two months ago?"

"Why do you ask, Detective Miller?" I said, tossing his question right back at him.

He said, "Well, they seem rather, ummmm, intimate, if you grasp my meaning."

"They only met a few days ago," I said, despite recalling the text messages I found in Susan's cell phone earlier.

His gray eyes lit up.

"That so," he said. "Extraordinary. Perhaps they've been soul mates for all eternity and only now found each other."

"Maybe," I said.

"Enjoy the beautiful summer weather, Mr. Forrester," he said, as he slid open the glass door. "Before you know it, it will be fall and apple picking season."

"That's right," I said. "An apple a day keeps the coroner away."

"Very good," he said. "You like apples, Mr. Forrester?"

"Who doesn't?"

"Some people consider them the true forbidden fruit."

"Adam and Eve."

"A God-*damned* pair if ever there was one," he said before stepping through the door, sliding it closed.

I turned and looked out onto the dark yard, and nearly collapsed from the sheer weight of my guilt.

CHAPTER 41

SAT outside as the police and the EMTs left the scene along with John's black-bagged body. The night was warm and clear and my eyes were attracted to the moon. It was a waxing moon. I stared into its luminescent whiteness and I saw the face of Detective Miller. The hard, lifeless face told me in no uncertain terms that he wasn't buying into the Cattivo suicide story for even a minute. Or, he wasn't about to buy it until he'd exhausted every possibility of foul play first. Christ, how was I to know his two front teeth would break when I shoved the automatic into his mouth? And what about that blood stain on the floor? What if tests come back proving I was standing in that room hours earlier? It might prove that I had planned out the murder to look like a suicide. That would be murder one. Premeditated murder.

No choice but to keep playing dumb.

"It's a suicide until I say it ain't..."

The door slid open and Susan stepped out. She was holding a beer in her hand, which she handed to me. I stared down at it, feeling its coldness against my palm and the pads of my fingers. At this point, it seemed like a gift from God even if it was a small offering from my wife. But at least she was being nice to me now.

"How's Lana?" I said. "Or don't I get to ask?"

She folded her arms, as if she were cold.

"Taking it badly," she said. "But then, you're already aware of that."

I popped the tab on the can, took a drink.

"I'm confused," I said. "Did she or did she not want to see her husband dead? Did she or did she not set him up to die by placing a bullet inside the chamber of that Colt .45? Did she or did she not insist that I encourage him to demonstrate precisely how a suicidal cop eats his piece? Was she or was she not convinced John was going to kill her... kill her tonight?"

She exhaled, nodded, stared down at her sandaled feet.

"Be careful what you wish for, Ethan," she said. "As bad as he was to her, he was still her husband. She knows you've fallen in love with her. I know you've fallen in love with her."

"You've fallen too. But I love you at the same time. Do you think she loves us back?"

She raised her head, looked me in the eyes.

"I try not to think about it. I only know that as strange as the whole thing sounds, it's happened."

I thought about Susan's cell phone and the many texts she and Lana had been sending one another over the past few weeks. But now was not the time to start lobbing accusations that would only make my wife angry with me and put Lana on the defensive. Better to let things play out for a while. I had bigger fish to fry than worrying about who's been screwing who for the past two months. Like keeping myself off death row, for instance.

I said, "That plainclothes cop who just left... Detective Miller... he isn't so convinced it was a suicide."

"Well, it wasn't a suicide, was it?"

I shot her a look while she bit down on her bottom lip. I wanted to slap her face. But then, she was right. It wasn't a suicide. Not at all.

"Miller admits John was a real asshole," I said. "But not the type of asshole to blow his brains out at this stage of the life and career game, even though he was married to a woman with a known history of adultery."

She stared down at me with unblinking eyes. "There's no way he can suspect anything. It's a clear case of negligence. He was playing with his gun and he shot himself. Happens all the time. That's our story before and that's our story now."

Earlier inside the house, you and Lana made me feel like you were double-crossing me, blaming me not for John's suicide, but his murder...

She looked away, silently for a moment, the quiet filled up with the buzz of mosquitoes and the squirrels in the apple tree. But then she did something that made me feel a little better. She reached out, placed her hand on my shoulder. Tenderly.

"Don't worry," she said. "It's all going to be okay. Soon this will all be behind us and we can move away from Orchard Grove forever."

"Who exactly will move away from here? Just you and me?"

"You, me, and Lana," she said. "Just like we planned."

In my head, I heard and felt the report of that automatic and the back of John's head spattering against the window and the wall.

Susan turned, went for the door.

"Susan," I said.

"Yes?"

"Earlier on," I said, "why were you so cold to me? You made me feel almost guilty... Guilty of cold blooded murder."

Her beautiful face lit up in the moonlight.

"But aren't you, Killer?" she said.

CHAPTER 42

MY foot throbbed. I should have had it elevated and iced. Instead I was drinking beer out on the porch of the man I murdered. Who the fuck was I fooling? Myself, and that's all. At least, that's the way I felt. Sure, Lana helped me plan out John's death. She even instigated it. She needed John dead or face her own demise. And sure Susan knew all about it. But I was alone in this thing. What's more, if it ever came out that John had forced my wife to perform some particularly dirty deeds with Lana at gunpoint, Miller could peg me with motive. Motive and means.

After I finished my beer, Susan came back out, told me she would be staying with Lana tonight to keep her company. I asked her how Lana could even contemplate staying in that house of horrors for one more minute. But my wife just shook her head and explained that it's precisely what she wanted. Even stranger than the thought of sleeping in that house where her husband's brains were just blown out the back of his head, Lana wanted to reenter the gunroom to clean up the carnage. Wipe it clean of blood and brains. According to Susan, it would somehow make Lana feel better to play an active role in cleaning the place up. It would make her feel as though John's death were real and not some bizarre dream that occurred earlier this evening. She could deal with the real. Put it behind her, eventually.

I might have suggested to her that Miller wouldn't think highly of her messing with a probable crime scene. But then, forensics had already scoured the place, so their evidence, whether it proved fruitful or not, was already collected, the necessary photos, already snapped. I also recalled Miller stating explicitly that his job was already "done here." My guess is that the detective was throwing Lana a bone, cop to cop-wife. Otherwise, no way he'd allow her to sleep in the house.

"Why don't you go home and get some sleep," Susan said. "In the morning, everything will seem more optimistic."

"Optimistic," I snickered. What I wanted to tell her is I felt like my balls were trapped in a vice that was only getting tighter. No optimism in that.

"Goodnight," I said, pulling myself up by my crutches.

"Goodnight, Killer," she said, leaning into me, planting a kiss on my cheek that might have come from my sister if only I had a sister.

But I didn't leave right away.

When she was gone I stood outside on the deck looking into the dining room and kitchen through the big picture window. I saw something that shocked me, but given everything that had gone down that day and during the previous two days, shouldn't have shocked me at all. I saw my wife take Lana into her arms and hold her tightly. Lovingly. For a time, Lana just seemed like she needed a shoulder to cry on. Someone strong and understanding. At least, that's what the once-upon-a-time-dedicated husband in me wanted to believe.

After a few beats, I saw Lana lift her head and open her pouty mouth just a little. She and Susan gravitated toward each other, their mouths connecting. They kissed as passionately as two lovers can possibly kiss, each of them running their hands through one another's hair, their tongues connecting, playing, exploring. After a time, Lana began to unbutton Susan's blouse, while Susan lowered both her hands down to Lana's bear thighs, and then slowly drew them up and into the underside of her short skirt.

I turned away then, hiding myself from the window. My heart was beating fast again, and my throat felt like a rock had lodged itself inside it. What in God's name was going on here? It was one thing for two girls to make out while their men were present and a loaded gun was involved. Or, *a* man, at least. But it was something else when they decided to enter into the sexual act on their own without the man or men.

Susan… *"I'm falling for you."*

Lana… *"Go with it."*

In my overheated brain, it meant only one thing: Not only were they falling in love, but they were already in love, and what's more, they were cutting me out of the equation.

I made my way across the two fence lines, my foot throbbing, pulsing. Entering into the house by way of the back sliding glass doors, I flicked on the overhead lights, navigated the couple of steps up into the dining room, and poured a shot of whiskey. I downed that and poured another and drank that. Then I made my way to the bathroom off the master bedroom. All I wanted to do was wash up, clean my hands and face of John Cattivo's blood, then get in bed and sleep a dreamless sleep for a thousand nights.

Pulling off my button down shirt without bothering to unbutton it, I stood at the bathroom sink in my white undershirt and stared at myself in the mirror. I stared back at tired, bloodshot eyes, and a scruffy face that had seen better days. The roundness of my face that once upon a time seemed so youthful was now the precise feature that made me appear worn and old. The weight of guilt is said to be unbearable given time. But only a few hours had passed since John blew his brains out…rather, I blew them out for him…and already I felt like I was hefting ten times my own weight on each shoulder. That was the first time it occurred to me that it might be a good idea to give Miller a call and confess the whole damned affair. A confession might put me, Lana, and Susan behind bars for a lot of years, but at least the guilt would be gone.

I turned on the cold water, splashed my face with it. My reflection stared back at me, dripping with water. I was the drowning man. Drowning in my own guilt, greed, and paranoia. Maybe I should have added a little anger to the soup as well. More than a little anger. Anger at Lana and Susan.

At myself.

I'd bitten the apple, and one way or another, I would pay the price. Maybe not in this life, but in the next.

Turning off the water, I pulled the towel from the rack beside the sink, dried my face. Tossing the towel onto the counter, I looked back up into the mirror. It was then I made out the reflection of a second face framed inside the glass.

SNAPSHOT

THE beam of Maglite shines into the Culvert. But with her eyes closed, she can't see it, so much as sense the powerful light seeping through the water and through her thin-skinned eyelids. The water is foul, and it seeps into her nostrils. She can't hold her breath forever. She needs oxygen. She can't help herself. She begins to gag and choke. No choice but to lift her head from out of the water.

"Help me!" she screams.

Brad the cop is startled to hear the voice and see the female body it belongs to.

"Detective Miller!" he shouts. "You'd better get down here right away!"

CHAPTER 43

FOR a guy with a bum foot, I swung around fast.

He was standing just outside the door to the master bedroom in the dark.

Detective Miller.

"Hope you don't mind my intrusion," he said. "Your wife said I'd find you here. I rang the doorbell, called your cell. No answer either way."

Once my pulse leveled off, I slid my crutches under my arms, hobbled out of the bathroom, my face and hair still damp.

"You gave me a real start," I said, wondering how he knew he might find Susan next door. Perhaps he simply deduced it. Or maybe he wanted to check out the gunroom one final time.

He smiled that smile again. The one that wasn't really human.

"You must be pretty jumpy after this evening's drama," he said, his hands shoved in his trouser pockets, the grip on his service automatic visible. Then, "Got anything to drink in this place?"

"Thought cops weren't supposed to drink on duty."

He looked at me with that cold, gray-eyed stare.

"Wouldn't you?" he said.

We sat down across from one another at the dining room table. I set a drinking glass in front of him, and one in front of me. Rather than drag myself up and out of my chair every few minutes, I set the bottle of Jack on the table between the typewriter and the bowl of apples, easy access. Sitting myself down clumsily, I grabbed the bottle by its neck, poured the first round, set the bottle back down, hard.

He said, "Must suck having a leg banged up like that, bleeding all the time. How'd it happen?"

"Blame the mileage," I said. "The football came back to haunt me. So did all that jogging. I split the plate down in the Amazon doing some research for a script. They put four permanent screws in the plate and removed a portion of the index toe. But they tell me I'll be as good as new when I heal."

"Try and stay off it," he said.

"Thanks for the advice. But you ever gonna tell me what this surprise visit is all about?" I said, after a beat. "I just got through talking to you."

He drank his shot, went to pour another almost immediately, as if the act of emptying your glass and refilling it were not two separate acts but instead, one single fluid motion.

"You mind?" he said, taking hold of the bottle.

"You're the cops," I said. "Why should I mind?"

More of that steely smile.

"I like you, Ethan," he said. "You've got spunk. Wish more of my support staff were like you."

"We're back to a first name basis. You must want something from me."

"Course I do. Me and the great Empire State of New York." He poured a shot, glanced at my glass, saw that it was full, capped the bottle and set it back down in the same exact spot in which it previously rested. "Why else would I be here?"

We were dancing around one another and he knew it. Feeling one another out, waiting for someone to take the first jab. How did the old saying go? Sometimes in life you're a hammer and other times you're the nail. I don't have to tell you what I felt like sitting there across from him.

I drank some whiskey. Half the shot. The booze sank into me, warm, strong, and good. But the man who sat before me didn't make me feel so good. Considering the circumstances anyway.

"So what can I help you with, Miller?"

"Ethan," he said, "how well have you and your wife been getting along as of late?"

I could almost feel my eyes go wide. I was sure he noticed them, since he was no doubt trained to notice such reactions. It was exactly the kind of involuntary response I needed to get under control if I was going to weather what was surly going to be a prolonged storm of police questioning over the course of the next few days and nights. That is, until Miller was convinced without an ounce of a doubt that Cattivo's death from eating his piece had been an unfortunate accident. Or perhaps a fortunate one, depending upon whom you asked.

"You want the truth?" I posed.

"Like you said, I'm the cops. Downtown, on the State Street hill, the fat guys in the black robes locked inside the white marble building with the big pillars out front, those are the judges."

I sipped a little more Jack, thought about Susan in bed with Lana right this very second.

"Okay, Miller," I said. "Have it your way. Susan and I have seen better days. Feel better?"

"And why are the better days behind you? She's an awfully attractive woman, if you don't mind my saying."

Miller, dancing, jabbing, provoking…

"Do I have to tell you this stuff? What's it got to do with Cattivo?"

"Who said it has to have anything to do with it?"

"Isn't that why you're here, interrupting what I hoped would be a week-long coma?"

He nodded. "In part. You see… and you might appreciate this as script writer who's written a few shoot 'em-ups for the silver screen… but in order to get at a certain truth, a detective needs to more or less skirt around the issue, kind of like the Indians will circle the wagons, hoping to force someone or something out in the open."

"In this case, a truth or something directly related to the truth."

He slapped the table, shocking my system. "Exactly. Only in this case, the truth is not established. The truth is still a question. The truth is still a question. That question being, did John Cattivo really, truly, kill himself? Or was he somehow coerced or set up?"

"I see," I said, my beating heart inching its way back up into my throat.

He drank the rest of his drink. I drank mine. He poured us two more.

"Now," he said, "why are you and the wife not getting on so well lately?"

I stared into the golden brown booze, wishing I could drown in it. Since I had no choice but to sit there and take his jabs, I decided to play a little rope-a-dope and give him what he wanted. I'd stretch the truth just a little to maybe get his mind off me and me alone. Maybe if I spread around a little of the suspicion, all eyes wouldn't be on me. After all, it was Susan who was sleeping with Lana right now. Not me. Not after what I'd done for the blonde beauty. Not after putting my life on the line. I was getting screwed over while Susan and Lana gladly screwed one another.

"Why else do couples start to fight?" I said. "Money, or the lack of it. House in foreclosure. My work in the crapper. Not much to say to each other anymore that doesn't end up in an argument. The wife screaming at me, hitting me, clawing at me, telling me I'm no good. Can't even support her. All washed up. Useless. Telling me she's gonna find someone else to give her multiple orgasms. You know, the usual shit."

He nodded like I'd gone all TMI on him.

"My wife died on the operating table," he said. "I wouldn't know."

"I'm sorry," I said.

"Don't be. Because you're not, and that's okay. Why should you be? You didn't know her. You don't know me. You had nothing to do with it."

"Do I want to know you, Detective Miller?"

"Like they say in law school, the question's moot, ain't it?"

"Yeah, I suppose it's beside the point anyway."

"Why so broke?" he asked, grinning through his teeth. "I thought writers who make movies do pretty good. I worked a case not long ago that involved a writer lives not far from here. Crime writer by the name of Reece Johnston. He also happens to be a pyromaniac in remission. Maybe you know him. He seems to do okay."

As a writer, even a script writer, I hated to be compared to other writers, especially when it came to success. I'm sure that as a detective, Miller could see the bitterness painted on my face at the direction this conversation was going. Never mind that I stood the chance of going to prison for John's murder. When it came to my writing, my skin was thinner than Saran Wrap and just as transparent.

"William Kennedy lives in Albany too. So did Herman Melville and Nathanial Hawthorne. So what? Sometimes writers do great, other times we don't make squat. I happen to fall into the latter category these days. Satisfied? What's your point in all this, Miller?"

He sat back, exhaled.

"Just trying to fill in some holes in my line of questioning is all," he said. "Now then, Ethan, tell me, how long have you known the Cattivo's exactly?"

"Since they moved in, I guess. Early June. I didn't get to know them at that time. I just knew *of* them."

"Almost two months," he said. "It's taken you and your wife all this time to get together with them socially?"

"We bought a fence for a reason. Fences make real good neighbors."

"Now you didn't write that line, Ethan, did you?"

"I abide by it nonetheless."

"That why you've been spending your days lately looking over the fence at Mrs. Cattivo while she sunbathes?"

I thought the floor was going to open up like one of those sink holes down in Florida, swallow me whole. He reached into his pocket, pulled out a few sheets of standard copy stock that had been folded down the center. He opened it up, set it on the table so I could see it. The top sheet was a digital photograph of me staring out my master bedroom window, crutches planted under my armpits, my eyes staring intently out onto something which we both knew was a topless Lana. I went for the sheet directly underneath it, but then hesitated.

"It's okay," he said. "Be my guest."

Pulling the top sheet aside, I eyed the second image. It was a doozy. Lana and I locked in embrace on her back deck. It must have been taken from directly inside the Cattivo residence. Now I was *wishing* for the floor to drop out from under me. Laying that page on the typewriter, I checked out the third picture. It was snapped from outside the front living room window in the spot where Susan had eyed Lana and me sexing it up on the dining room table, which made for a damn nice photo. I put that aside and looked at the fourth and final shot. It showed me standing all alone inside John's gunroom, where I'd just thumbed the clip release on the very same Colt .45 that blew his brains out.

Miller sipped more whiskey.

"Oh, Ethan," he said, with all the casualness of someone discussing a recipe for apple pie, "and as for that last picture of you standing inside Cattivo's private firearms collection room just this morning, we have a series of about two dozen pictures that prove you were not only interested in the now late detective's guns, but interested in one gun in particular. The same Colt .45 Model 1911 that made his brains do spin art on the window behind the desk."

"The blood stain," I exhaled.

"I'm guessing that would explain that," he said. "Seems to me there's a bit of a contradiction in your testimony. After all, you never mentioned having previously visited the gunroom."

I stared at the photo hoping it would spontaneously dissolve right there on the table or that maybe I might suddenly wake up in my bed from this nightmare. But it was not to be.

"How do you know I was there this morning?" I said. "Maybe those pictures were taken just prior to his committing suicide? At a time when he was willingly showing me his collection."

"Well for one thing, you're wearing a different shirt. For two, we've already determined the blood on the floor to be more than six or seven hours old, if not more. For three, you can tell by the light coming in through that east-facing window that it's morning, and for four, you can tell by the digital alarm clock on John's desk that it's ten in the morning. On the *dottimundo* in fact."

Dottimundo…funny guy.

I sat back in my chair, hard. Just a few minutes ago I was considering placing a call to the very detective who now sat before me, and spilling my guts. But now my defense mechanism was kicking in… my survival of the fittest… and I not only wanted to kick Miller out of my house, I wanted to kick him in his perfect white teeth.

"So do I get to ask who exactly captured these pictures? Or is secrecy just another one the many police privileges?"

"You can ask, Ethan. But I'm not sure what difference it would make. We'll have the blood tested for DNA and for certain, it will have your blueprint on it."

Maybe the person I saw standing outside the picture window in my living room was my wife, Susan, but in my head, I suddenly saw a tall, well-built man, with a black goatee, and Ray Ban aviator sunglasses masking his eyes. After all, I'd never known Susan to go around carrying a camera. And I doubt very much that she pulled out her smartphone and started snapping away while Lana and I were locked in embrace on the dining room table. Carl, on the other hand, was trained in the art of surveillance. He was cop after all. A detective. He must have snapped the shot and then hid around the side of the house when Susan pulled onto Orchard Grove.

"Try me," I said.

"Cattivo's partner, Carl," he said.

Bingo…

A slow burn began in my bum foot and quickly spread out throughout my entire body. I decided the time had come to go for broke.

"You aware that your boy, Carl, is sleeping with Lana?" I said. "And that it's possible John was so angry over it, he threatened Lana's life?"

"That so?" he said. "She tell you that? Aren't you the nosy little neighbor. Not getting a lot of writing done these day, I guess."

"Lana told me she overheard John speaking to someone on the phone. According to John, Lana was going to pay for sleeping with his partner. He was going to wait until nightfall… tonight… to throw her down the basement stairs. Make it look like an accident."

"Now let me get this straight," he said. "That's your story or Lana's story?"

I stared down at the pics, mind spinning out of control. Had Lana lied to me about John's threat?

…Of course she did, you dumb son of a bitch… She saw you coming, Ethan, and snagged you hook, line, and fucking sinker…

"Okay, I'm having a bit of an affair with Lana," I said, raising my voice. "But it turns out I'm one of many, which also includes my wife. There, happy now?"

He cocked his head, pursed his thin lips.

"Happens all the time," I went on, "all over this great country of ours. Christ, all over the planet. And John was crazy angry over it all. But it doesn't mean I stood over him and pulled the trigger for him. He did a good job of that all on his own."

…In my head, I'm grabbing his hair, jamming the barrel into his mouth, breaking his teeth…

"With a Colt .45 that you were interested in."

"Yes, I took a sneak peek at his guns this morning while having a friendly coffee with Lana. Again, so what? I'm thinking about writing a script about a detective who carries a Colt .45, Model 1911. Of course, I'm interested in it." Running my hands down my perspiring face. "You know what, Miller? Maybe it's time I got myself a lawyer."

He smiled the robotic smile once more, teeth grinding, cheeks concave. "Let's just say this is one of those situations where we're still circling the truth, only now, we're closing in on the truth as it begins to expose its ugly head." He stood up tall, seemingly unaffected in the least by the drinks. But then, quite suddenly, he trembled, like the frigid ghost of Detective Cattivo passed right through him. "God, sometimes I scare myself I'm so good."

Positioning my crutches, I pulled myself up, my head spinning. Turns out, I was a lightweight drinker compared to the homicide detective.

"None of this means a thing, Miller," I said, trying my best not to raise my voice a second time.

"You're right," he said. "Doesn't mean shit. That is, you had no reason not to want to see Cattivo dead."

…Cattivo, standing over Susan, a gun pointed at her skull…

"As of this point, I don't speak without a lawyer present."

"Sure you can afford one?" he said, lifting his glass, draining what was left. He leaned into me, not unlike the way he'd done it outside on the Cattivo back deck when he interviewed me earlier. "You'd have to move quite a bit of that pot back there to afford a damn good attorney, believe you me." He burst out laughing, reached out and slapped me on the arm like we were old buddies. I nearly fell over onto my side, but managed to plant my hand on the tabletop. For a quick second, I thought he was John's spirit, having taken over a different body. "Don't sweat it, Ethan. I won't tell anyone. Besides, I'm an officer of the law. Who else is there left to tell? Your mom?" He stepped back from the table. "But allow me to pass on a little advice. Go get that lawyer, no matter what the cost, and don't leave town."

"What's that supposed to mean?"

He straightened out the ball knot on his blue tie, then stuffed his hands in jacket pockets.

"What it means, Mr. Forrester," he said, "is that if you're innocent, you have nothing to worry about. But if you're guilty of a homicide, no matter the degree, no matter the motive..." He lifted up his hands, pressed his lips together, eyes wide. "Well then, due justice will take its course."

"We through?"

"Thanks for the drink," he said, turning for the front door. When he got there, he about-faced. "Please don't take this the wrong way, Mr. Forrester... *Ethan*... I'll say it again. I like you. I really do. But it's just that I have a job to do and quite possibly a crime to solve. Doesn't matter that I thought Cattivo was an asshole and a reckless asshole at that who probably would have ended up shooting himself in the end anyway. It's just that there have been some strange things going on here on Orchard Grove, and I aim to get to the bottom of them. It's all a part of the serve and protect program you personally pay for with your tax dollars."

"That what you're doing, Miller? Serving and protecting?"

Bringing up his right hand, index finger high, he made a twisting motion with it.

"Circling the wagons, my friend... Circling the wagons."

Opening the front door, the cop let himself out, the same way he'd let himself in.

CHAPTER 44

THE whiskey bottle sat on the table, begging me to pour another shot.

I obeyed.

I drank it down fast, then poured another and drank that too. For a brief moment I felt like the entire world was spinning out of control.

…Carl was there, the whole time. He saw everything. He knows everything. Maybe Susan was standing right beside him when he took that picture of Lana and me on the dining room table. Maybe he's over there right now with Lana and my wife. Maybe he's in bed with them…

Sitting back in my chair I tried to sort all of this out in my mind. My eyes locked on the full color digital printouts of my image engaged in a whole lot of illicit activity with Lana. The new neighbors move in and my life turns upside down. I fall in love with a woman I don't know and I can't even function like a productive human being. That's how obsessed I'd become. My wife falls for her too and decides to keep it a secret, as if she wants Lana all to herself. But she can't have her all to herself. They need something from me. They need me to kill John so that the three of us can live happily ever after on the cop's pension and insurance money. But then, I'm stupid… dumber than a box of rocks. The third man Lana and Susan had in mind isn't me at all. It's Carl. I'm along for the ride as the murderer.

The killer.

John wasn't about to kill Lana. It was all a fabrication. A lie designed to lure me in for good. I'd already wanted John dead for what he did to Susan on our back deck. It wouldn't take a whole lot more to get me to agree to Lana's plan. Only the promise of her murder, and quite possibly my own, if I didn't go through with it.

I sat there shaking, shivering. Maybe from fear, maybe from anger. Maybe from I don't know what? I wanted to ask myself, *Why me?* But the little voice inside my empty gut only laughed, lit up a smoke, and said,

"*Why not you, asshole? You see, Ethan, it's like this: Lana, Susan, and Carl… they all needed John dead. That is, they wanted to enjoy a nice life together while you rotted away in prison or worse, faced lethal injection. Lana saw through you. Saw how in love you were with her. Obsessive love. Possessive love. Manic love. The kind of love that hurts worse than a heart attack. The kind of love you cheat and steal for. The kind of love you kill for. How gullible can you be, Ethan? How much of a chump? So yeah, why the hell not use your ass to take the fall for John's murder? You're so blind with love you can't see past your own crooked nose.*"

Then, a sound coming from the kitchen.

Water dripping from the leaky faucet into the metal sink.

Drip, drip, drip…

But that wasn't it.

I turned, saw a face in the picture window. A man standing out on the back deck.

Carl.

I bounded up, my crutches slipping from my grip. I lost my balance, went over hard onto my side.

"You fucker!" I screamed, feeling a shot of pain shoot up my right leg. "I know what you're doing!"

I cocked my head, saw him in the window, smiling. Lifting up his right hand, he made a pretend pistol, shoved the barrel into his mouth, brought down the thumb, shouted, "Bang! Bang!"

I rolled over onto my stomach, started crawling toward the sliding glass doors. When I came to the steps leading down into the playroom, I tried to pull myself up onto my feet. But my right foot was too tender, too swollen, too raw with pain. I dropped down, rolled down the steps.

When I caught my breath, I once again looked out the window.

Carl was gone.

Tears filled my eyes while I sat myself up. Rolling back onto all fours, I crawled my way up the two steps, and then pulled myself up into my chair. I grabbed hold of the whiskey bottle, didn't even bother to pour a shot. I just drank from the bottle while droplets of sweat poured from my brow into my eyes and my foot throbbed like a beating heart. What the hell was the temperature outside? A comfortable sixty-eight degrees? Inside this house it was a sweltering two hundred. It felt like hell, and I supposed I'd better get used to the idea.

How could I have been so blind that I couldn't see through the ploy?

The sunlight that reflected off a dame like Lana Cattivo was blinding. It also sucked me in like a black hole. I'd been damned from the moment she moved in and I was more damned now that they were all plotting against me. Christ, for all I knew, Miller was in on it too.

Leaning over, I picked up my crutches, but then in a spontaneous burst of anger, tossed them across the room. I could either sit there and wait for Miller to build his case against me or I could do something about this mess right now. I could head back over to Lana's and demand that she tell the truth about the plot to kill her husband and make it appear to be an innocent suicide. She wasn't about to willingly confess to Miller about what she cooked up, but if I could somehow record her confession, I'd have the fuel I needed to at least save my tortured ass from frying.

But in order to pull this off, I needed a bit of a convincer.

Looking down at my foot, I saw the fresh blood that stained the sock.

"Screw you and the horse you rode in on," I said aloud.

Limping into kitchen, I went to the silverware drawer. Pulling it open, I found the big French knife. If Lana, Susan, and Carl wanted to play rough, then so be it. Gripping the blade by the wood handle, I hobbled back down into the family room and, opening the sliding glass doors, made my way back out into the dead of night.

CHAPTER 45

WHEN I got to the Cattivo's back deck, I heard music playing. Although the lights in front were extinguished to make the place appear locked up for the night, the lights were still burning in the kitchen and the dining room. I could easily make out slices of electric white light as they spilled out through the partially open horizontal slats on the venetian blind that covered the big picture window. I made out the noise of laughter. People enjoying themselves. Partying. I listened for a male voice to cut through the female chatter. I couldn't make anything out. But that didn't mean Carl wasn't in there with them.

The French knife in hand, I limped over to the window, peeked in through the narrow space between the shutter slats. What I saw felt like a quick, unexpected jab to the face. Lana and Susan were dancing in the middle of the kitchen floor. They'd both stripped down to their panties, and they were dirty dancing to some sort of free form jazz that was blaring out of the home speaker system. Lana was stealing a toke off a joint while Susan gripped a long neck beer bottle in her right hand.

This wasn't the way people acted when death touched a close family member. But then, I guess Lana and John didn't have any family to speak of, other than each other. Their bond wasn't blood, but it certainly ended that way. At that moment, I wanted nothing more than to find a big rock and shatter the picture window. I wanted to jump on through the window and strangle them both, then use my knife on them.

Whiskey muscles.

The better move would be to head back home, get my shit together, and try to find a way out of this mess. Legally. No more violence. In the morning I'd confront them both, make them admit that they, along with Carl, set me up to take the fall for John's murder. I'd bring along my cell phone and record Lana's confession, which I would deliver directly to Detective Miller. No one saw me shove that pistol into John's mouth. No one saw me press the trigger. Only he saw me. He and God and the Devil.

I wasn't the least bit aware of it when my grip on the knife loosened and it fell onto the wood deck. As if on cue, Lana and Susan both stopped dancing. They looked into each other's eyes without saying a word.

"You hear something coming from outside?" Lana said.

"Not sure," Susan said. "Maybe it's that Miller cop guy again."

The jazz was still going strong. Trumpets, bass, and drums. Something from the Fifties or Sixties maybe. Miles Davis or Cliff Brown. Sexy music from a black and white era. For a split second I thought they might both head outside to investigate, or the very least approach the picture window to get a good look out on the deck.

I bent over, clumsily, picked the knife back up, then pulled back and shifted myself away from the line of sight.

"Maybe your husband is spying on us," I overheard Lana say.

"He'll be passed out by now," Susan responded. "He was half drunk when he left here. There's whiskey at home. He's no stranger to the bottle. Seems it's all he's capable of these days is getting hammered."

"Maybe we just heard an animal," Lana said. "A raccoon. Or maybe it's the asshole's ghost."

"I'll go with the animal," Susan said. Then, "Let's go to bed, baby. If the police come back tomorrow to ask more questions, we'll want to be well rested."

"Carl said there'd be no more questions," Lana said. "He'd make sure of that. No more Q and A's with that pinhead, Miller. But I agree. We should go to bed. But…" Her voice trailed off.

"But what, baby?"

"I'm not sure how much sleep we're going to get."

I made out the distinct sound of an ass cheek being slapped. Then I made out more laughter. Susan's laughter.

"You naughty girl," my wife said.

Then Lana said, "We did it, didn't we? We got rid of the bastard and other than Miller, the cops don't have a clue."

"Not about us," Susan said. "Can't say the same about my husband."

"He'd be in the way anyway. Did he really think we were going to live as a threesome together? If he did, he's more insane than John was."

"What about Carl?"

"We need Carl," Lana said. "Carl is the cops. He brings something very special to the table." Then, she said. "By the way, sweetie, I'd like to congratulate you on your acting skills. Ethan truly believes we only really got to know one another just this week."

"You took a real chance sending me those gifts," Susan said. "I had to flush the card that came with the panties down the toilet after Ethan found it."

"But he never would have guessed we've been together for weeks now. He's the blind leading the blind."

"He's gullible. Always been gullible. It's why he bailed out of Hollywood. Some drunk producer would kiss his ass, tell him to write a script that he'd produce no questions asked, and of course it wouldn't happen. Ethan would be left holding onto a ream of worthless paper. Now he's broke and unemployable. A loser."

My head was filling with adrenalin. My veins felt like hot electrical wires. My foot throbbed in thunderous jolts of pain. The voices stopped for a few moments while the jazz kept on playing. I knew they were kissing then. Caressing and holding each other.

Then Susan said, "Let's go to bed, baby. I can't wait any longer."

After a minute, the music stopped, the window closed, the slats on the venetian blinds drawn all the way, the lights in the kitchen and dining room extinguished. The pain in my foot was getting worse, along with the bleeding. But I didn't care. Right then, pain was the only thing keeping me from breaking into the house and killing the women I loved most in the world.

Loved *and* hated.

I love you. I hate you...

I felt the knife in my hand, gripped the wood and steel so hard I thought it might melt. Taking a gimpy step or two backwards, I looked over my right shoulder. I saw a light go on in the master bedroom. Like the rest of the windows in the single-story house, the slider window was open, so it was easy to make out the giggling. Giggling that lasted for a few minutes until the light was extinguished and I began to hear the sound of something else.

It was the sound of passion and pleasure. Moans and wails of two people who could not get enough of each other.

All the oxygen in my lungs emptied out. All the blood in my veins spilled out onto the wood deck. I turned for my house, but as I passed by the sliding glass door, I put my hand on the opener. When I yanked on it, I found, much to my surprise, that it hadn't been locked. Locking up the house at night must have been John's job. But John was no longer around to keep his wife safe. John was dead, because of me. Me and Lana.

I looked down at the knife gripped in one hand and my other hand gripping the slider.

"*Go home,*" insisted the voice inside my head. "*Go the hell home now.*"

"Kiss my parched ass," I whispered to the voice.

CHAPTER 46

I **DIDN'T** bother with checking the time when I got back to the house. I just gravitated toward what was left of the whiskey bottle, and drank it all down. Then I found another bottle and started in on that one. I drank and I cried and I cursed myself for playing the fool. After a time, I began to laugh hysterically, because I was nothing more than a clown. A stinking, filthy drunk clown.

At one point, my eyes connected with the bowl of apples set out on the table. In my alcohol-soaked head, my mind shifted from the apples to the memory of my making love to Lana on the table, back to the apples again. The French knife was set on the table. I took hold of it and began to stab at the apples, feeling the blade slicing through the fruit's skin and flesh, knowing all along that the sensation could not have been more different than the feel of a blade slicing through human skin and meat.

I didn't realize it at first, but there was blood all over the knife.

Last I'd heard, apples didn't bleed.

It had to be *my* blood. I released the blade and looked at my hand. Somehow, in the process of drunkenly stabbing at the apples, I'd cut it up. Cut

210

my fingers when my sweaty hand slipped from the moist grip and slid along the sharp edge of the blade. I was too drunk to feel any real pain. Tossing the knife against the wall, I limped my way to the master bedroom, where I collapsed onto my back.

In my head I once more felt my finger pushing John's finger against the trigger, heard the gunshot, saw the brains spatter against the window behind him. Then I heard the jazz music that had been playing inside Lana's kitchen, and I saw my wife dancing with her new lover. My head did somersaults as I lay prone on the mattress, fully clothed. I felt like I was spinning out of control while dropping at breakneck speed into a bottomless black pit. I dropped and I dropped until sleep overtook my soul, and I found myself in a different place altogether.

I'm walking a city street in the dark of night. It's cold and the city is empty, entirely devoid of life. The scene is desperate, post-apocalyptic. I'm walking without the aid of my crutches and the pain from the incisions in my foot are shooting up and down my right leg. The colorless atmosphere is black and white, but when I look down at my foot, I can see that I'm leaving a trail of crimson blood on the cracked macadam.

A wind blows and sends a shiver up and down my spine. I feel eyes on me. Multiple sets of eyes. Then, appearing before me in the distance, two women. It's Susan and Lana. They're standing in the middle of the empty city street. Although they are far away they begin to approach me at the speed of light. They haven't moved a muscle but suddenly they're standing only inches away from me, staring at me. Into me.

They look so beautiful. Angelic in their matching white dresses, their soft, olive-colored skin, and their deep-set eyes. Lana is holding a bright red apple. Bringing it to her mouth, she takes a bite out of it, then hands it to Susan who does the same. I'm trying to speak to them, but it isn't easy. It's as if my jaw is partially wired shut.

When finally the words come to me, I say, "Why did you stab me in the back?"

But the women just stand there chewing while a cold wind blows up and down the empty city street. But soon something starts coming out of their mouths. It's blood. The blood flows dark red against the black and whiteness. It flows out their mouths, down their chins, and onto their chests, staining their white dresses. They're no longer sharing an apple. Instead, they're eating John's severed, bullet-damaged head. The thing is, he isn't dead. His blue eyes are wide open and he's smiling that devil grin that I've come to abhor.

"You know for a screenwriter," he says as Lana takes a big bite out of his exposed brains, "you sure are a stupid fuck, Hollywood."

That's when I'm startled awake.

I bounded up into sitting position, as if my backbone were a heavy-duty spring. I breathed in heavily, the sweat soaking my face, soaking through my clothing. My head was filled with chunks of concrete and rusted barbed wire, and my foot felt like someone chopped it off while I slept, leaving only a bloody stump. I glanced at the time on my watch. Four in the morning. I'd been out cold for four hours.

My hands felt strange. My fingers stung, and the skin on my palms was sticky, like I'd dipped my hands in a bowl of maple syrup before collapsing onto the bed. Flicking on the light beside the bed stand, I saw that the insides of both hands were nearly covered in dried blood. Then I remembered that I'd cut both hands with the French knife when I was stabbing the apples, and now the cuts had bled out and cauterized themselves while I slept off the booze.

That's when I began to hear the sirens.

Soft at first, but then louder the closer they came to sleepy Orchard Grove. In all honesty, the sirens were only now registering while surly I'd been hearing them even in my sleep. It must have been the sirens that woke me up in the first place. It wasn't the first time I'd heard sirens in the middle of the night, but there was that voice inside my gut again, trying to tell me something. It told me the sirens were meant for me. It told me the digital photos Miller laid out on the dining room table were just the start of something bigger and more sinister. Somehow I knew that he had enough evidence by now to take me into custody, and that custody would lead to indictment and an arrest for Murder in the First.

I bounded out of bed then, feeling like my head was split down the center. I went to the bathroom and urinated. Spotting my shirt on the floor, I knelt down without falling down, picked it up and pulled it over my head and shoulders. Limping as fast as possible into the kitchen, I went to the sink, opened up the hot and cold spigots and washed my hands with soap and water until the blood fell off the skin and circled the aluminum drain. The sting from the many cuts was enough to make my eyes water. But they were only surface cuts, and nothing to worry about.

Splashing some water onto my face, I then dried it with the dishrag, which I dropped to the floor. I located the keys to a car I hadn't driven since my foot had been operated on. For a brief second, I thought about heading down to the pot patch to grab the coffee can I'd buried there weeks ago. A can that contained five thousand in cash. Cash I'd been hiding from Susan. But the sirens were getting louder. There was no time for hobbling down to the tree line. Not with my gimpy foot. I would just have to grab some cash from an ATM.

Snatching my cell phone off the kitchen counter, I shoved it in my jeans pocket. I pulled my Levis jean jacket from the closet, and left the house through the front door. I got into my ten year old, top-down Porsche-Carrera that was parked in the driveway, and turning the key, set my left foot on the gas.

It started up right away.

Backing out with the headlights off, I shifted the auto-tranny into drive and toe-tapped the gas. I was hooking a left onto the cross street that would take me away from Orchard Grove, just as the blue-and-whites turned into the neighborhood, lighting the joint up in their red, white, and blue LED flashers.

By the time they pulled up into my driveway, I was already gone.

CHAPTER 47

DESPERATELY needed a place to go. A safe house. A friend.

But who the hell would take me in?

I had no friends. Susan had been my friend. Now she was gone.

Options.

I might head into the city, hide in my writing studio. But then, that would be the second place the cops would look for me once they'd finished up with the Orchard Grove house. I could hit the northbound highway, head for the Canadian border two hundred fifty miles away. But I'd never make it past the border without getting busted on the spot. Plus I didn't have my passport on me, or one of those special digitally enhanced new driver's licenses.

Going south was always an option. Mexico. But that would take two or three days of nonstop driving. By then, my disappearance would be broadcast all over the social media sites. Miller would send out an APB, the Staties and the FBI would grow massive hard-ons that pointed at me, and then the roadblocks would go up. I'd be lucky to make Ohio.

I drove away from the city, knowing that they'd comb every street and alley for me. No choice but to hit the highway until I was beyond the city limits. From there I'd hit a back-country road, maybe find a motel-no-tell where I could hold up for the night until I scripted my next move. It wasn't much of a plan, but then, I'd never run away from anything before. Never run for my life.

Dead ahead, the entrance ramp to New York State Highway 90.

I swerved into the right lane and drove onto it, then started heading east along a back- country road. The dark of night hung over me like a black shroud. The humidity was so thick; the air that blew against my face as I drove with the top down had little effect. Or maybe my foot was infecting, causing a fever from which I would never recover. Maybe it's what I deserved for what I'd done to John. Or what the hell, maybe I deserved a medal.

I went as far as the Nassau exit and got off.

To say the place was sparsely populated was saying a lot. It was nothing but wide open farm fields and the occasional farm house. Without a roof over me, the smell of cow shit tainted the every single ounce of oxygen I breathed.

Up ahead on my right, a twenty-four hour gas station/convenience store. My gas tank registered three quarters full, but I was in desperate need of cash. I could have kicked myself in the ass for not digging up my coffee can from out of the pot patch before I split Orchard Grove. It would have taken only a few minutes at most and I'd be five grand richer for it. If only I'd woken up just five minutes earlier, I might have had the time to grab the money and avoid the police. Now I was a prisoner to whatever was left in my joint checking account with Susan. That is, she hadn't already emptied the sucker out. I also knew that the cops would attempt to trace every credit card transaction I made prior to putting a hold on all my accounts. Which meant speed was of the essence.

Pulling into the convenience store lot, I parked around the back of the small wood building near the dumpster and killed the engine. I exited the car and limped around to the front of the store, entered into it through a front glass door that sported a picture of a giant green bass breaking the water's surface in a flying leap, the words, "Fresh Night Crawlers for Sale!" printed in big black letters below it. That's what I was to the Albany cops. A night crawler. A worm. A slimy insect.

There was an old man sitting behind the counter on a stool. The scraggily gray beard he wore made him *look* old anyway. He was watching a television that was mounted to the wall above the counter, directly beside the overhead cigarette racks. It was still dark out, yet he barely acknowledged me as I stood by the now closed door.

"ATM?" I asked, trying not to look at him directly.

He slowly peeled his eyes away from the tube, nodded.

"Behind you," he said.

"Thanks."

I turned, eyed the gray cash machine set up against the exterior wall by the window. Pulling out my wallet, I slid out the red ATM card, entered it into the card slot. When the screen came up asking me for my PIN, I entered it and waited. That's when the silence was broken by the sounds coming from the old man's television, as if something he'd just witnessed on the screen caused him to dramatically turn up the audio.

"This is your news on the nines for the top of the five o'clock hour. Police are on the lookout for a North Albany screenwriter suspected of murdering a local APD detective in a bizarre homicide-made-to-look-like-a-suicide plot only Hollywood could cook up."

My knees grew wobbly, my foot throbbing with my every pulse, the skin that surrounded it feeling too small for the swelled, sutured flesh... feeling as if it was splitting apart. I made the mistake of looking over my right shoulder at the old man who shifted his eyes from the television to my face. I quickly turned back to the machine, hoping against all hope that it would disburse my cash immediately. Instead it asked me if I'd be willing to pay three dollars to access my cash account. I pressed Yes. As if I had a choice in the matter.

Then it asked me how much I wanted to withdraw. The most it offered up was two hundred bucks. But there was another option called "Other." I chose that one. Meanwhile, the bad news continued to spill out of the television just three or four feet away.

"The body of APD Detective John Cattivo, forty-one, was discovered last evening by his wife immediately after she heard what was described as a gunshot coming from one of the rooms in their North Albany home. Initial reports indicated that Cattivo died from a self-inflicted gunshot wound to the head while alone in the room. Later on, however, it was reported that Cattivo had been accompanied by his next-door neighbor, local screenwriter Ethan Forrester, into the room only moments prior to the suicide. After careful questioning by APD Senior Homicide Detective Nick Miller, it was determined that Forrester either tricked Cattivo into acting out a suicide on behalf of research he was said to be conducting for an upcoming Hollywood production or, Forrester actually pulled the trigger himself. Preliminary ballistics reports indicate that Forrester's prints were not only discovered on the suicide weapon, but also on the single bullet casing that, by all appearances, had been secretly loaded into the otherwise empty automatic's nine round magazine.

"A second source for the APD, Sergeant Carl Pressman, who is also reputed to have been the deceased's partner, reports that Forrester who, it should be noted is on crutches after a recent foot surgery, had been harassing Cattivo's wife, Lana. According to Pressman, Forrester who lives next door to the Cattivo's on Orchard Grove, has shown up on numerous occasions to their home uninvited. Mrs. Cattivo has also lodged several complaints with the APD after discovering Forrester spying on her from a window that looks directly out onto their next-door home and backyard.

"Miller, who is presently in charge of the on-going investigation, told Channel Nine that he was able to obtain a bench warrant for Forrester's arrest only a few hours after the fatal early evening incident. However, when the APD made a raid on Forrester's Orchard Grove home at approximately three-thirty AM this morning, the screenwriter had already fled the scene, perhaps acting on a tip-off from some unknown party."

I could feel the old man's eyes digging into me as I typed in the numbers, 1-0-0-0 into the ATM, pressed Enter. When it spit out an electronic beep and flashed the words, "$500 Maximum Withdrawal," I was left with no other option but to cancel my request and type in 5-0-0. I bit down on my bottom lip so hard I thought I drew blood, pressed Enter and waited for the ATM to cough up the cash. I tried to turn off the voice on the television and concentrate instead on the mechanical workings of the machine, the bills being electronically counted and collected by the wheels and gears.

"Excuse me," the old man said. Just the sound of his old, gravelly voice sent a jolt of electric sparks throughout my nervous system.

A stream of cash began dispersing into the gray plastic tray in twenty-dollar denominations. It spilled out like green blood.

"Hey you," the old man pressed. "That's you on the television, ain't it? Ain't…it?! You're the killer. "

I tried to ignore him. But my head was filling with the sound of a thousand blaring trumpets and beating, pulsating bass drums.

"Hey you, killer!" the old man repeated, his voice louder, more insistent, more threatening.

I grabbed my money, shoved it into my jeans pocket. It wouldn't be enough, but I was on the run from the law. Somehow I would have to find a way to get to that coffee can in the pot patch. But for now I had to stay away or else risk getting snatched by Miller and his blue knights. I was floating alone in a great big wavy ocean, and there were storm clouds overhead, lightning bolts striking all around me. A fugitive from a kind of half-baked justice where a cop gets to wave a loaded gun at my wife's head while forcing her to get half naked and perform sexual acts with his own wife. Doesn't matter if it turns out that both women surly enjoyed the act. Right is right and wrong is fucked up. So what if the end result was my helping him kill himself? He had it coming. The only thing I did wrong was not finding a way to kill him when he was still holding a gun on my wife out on my back deck.

I turned, faced the old man.

He was wearing a wife beater that had turned fifty shades of gray. His gray hair was over grown like a patch of weeds, except for the very center of his skull that was egghead bald. His eyes were bloodshot and wet with decades of accumulated rage. Now was the moment he'd been waiting for his entire life. He reached under the counter and came back out with a pump-action shotgun. He pointed the barrel at my chest.

"You don't want to do that," I said. "You have me confused for someone else."

"The hell I do," he said. "I want you to put them hands over your head, and drop down to your goddamned knees. I'm gonna call the cops and they're gonna cart your fancy cop killin' ass to jail. You hear me, movie star?"

"I write film scripts," I said. "I'm not a movie star. And you're making a big mistake."

"You're making the mistake by opening your mouth. You don't care about people. You care only about yourself. You put a bullet in that police officer's gun and you blew his brains out. That's murder and you die for murder. That's the law."

The pulse pounded in my foot and in my brain. Okay, I pulled the trigger on John Cattivo. Sure I wanted him dead, and sure I agreed to arrange his suicide. But I was set up to be the lone murderer.

I began to raise up my hands, like I was surrendering myself when in fact I was stalling. At the same time, I began to lower my body. But that's when I caught sight of the stack of Campbell's Chicken Noodle Soup cans over my right shoulder. There was a cardboard sign Scotch-taped to the pyramid-like stack announcing a ninety-nine cent per can sale.

"Get down!" he barked, pumping a fresh shell into the shotgun chamber. The tight mechanical metal-workings of the shotgun filled the store.

Reaching out quick, I snatched up my ninety-nine cents worth of soup, sending the rest of the stack tumbling to the floor, and tossed it at his head. He ducked and triggered the shotgun, blasting away the cigarette rack. Cigarettes rained down onto the floor as I speed-limped the couple of steps to the counter.

Extending both arms, I lunged forward off my good foot, caught the counter with my left hand while grabbing hold of the shotgun barrel with my right. As we struggled, he managed to cock another round into the chamber. He fired again and the blast sent me sliding off the counter and onto my back while a chunk of plaster ceiling came raining down on me. He bounded up onto his feet like a man years younger, and came around front, aiming the barrel down at my head. Pointblank. At that range, he would vaporize my face.

"You attacked me," he said, cocking his head up toward a video monitor. "I got it on film. You attacked me, and you killed that officer of the law and now I'm gonna blast you away in self-defense."

The old man meant business. I saw the death in his eyes. It was as plain and despairing as the broken blood vessels that streaked across the wet whites.

I recognized his dire need to kill me. His hatred and his lust for what he was about to do. Like he'd waited for this singular moment in time for his entire life, and that once accomplished, he could die without a shred of remorse. He didn't just want to kill me. He wanted to kill himself, and all of mankind. In a word, he'd had enough already. He pumped a round into the chamber and he smiled the smile of a man who had finally found peace.

"Give my love to the devil, asshole," he said, as his finger slithered onto the trigger.

But I reached out fast. Grabbed hold of the barrel, pulled it out of his hands. Leaning up, I swung the stock against his knee, dropping him on the spot like a scarecrow made of twigs. Then I swung it in the opposite direction, connecting with his head. I felt the crack of his skull more than I heard it, as its energy travelled from the wood stock along the length of the metal barrel, into my hands and arms. It was no more or less an act of nature than if I'd just cracked open an egg. Surrendering the devil that possessed him, he collapsed, while the blood that tiredly poured from the split in his head made a thick pool on the filthy wooden floor. He was a dead man now, and there was no question in the world about who killed him and why.

I used the shotgun like a crutch to pull myself up off the floor, before I got soaked in blood. My head pounding, the wound sutures in my foot no doubt having split open, I limped over the old man, went around the back of the counter. The register was closed, and I had no idea how to open it. I did the only thing I could think of which was to raise up the shotgun, slam the stock end down on the machine.

The drawer shot open.

I grabbed up what little cash there was, stuffing it into my pocket. Then, peering down under the counter, I located the open box of 12-gauge shells. Grabbing a fist full of them, I filled my jeans pocket. As my final act in the Godforsaken place, I searched the narrow cubby behind the register for the security system tape loop. When I located it, I pulled out the plastic cassette tape, and shoved it into my pant waist.

Making my way back around the counter and the front door, I made sure not to step in any of the old man's blood. After all, I was leaking plenty of the stuff myself. On my way out the door, my eyes caught sight of wooden hat-rack that was screwed to the wall and that displayed maybe a dozen baseball caps. One that bore the letters NRA on the brim in big white letters caught my attention. The tag attached to it read eight dollars. For a brief second, I thought about digging into my pocket for a ten spot, setting it onto the counter.

"How stupid is that?" I whispered aloud.

I was already a killer who'd just robbed the till. What difference did stealing a cheap baseball cap make? Pushing the door open, I made my way out of the store, a desperado whose time was about to run out.

CHAPTER 48

I was still dark out. But dawn couldn't be that far off on the horizon.

I was sure no one had seen me or heard the shotgun blasts. But that could have been wishful thinking, like believing Susan, Lana, and I could have lived together happily ever after. The world was getting smaller. Even in a remote area like this one. For all I knew, the state police had employed a drone to scour the countryside for me. I'd written one into a script once, just to keep up with modern tech. But I'd never really seen one in person. Looking up at the sky, I listened for the buzz and hum of tiny propellers. I didn't hear any. But that didn't make me feel any less vulnerable. Peeling the round gold price tag off the cap's brim, I put it on, yanking it down over my brow. It wasn't much of a disguise, but it would have to do.

Back at the car, I tossed the shotgun onto the passenger seat, and pulled the security tape out of my pants. I stuck my fingers into the cassette, yanked out the tape, snapped it in two, then tossed the whole thing into the dumpster. Slipping back behind the wheel, I fired up the Porsche and, once more pressing my left foot on the gas, drove out of the lot with the headlights extinguished.

I had no right in the world to pray. Rather, I had no right to pray and believe that Jesus, if he could actually hear me, owed me a solid. And I sure as shit knew that I would never see nor get to know him after the two men I killed in a single day. Correction…two men who might have killed me first given the opportunity. Technicalities. But regardless of how Jesus or God or Buddha felt about the death trail I was leaving behind, praying felt like the right thing to do for a man who was wanted as much by the police as he was Satan.

"Our father who art in heaven," I said aloud into the wind, "please save my sorry ass."

Hooking up with Route 9-and-20, the old road that used to connect Albany with New York City before the construction of the New York State Thruway, I drove for another twenty or thirty minutes through the desolate countryside. Other than sleeping off a few hours of a whiskey drunk, I hadn't had any decent sleep in close to forty-eight hours. I was dead tired. Tired and wired and afraid of what awaited me around the next corner. I knew the right thing to do was to keep going until I at least made it to the Catskill Mountains where I could find a place to hide in the woods. Maybe an old wintertime hunting cabin I could break into. But I was driving with my left foot while my right foot was bleeding badly and my eyes were closing involuntarily. The immediate danger I faced was running off the road due to exhaustion. I'd be lucky to make it another five miles without crashing.

I recognized the area as a once popular tourist destination back in the Forties and Fifties for the World War II generation who returned from the battleground looking for cheap getaways. No one used the area for vacationing anymore now that Cape Cod and the New Jersey boardwalk were all the rage, but the old motels still remained, mostly as overnight beds for sleepy truckers.

Forcing my eyes to stay open, I drove until I came to the first roadside motel I could find that looked somehow inviting. The one I found had a few pickups and a couple of semis parked outside in the gravel lot. There was a big, vertical neon sign that said Motel in descending letters, only half the red and green neon in working order. But the lights were on in some of the rooms. Rooms that belonged to truckers looking to get an early start on the day.

I pulled up outside the front office and turned the car off. Before I got out, I laid my jean jacket over the shotgun. Last thing I needed was someone spotting the weapon used to kill a man, even if that killing were conducted in self-defense.

Standing outside the car, I looked to the east and made out the vague hint of sunlight as it was starting to rise over the mountains. A quick glance at my watch told me it was going on six o'clock in the morning. In a few minutes, daylight and humid summer heat would wash over this motel like a filthy, cum-stained bed sheet. When it came, I wanted to be secured behind the dead-bolted door of an anonymous room, the blinds closed, the air conditioning unit blasting cold, manufactured air.

I needed time to think.

To plan.

To figure a way out of this mess or at the very least, expose Lana for who she truly was. Whatever the case, I was starting to think that turning myself into Miller before somebody else got killed might not be the stupidest of ideas. At the very least, I'd be able to get my foot looked at. At this rate, I was risking the onset of gangrene. Once that happened, the foot was as good as gone.

The sound of two or three electric jolts filled the air, and the neon sign went dead for yet another day. Must be on a timer. I wondered if that's what an electric chair sounded like. Turning, I limped up onto the concrete sidewalk and approached the glass door, the words OFFICE stamped on it at eye level in white paint that was chipped and browned with age and over exposure to the sun. Opening the door, I approached the empty Formica-covered counter. Maybe we were living in the digital age, but there was a good old fashioned bell set out on the counter. I slapped it, the ring so surprisingly loud, it took me by surprise.

After a slow couple of beats, a woman stepped through a door-sized opening that was partially covered by a brown curtain. She was old, and she looked even older in her baggy housedress, worn slippers, and head of dyed black hair that had been put up in curlers. Her face was covered in a mask of translucent crème that belonged to the bedtime routine of a woman who, many decades ago, might have been as pretty as a movie poster. Now she seemed as aged and broken as the sign out front. Maybe as aged as the motel itself, her wrinkled body a worn casualty of the greatest generation that was now mostly dead.

"Can I help you?" she said, forcing the words from the back of her throat along with a generous chunk of phlegm.

"Sorry to wake you," I said, knowing full well that the day would soon come when she wouldn't wake up at all.

"I was just about to get up anyway. You look like you need a room."

"That good, huh?"

"Would you prefer an ocean front view?"

I just looked at her, perplexed.

"That's just a joke. What's the matter, mister? Too tired for a sense of humor?" She looked down at my feet. "Take a step back," she added.

I did it. Her eyes went wide.

"That foot looks like hell. You're not bleeding on my floor I hope."

"It stopped," I said, hoping that it had. I was leaving a blood trail all over upstate New York.

I pulled the baseball hat farther down my brow so that my eyes were entirely hidden.

"You should be on crutches."

"I forgot them."

She looked up, cracked a sly grin.

"Booze will do that," she said. "Or is that Jack Daniel's toothpaste I smell on your breath?"

I tried to work up a smile, but my face felt like I was wearing a mask of concrete. I also felt relieved. If she'd only just woken up, then she wasn't yet aware of the cop I helped kill in Albany or that old man I put down thirty miles back in Nassau. To her, my face was just another face in a lifetime of faces. No more or less important than a manikin.

"Been on the road all night. Need some sleep. You have a corner room available? A quiet room?"

Mounted to the wall behind the desk was a square unit that had been divided up into about thirty or so separate six-inch-by-six-inch cubbies. She gazed at the boxes until she found the key she wanted. Pulling it from the cubby she then slapped it down onto the desk.

"You got some plastic for me?" she said, digging into the pocket on her housecoat for a pair of reading glasses. The fifteen-dollar jobs you can buy without a prescription in the drug store. She slipped them on and stared uncomfortably at the screen on her computer.

Without thinking, I dug out my Amex, handed it to her. It took a few beats, but it wasn't until she had the card in hand that I realized what I'd done. I felt my stomach tighten up and my pulse take on an added velocity. The one thing I didn't need was for her to get suspicious, so I let it go and hoped the card wouldn't be traced. At least, right away.

She swiped the card in the little credit card machine and waited, her eyes glued to its small digital screen. After a few long seconds she shook her head, whispered, "Declined."

A truck started up in the lot, startling me. From the sound of it, a big semi.

"Jumpy this morning, aren't we?" the woman said without ever looking up from the little credit card machine.

She ran the card again.

"Just not your day," she said. "Declined again." She pulled off her glasses, peered up at me. "Got anymore plastic that's willing to cut you some slack?"

"How do you feel about cash?"

She smirked, handed me back my card.

"Your ball cap says NRA, but you don't by chance work for the IRS, do you?"

I shook my head, returned the card to my wallet.

"Cash is fine as wine," she said. "Forty for the room. Ten extra for towels and maid service. Daily tip is up to you. You pay for the entire stay in advance." Reaching under the desk, she pulled out a white index-sized card that had some black print on it. "Fill this out, if you please," she added, setting a Bic ballpoint on top of the card.

My eyes peering down at the black space where the word NAME was printed, I made the split second decision to go with the first fake name that came to mind. Jim Summers. After all, it was summertime. I wrote down a fake license plate number and a fake phone number in the spaces provided, and simply didn't bother with an email. When I was done, I slid the card back toward her. She picked it up, read it.

"How long will you be staying with us... Mr. Summers?"

I figured I wouldn't be using the motel for more than a few hours. Four hours at most, depending upon how close the police were to picking up my trail. Just enough time to get some rest, maybe eat some takeout, catch a shower, clean my foot, and figure out my next move.

"Just a day and a night," I lied, reaching into my pocket, shaving off two twenties and a ten, handing the bills to her. She didn't store the cash in the register, but instead stuffed them in her housecoat pocket.

"Enjoy your stay, Mr. Summers," she said. Then, "Oh, and before I forget." Once more she reached under the desk, came back out with a business card that she set out onto the desktop. The printing on the card said, "Catskill Escort Service" in big block letters. Under that it said "Discreet and Affordable." A phone number was printed below that.

"Listen," she said, "I know how all you guys on the road get lonely, and since I don't want no strangers coming and going at all hours, I only allow one escort service to operate here. Understand, Mr. Summers?"

I took the card, slid it into my pants pocket with my cell phone.

"Gotcha," I said, nodding. I added, "What, no bellman to assist me with my luggage?"

"So you do have a sense of humor after all," she said. "I'll have you know the bellman was my husband and the son of a bitch took off ten years ago with a cocktail waitress and never came back."

"Men are jerks."

"He wasn't very well endowed anyway. And even if he was, he had no idea how to use it."

"Maybe you're better off."

"You're right. Just look around you. I live in Camelot now."

She exhaled, turned, then disappeared back behind the curtain to be alone with her memories of far better days.

CHAPTER 49

I GOT back in the Porsche and drove it the short distance across the lot to room 30 which, it turns out, was the far corner room, just like I'd requested. I wasn't sure how good an idea it was to park directly outside the room, so I drove around the side of the motel and parked it behind the blue dumpster, entirely out of sight. There was a good-sized patch of second growth woods directly beside my room which would come in handy if the state cops or local sheriff made a visit. I could only hope that I'd had enough of a head start on them to earn me at least a few hours peace. Picking up the shotgun along with the jacket that concealed it, I got out of the car, and headed for room 30.

Slipping the key into the lock, I opened the door and closed it behind me, engaging the deadbolt. I flicked on the air-conditioning unit, which was installed in the wall directly beneath the curtain-covered picture window and laid the shotgun out onto an easy chair that was positioned immediately to the left of the door. While the big cooling unit spit out red/orange sparks along with something that smelled more like an oil slick than air, I hobbled on past a kitchenette efficiency unit that contained a small gas-fired stove, and stole a peek inside the bathroom. There was a sink, a toilet, and a shower stall that was covered in a bone-colored curtain that had green and brown mildew stains on its bottom. A narrow slider window was installed over the toilet. It was too small to push myself through if I were to suddenly require a second means of escape, which meant I was leaving this place through the front door, one way or another.

Coming out of the bathroom, I went around the side of the bed and took a painful load off. To my right, at the end of the bed sat a television. The old kind with the big tube in it. I could turn it on, check the news, but it was the last thing I wanted to do right now. What's the saying? Ignorance is bliss. Well, I don't know if what I was experiencing was blissful, but it seemed somehow better than knowing precisely how screwed I was at the moment.

The nightstand contained a phone and a laminated card that advertised local services like twenty-four-hour pizza delivery and a Chinese food takeout joint. I realized that I hadn't eaten since yesterday's breakfast of toast and butter. Without having to look at it, I knew my cell phone still had power, but something told me not to use it unless it was absolutely necessary. Cell phone calls could be tracked. I also knew the phone itself could be tracked with GPS, but I was betting on the APD not being sophisticated enough to sport that kind of high tech.

FBI would be a different story, however. I would need my phone later on down the road so hanging on to it was a chance I had to take.

In the meantime, I'd turn it off to conserve power. But before powering down, I'd check it for any texts or messages. There were none, telling me two things. First, that Lana and Susan were avoiding me like the plague. And two, Miller wasn't ready to make direct contact with me for whatever reason. Maybe he assumed I'd do something even more stupid than killing a convenience store clerk. Maybe he thought that by calling me, he'd scare me off even more. Make me run faster and farther. Who knows? Maybe Miller who was waiting for me to call him. What did the cops call that? A passive/aggressive apprehension tactic? Now I was back to being the scriptwriter, making shit up as I went along.

I did know this: When the time was right, I would call Miller and make a few demands. That is, he wanted me to turn myself in. But just when that time was and what precise demands I would make had yet to reveal themselves. They would have to wait while I sorted things out and gave my head and bad foot a rest.

Depressing the small narrow button on the side of the phone, I powered it down. Then, I picked up the receiver on the room phone, dialed the pizza place and waited for an answer. When someone picked up, I told him I wanted a delivery.

"This early?" the kid said. A young man. A boy from the sounds of it. "It's not even seven."

"Says on your advertisement you're open twenty-four hours a day."

"We just say that shit because it sounds good."

"Tell you what I'm gonna say because it sounds good," I said. "You bring me a cheese pizza and a pint of Jack Daniels and a can of Flex Seal, I'll make sure your wallet is glad it got up with you today."

"Did you say Flex Seal?"

"Yup, as seen on TV. The twenty-four-hour chain drug stores should have it in stock."

"Okay. Might take a while. I gotta heat up the ovens and then I gotta find the nearest CVS."

I told him my address at the motel. He said he knew the place better than the back of his hand.

"Who really knows what the back of their hand looks like?" I said.

He hung up.

I stood up, heavy on the good foot, light on the bad, shoved the cell phone in the pocket opposite the one that held three or four shotgun shells. When I pulled my hand back out, something fell out onto the floor. The card for the escort service. Ever since the woman at the front desk had given it to me, it had been burning a hole in my pocket.

I peered down at the card where it rested on the floor, read the words Escort Service yet again. No matter how many times I read them they didn't change. Some people's bodies shut down under severe stress. But I was one of those rare men who needed a stress release.

Committing the phone number to memory, I picked up the landline again and punched it in. A woman answered. I told her who I was and where I was.

"What did you have in mind?" she said. The raspy voice was young, but not that of a child. More like a woman in her thirties or forties who was no stranger to cigarettes.

"I didn't know I had a choice," I said.

"You always have a choice," she said.

In my head, I pictured precisely who I wanted, but could no longer have.

"Do you have anyone who's blonde? Naturally blonde? Well built, but doesn't look like one of those female bodybuilder types? I want someone who's feminine and proud of it."

"I think we can do that for you," she said. "Anything else?"

"Can she wear a red robe?" I said. "Like a Japanese kimono."

She giggled. "That's pretty specific. But I'll see what I can do."

Then she told me the woman I requested would be there within the hour.

I suddenly felt happy. Lana was coming to see me.

Sort of.

Her company would do me good before I had to resume running for my life.

When I hung up, I laid back on the bed and put my feet up. One good foot, one bad foot … a foot bloodied and throbbing and soon to be smelling of gangrene. Or so I was convinced. It desperately needed cleaning. Correction… It desperately needed an emergency room. But I was too tired and too wanted by the cops to even think about cleaning it right now, much less risk exposing myself to the medical staff of an emergency room. The second I walked in through the sliding glass doors of a hospital ER, it would be game over.

Silence seemed to surround the motel. It was almost unnatural. A serene quiet where there should be sirens and the locking and loading of firearms, all of them pointed at me. Maybe I was already dead and didn't even realize it.

Looking around the motel room, at the TV, at the old, clunky AC unit, and the kitchenette, I was reminded of the week long sea-side summer vacations my family would take on Cape Cod, back when I was a little kid. How much I looked forward to digging in the sand, swimming in the sea and the hotel pool. Going to bed at night to the ocean breeze and being lulled to sleep by the ocean waves that steadily slapped the shoreline. I remembered how as a skinny, undersized seven-year-old, I stepped into the ocean one morning and immediately felt something stab my foot. It was like a pair of heavy-duty scissors sliced my big toe off. My dad picked me up by the waist, only to discover that a crab had clutched me in its claw. I screamed and cried, more filled with fear than actual pain. A million years had passed since that bright summer morning, but somehow it all seemed like moments ago.

Soon I began to doze off. I tried like hell to think about nothing. But as soon as the lights went out in my brain, I thought about Lana. When I thought about Lana I automatically thought about Susan. Thought about the two of them together. I saw them naked and I saw them making love to one another in the heat of the long night. I saw myself making love to them at the same time. Even though they were dozens of miles away from me, I could feel their presence inside my chest and my sex as if the two of them were somehow crawling around inside my flesh and bone.

It was the strangest thing, but now that they'd set me up to take the fall for John's killing, I wanted them both more than ever. Rather, I wanted Lana. Have you ever wished you could open up your skull, extract the piece of brain that holds the memory of a woman who controls you more than you control yourself? That's precisely what I would have done, if only it were possible. But thus far, the only one who'd made out fine as red wine in this mess was John Cattivo. He might be dead, his brains blasted all over his gunroom wall, but at least he was free of Lana.

As sleep began to take over, the events of the past couple of days took on a new clarity. It was as if I had a tumor growing on my liver and somehow I could see the big pink lump like my skin had turned translucent as glass. The world loved to see a big man fall. But then, I wasn't a big man in any sense of the word. Sure, I was a screenwriter who'd had some films produced. Sure, I once had a name and reputation. I had friends and was invited to parties in LA that other screenwriters and movie stars also attended.

Here's one for you: I once got high with Brad Pitt back in '90 or '91 out in the turnaround of the Avalon Hotel in West Hollywood. I did shots with George Clooney in his trailer on the Universal Studios set of *Out of Sight* for which I was the writer's assistant. I even hitched a ride with Johnny Depp to a 7-Eleven on the corner of Olympic and Reeves when he needed a pack of cigarettes and I needed a sixer of beer. On the way back to a mutual friend's townhouse on Santa Monica Boulevard, he stole one of my beers and I stole one of his butts. We blared Nirvana and laughed at the stupidest shit.

Now I'm not sure Johnny Depp or George Clooney would have the slightest clue who I was. That's how long gone I'd become. How positively yesterday I was. Like an old T-shirt that had been ripped and shredded and tossed into the corner of the garage to collect dust and spider webs.

But I was still a writer.

No son of a bitch could ever take that away from me. But what if I turned myself in? Would the cops believe me when I told them I just wanted to see what it looked like when a man ate his piece? That I was conducting research at the time? That I had no idea his wife had planted a bullet inside the gun? That John insisted on demonstrating how it was done. So what if his teeth were broken. Maybe he did that by mistake when he shoved the barrel inside his mouth on his own. Just because his teeth were broken didn't mean I shoved the gun in his mouth and pulled the trigger.

It's how I would explain it to Miller. But chances are, he wouldn't believe me. Or maybe believing me would be beside the point. A man was dead and it was my fault. There was also no getting around the fact that it was my prints on the bullet casing and no one else's.

But John Cattivo was just the first in what would become two dead bodies in less than twelve hours.

Would Miller believe me when I said I was defending myself against a raging convenience store clerk? It wasn't likely. Even when forensics scoured the place and discovered he shot at me first, they'd come up with a scenario that proved I was physically threatening the old man. In the end, they'd work it out so that he was the one acting in self-defense. Not the other way around. After all, I'd already killed a cop.

The future looked black and bleak.

And now here I was lying on my back inside some roadside motel, filled with fear and exhaustion so deep, I could feel it in my teeth and in the core of my bones. What I should have been doing was heading south to New York

City where I could ditch the Porsche in the East River and then blend into the crowd. At the first chance I got, I could either steal away on a cargo ship bound for South America, or I could somehow figure out a way to pay off some Chinese smuggler for safe passage to Asia where I'd disappear forever under a false ID.

Maybe, just maybe, if I had even an ounce of luck left inside me, I would end up in Burma or maybe Vietnam where I could tend bar and write novels under a pen name, open up a Swiss bank account where I'd receive my royalties. It wasn't a likely outcome for a man who'd fallen off the bitched-for-life tree and hit every branch on the way down, but just the thought of it offered me a smidgeon of hope.

Hope… Hope floats like a bloated carcass…

I closed my eyes, felt myself drifting off, sinking down and down until the world turned black.

CHAPTER 50

THEN a knock on the door.

I shot up, sweat dripping off my forehead into my eyes. Damned A/C didn't work any better than my luck. How long was I out? Ten, twenty minutes at the most. I slid off the bed, limped the few steps to the door.

"Who's there?" I said.

"You called the escort service," spoke the voice, which was clearly female.

I nodded, as if she could see me through the wood door. Side stepping to the window, I peeked out through the slim separation between the glass and the filthy fabric. I made out a slim, woman dressed in cut-off shorts and a tight T-shirt that ended half way down her slightly soft belly. She sported ample breasts and her smooth, straight blonde hair was thick and trimmed maybe an inch or so above her shoulders, just like Lana. From where I was standing, she didn't look any older than nineteen or twenty, but I could have been mistaken. The important thing was that she was here now, hadn't brought any cops along with her, and that she reminded me of Lana.

Tossing my jacket back over the shotgun, I unlatched the chain, unlocked the deadbolt, opened the door just enough to show my face.

"Good morning." She smiled. "Or is it still good evening?"

I just looked at her, at her blue eyes and her beautiful young face veiled by blonde hair. She wasn't Lana but she was my Lana for now. She held a plastic shopping bag in her hand. The bag was stuffed with something.

I opened the door wide enough to allow her to slip on through. When she was in, I took a quick look around outside and saw that the coast was clear. For now anyway. Closing the door, I put the chain back on and reengaged the deadbolt.

She turned to me, held out her free hand, like we were meeting for the first time at a fundraiser.

"I'm Casy," she said, all smiles. "Casy without an E before the Y."

I tried to picture in my head how I might spell Casy. I would have put an e before the Y, as in "The Great Casey at Bat." A silly poem my dad would recite every time he'd get plastered on Genesee Cream Ale while watching a Yankee game on TV. Seemed to me the name should be pronounced Casy with a hard a, as in Lassie.

I pulled my hand away.

"Your name is Lana for now," I said.

"Oh yes," she said, holding up the shopping bag. "They told me what you want." Then, turning for the bathroom. "Do you mind if I slip into this?"

"How old are you?" I said.

"Old enough," she said, unbuttoning her shorts, allowing them to fall to the carpet.

"You in a rush?" I said. "How much time do I have?"

She stepped into the bathroom, out of sight.

"I go to the community college around the corner," she said. "I have a class in an hour. Hope that's okay?"

"You asking or telling?"

"Neither silly." She came back out, wearing a red kimono, and not much else. It wasn't exactly like the one Lana wore. And it was acrylic rather than satin. But it would do. "You're aware of the pricing?" she added.

"Remind me," I said.

"One hundred for the initial hour. Fifty dollars more for each additional hour. But that won't be a problem since I have to skedaddle."

My eyes were struck by her young blue eyes and pert breasts, which for now were covered by the kimono. She reached underneath with both her hands, went to pull down her thong panties.

"Don't," I said.

"Excuse me?" she said.

"Leave them on," I said. "And turn around."

She did it. "I have to ask you to pay in advance."

Digging into the pocket, which also housed my cell phone, I peeled off the correct bills.

"Would you mind being a doll and put the money in the left-hand pocket on my jean shorts? Say, what did you do to your foot?"

"I had it operated on a few weeks ago. Taking a while to heal."

"Ouch," she said. "People should learn to take care of their feet. You're bleeding."

Reaching down, I grabbed her shorts, stuffed the money into the left pocket as requested, then tossed them onto the easy chair by the door. She shuffled over to the television, turned it on. The tube just happened to be tuned into the local channel 9 news. The picture was clear and bright but the sound was muted.

"Hope you don't mind," she said. "I like to work with the TV on. Makes me feel more secure. You know, protected. Like someone is watching out for me."

"I don't mind," I said. "Sit down in the desk chair. Face the back wall. Lift your face up a little, like you're sunning yourself outside on a deck."

Pulling out the desk chair, she positioned it, and sat down, facing the back wall of the room. "Like this?" she posed. "To be honest, I'm not entirely crazy about turning my back on you. And I don't mean any disrespect. It's just that a girl has to be careful."

"You're doing fine," I said, feeling myself grow rock hard. I was looking at Casy, but in my head, I was seeing Lana sunning herself on her back deck. "You can trust me."

"Lots of nut cases out there these days. Killers. Did you know somebody killed a convenience store owner just last night out in Nassau? Crushed his skull with his own gun. I got friends live in Nassau. Scary shit."

I felt a slight start in my heart.

"You just never know when your time is up," I said, watching the back of her head, the way her hair draped the red kimono. "Now," I went on. "Slowly take off the robe."

She did it, slowly peeling it away from her shoulders and arms. I shifted myself so I could see her breasts, which were plump, the nipples erect, and pale.

"Do you want me to touch myself?" she said in a randy, sing song-like voice.

"No," I said, maybe a little too forcefully. "Just pretend you're sunning yourself."

"It's okay, mister. No problemo."

"You don't happen to have any sunglasses," I said, picturing the big rectangular ones Lana wore.

"I don't," she said. "Was I supposed to bring some?"

"It's okay," I said, knowing that I couldn't produce a pair of sunglasses for her any more than I could make her sport a red crying heart tattoo on her ankle. Still, she was doing the trick for me, fooling my brain into thinking I was looking at Lana. I was so hard I thought I might bust out of my pants. For the moment, I just wanted to watch her. I just wanted her to be Lana, even if only for a few peaceful moments. I wanted it to be like it had been before Lana and I met one another in person. Back when I would watch her from the window in the bedroom, and she appeared to have no clue about me. That was nature of our relationship then, and it was pure, and real, and lovely. Even if we didn't know one another physically, we shared an erotic and intimate relationship nonetheless. And it was beautiful.

After a time, my eyes filled, and the tears started to roll down my face.

"Are you crying, mister?" she said after a time. "Are you okay?"

I sniffled, wiped my face with the backs of my hands.

"Never mind," I said. "I'll be all right."

I watched her like that for ten more minutes, until I told her to get up and come to bed. I remembered my dream of Lana and the bed we shared in the forest. That was back when I had no idea about who the real Lana was. The evil Lana. For just a little while longer, I wanted to experience the good Lana. The Lana of my imagination. Of my fantasies.

With my eyes closed, I made love to the woman of my dreams.

CHAPTER 51

A **KNOCK** at the door. I got up, pulled on my pants as gingerly as possible over my impossibly swelled foot. I went to the chair, pulled the jean jacket off the shotgun, and grabbed hold of it.

"What the hell is that?" Casy barked.

"Relax," I said. "It's just that I'm not expecting anyone."

"I don't like guns," she said, wrapping her arms around her breasts. I recalled her telling me about the convenience store clerk. When she made the connection, she would naturally assume I was the killer.

I thought quick. "I'm in town for a trap shooting contest at the rod n' gun club. I'm a professional shooter. You can look me up on the web if you want."

Snatching up the baseball cap, I showed her the NRA logo stitched into the fabric. Setting it back down again, I peeked out the window, saw that it was the pizza I'd ordered. I'd forgotten all about it. The young man who was delivering it wasn't much older than Casy. Setting the shotgun back onto the chair, I covered it back up with my jacket.

"You might want to get under the covers," I said.

"Company?" Casy said, sliding under the white sheet.

"Pizza," I said. "Hope you're hungry."

"You sure are a strange one, mister," she said. "But kind of sweet too."

Unlocking the door, I let the young man in.

"Thirty-five fifty," he said, handing me the large, white-boxed pizza along with a plastic shopping bag which I assumed contained the whiskey and the sealant. I set it all on the round table.

"That flexy sealant shit is pretty expensive," the kid said.

Digging into my pocket, I pulled out a fifty, handed it to him.

"Keep the rest," I said.

"Sweet," he said, craning his neck to get a look at the girl.

"Mind your own business," I said.

He shot me a wink and left.

We sat back against the headboard and shared my pizza and my bottle. I'd almost forgotten that the television was on, until something slashed across the screen that captured my attention. It was a videotaped shot of the convenience store where I'd killed the clerk. There was a reporter standing outside the front door of the store beside the gas pumps, and she was talking into a hand-held microphone. With the sound muted I couldn't exactly make out what she was reporting.

The scene shifted to the interior of the store.

There was a black rubber sheet covering clerk's corpse. A few close-ups followed. One in particular of the now empty cash register. Another of the antiquated security monitoring system that was missing the cassette tape. Another shot followed that nearly sent me through the ceiling. It was portrait of me. A professional portrait snapped for me back in LA for my inclusion in the Screen Writers Guild.

I shot out of the bed, bad foot and all, hopping over to the television where I killed the power.

"What gives, Summers?" Casy said.

I inhaled, exhaled. By sheer luck or Providence, she hadn't noticed my picture on the screen.

"Gotta break up the party," I said.

She slid off the bed, glanced at her watch. "Oh my God, I should have been on campus a half hour ago. Well, looks like I'm missing my first class." She smiled. "But that was fun. Just hanging out in my birthday suit, eating pizza and doing shots. Ain't life grand." Looking at me thoughtfully. "Who exactly is Lana? And why aren't you with her if you love her so much?"

My sternum tightened.

"It's a long story," I said, pulling out an extra fifty, handing it to her.

She looked at the money in my hand, took it. I knew she thought I was crazy, and maybe I was. But I didn't care anymore. I might as well have had terminal cancer. It was just a matter of time until I was finished. Just a matter of when and how.

Casy got dressed, packed up the kimono.

"Listen, Summers," she said, "let me know next time you're in town for a… whatcha-ma-call-it… trap shooting contest." She leaned into me, planted a kiss on my cheek.

I'm not sure why, but I felt a pleasant wave of warmth wash over me then. It's the way I would have wanted to feel if I'd just spent the past hour with the real Lana. The Lana I dreamed about once upon a time.

But that hour would never come.

WHEN she was gone, I closed the door behind her, locked the deadbolt, slipped on the chain. Grabbing hold of the can of Flex Seal Clear, I limped my way to the bathroom where I sat down on the toilet, slowly removed the blood-soaked sock. Aiming the nozzle at the foot, I sucked in a breath, held it, then proceeded to spray the exposed wounds with the liquid rubber sealant. The cold sealant on the inflamed skin sucked the oxygen from my lungs. But as the material solidified and bonded, my bleeding stopped.

When I got my breath back, I raised myself up off the toilet, positioned the crutches back under my arms, and headed out of the bathroom. I wasn't two steps past the threshold when cops pulled into the motel.

SNAPSHOT

SHE *sits inside a concrete room with no windows. Only a big rectangular window that takes up much of the wall to her left. She's dressed in a pair of gym shorts and a gray sweatshirt that one of the smaller cops pulled out of his locker. The shorts and the sweatshirt bear the APD logo in big black letters. She also wears flip-flops on her feet, the tattoo of a red bleeding heart recently acquired at a downtown tattoo parlor plainly visible on her left ankle.*

After a time that seems forever, a man walks in. It's young Detective Miller. He's carrying a cup of tea in his left hand, the Lipton Tea tag hanging off the rim of the paper cup by its white string. He sets the cup down in front of her.

"How you feeling?" says Miller.

She stares down at her tea, feels the steam rising up from it clouding her view, coating the skin on her face. After a reflective time, she raises up her head, takes a good look at the tall, thin young man, at his full head of short cropped sandy blond hair and boyish face. She would never say anything about it, but she's pretty sure he doesn't have to shave more than twice a week, if that. A part of her is attracted to him, and another part... a more powerful part... wishes he'd answered one of her personals ads. How nice it would be to have him fall under her spell, then make love to him, and achieve climax by cutting him up. She would like to see that confused look in his eyes that always accompanies the first cut from the cleaver. The cut that doesn't cause pain so much as surprise and misunderstanding. Of course, the cleaver is gone now and so are her days of avenging her step-monster's atrocities.

"Think you can give me a description of the man who abducted you?" Miller says, his tone gentle and nonthreatening. Not the tone of a cop, like on TV. But of a man who really cares.

She steals a sip of tea. Then, "I told you, it's hard to say. It all happened so quickly. I was out for a walk and suddenly this man pulls me into the woods."

He looks at her forearms.

"Which arm?"

"What?"

"Which arm did he grab hold of? I'm assuming he grabbed you by the arm." She doesn't anticipate this question.

"The left," she lies.

"Funny he didn't leave a mark on your arm. A bruise. You ladies bruise easier than us men. Thinner skin."

"I think he was wearing gloves," she says. "He was all covered up."

"Maybe that explains it," he says. "But it's awfully hot out to be all covered up like that. Continue."

"Well," she says, "that dead guy was already there, down on his back." She takes a minute to work up some tears. Something she's not half bad at. "His throat was cut and there was blood all over. I tried to scream but the man's hand was wrapped around my mouth. Then you guys showed up. He let go of me, and I ran the opposite way. He must have run off too."

Miller sits back, digests her words. She's already described the man who abducted her as over six feet tall, heavy set, all dressed in black…"covered up." Amazing that a guy of that size didn't leave any marks on her, and what's more amazing, is that he was able to slip away undetected. Perhaps he's militarily trained. But even if he is, it all doesn't add up. If Miller's scientific profiling serves him right, the perp responsible for the killings… the beheadings… is almost certainly slight and quick and young. Someone who can get the jump on his victims, slash their throats. Someone who would more than likely dress and *uncannily present himself as a woman in order to fool his heterosexual victims into trusting him. If he did attack this young lady, she is almost certainly his first female victim, signifying a modification or mutation in his MO.*

…It just doesn't add up…

Still, he has no reason not to believe this girl. No reason to hold her. It's precisely what he relays to her in that same soft, gentle voice.

She takes another sip of her tea, works up a smile as she stands.

"Say, where'd you get that tattoo?" *he asks.*

She tells him.

"What's it mean?" *he says.* "Droplets of blood from a heart."

She reaches out, sets her hand on his hand.

"For me to know, Detective," *she says.* "And for you to find out."

CHAPTER 52

THE sound of sirens, the roar of engines, and the screech of tires as their brakes lock up outside my front door... It shattered the silence of my safe house.

I crutched my way back to the window, peeked out.

Three state trooper cruisers were parked diagonally in the dusty lot. A second unmarked cruiser was parked beside that one. The side passenger door on the unmarked car opened and out stepped Detective Nick Miller. He was holding his service weapon in his right hand, his left hand gripping the right wrist, combat position.

The troopers emerged from their cruisers, some of them holding automatics, a few others, short-barreled shotguns. One of them, a stocky woman, stood behind the open door of her blue and yellow cruiser, held a microphone up to her mouth. A black accordion style wire hung from the mic and extended into the open door of the cruiser.

"Ethan Forrester," she said, her deep unfeminine voice tinny and loud through the speaker. "You are under arrest. You must come out with your hands in the air."

There must have been a half dozen weapons aimed for my motel room. Some people began to gather behind the cops and troopers. I saw the old woman who owned the hotel. She was dressed in tan shorts, a black tank top befitting of a much younger woman. Her gray hair was no longer put up in curlers, but instead planted on her head like a dry, silvery bush. Out the corner of my right eye, I made out a tow truck that was only now coming into view. My Porsche was being pulled behind it. Now I had no way out of this place other than on foot.

One good foot… one foot not far from amputation…

I closed the blind, sat with my back against the narrow piece of wall between the window and the door, my shoulder pressed up against the easy chair. Was this it? The end of the road? Did the hooker give me away? The pizza boy? In answer to my own question, I shook my head no.

Those kids didn't give me away at all.

I gave myself away by not running away. Instead, I gave in to my obsession. My need to be with Lana. The law was standing outside my door, prepared to blow me away if need be simply because I left a trail too obvious to ignore. My blood and my prints would be all over that convenient store. So would an electronic record of my having used its ATM minutes before the established Estimated Time of Death for that old angry clerk.

In all my exhaustion and shock, I'd mistakenly attempted to use my Amex to pay for the motel room. By using a false name, I must have raised one hell of a red flag to the owner when, after all, she could plainly see that the name on the Amex, and the receipt for the failed transaction sported an entirely different name. A name that, sooner or later, she would connect with the man who was suspected of killing a cop in Albany and a convenience store clerk in Nassau.

You just couldn't avoid the news these days. If you didn't get it on your TV you got it on your smartphone. If you didn't get it there, then you got it on Redditt, Facebook, and Twitter. Drones filled the air, phones were tapped, security cameras were mounted everywhere. No one was safe anymore because there was nowhere to hide. The whole wide world could see up your ass and you had nowhere to hide.

I'd been screwed from the start. And I'd been avoiding the news…

avoiding the reality of what was happening on Orchard Grove and inside my brain. I guess I just wanted to escape, even if escape meant hiring a hooker to play the part of Lana... *Good* Lana. I just wanted out. To be free. To wake up in my bed and breathe easy, because this whole thing from start to finish had all been a silly nightmare.

"Ethan Forrester," the voice blared once more. "Come out with your hands up or we will remove you by force."

I knew what force meant. It meant they would come after me with smoke grenades, tear gas, and bullets. I turned around onto my knees. An electric pain shot into my right foot. Slipping the shotgun off the chair, I reached into my jeans pocket for the shells I'd lifted from the convenience store. I shoved the four shells into the shotgun and pumped a round into the chamber. Raising up the stock, I smashed a small hole in the bottom of the window pane.

The noise got the attention of the jumpy troopers.

The one on the far left triggered his semi-automatic. There was the explosion followed by a wallop in the wood door and a hole the size of my fist blown out of it. He missed by a mile.

Miller waved his arms in the air.

"Hold your fucking fire!" he screamed. "Forrester just wants to communicate with us!"

I liked Miller. He was a good cop. Under different circumstances, we might have been buds. Best buds.

I brought my face to the opening in the window, careful not to cut my lips on the jagged glass.

"I didn't kill that old man in the convenience store," I barked. "He tried to kill me. It was self-defense."

"Listen Mister Forrester," Miller said, taking a few steps forward on the gravel lot so that the space separating him from my room couldn't have been more than twenty feet, "...Ethan... just come on out and we can sort things out up in Albany."

"John's suicide... Lana planned the whole thing. She hated him. Despised him. He abused her and she couldn't take it anymore. He was going to kill her if she didn't get to him first. Do you understand me? She asked me to get him to eat his piece. But she put the bullet in the gun, not me. She must have covered her hands in Latex gloves. You have to believe me."

"I do believe you, Ethan," he said. "I *want* to believe you. But this isn't the place to be hashing out truth from fiction. This isn't one of your movies. But you know how it all works. Come out with your hands up and we'll leave this place peacefully." He took on a smile. "Hell, I'll even spring for some coffee and hard-rolls on the ride back to the city. Whaddya say?"

I rolled back over onto my ass, foot stinging, back once more pressed up against the wall. I felt the sweat dripping into my eyes, burning them. Making a fist with my right hand, I raised it up and swung it into the air conditioning unit, sending a stream of sparks flying out onto the table and the floor.

The idea came to me then, like a light bulb that illuminated brightly over my head.

"*Ah ha!*" came the voice of John Cattivo. "*I know what you're up to, Hollywood. Leave it to the crafty mind of a writer. You're gonna blow the joint sky high. That'll serve Miller, right, the pencil neck geek.*"

The dead cop was sitting on the bed, his head half blown away, chunks of flesh and brain hanging down off the sides, blood dripping out his nose, his eyeballs, and the corners of his mouth. For the first time, I got a real good look at his front teeth. Sure enough, the top two teeth were broken in half. Just looking at them made my own teeth feel strange and painful.

"Let me guess, John," I said. "You're too rotten even for hell."

"*Hey Hollywood,*" he giggled. "*Guess what? Hell can wait. I'm having a good time here just watching you panic. Why don't you just give up now? You can't outrun the cops. Even you, as stupid as you are, should know that. I mean, who kills a cop and a convenience store clerk, then stops at a motel for pizza and the company of a cheap whore? Where's the logic in that? My guess is you're already dead, pal, and you just don't know it. More dead than me even.*"

"Maybe I'm just in over my head."

"*Call it what you will, Hollywood. But you're done. D-U-N, done.*"

I shook my head, tried to shrug the vision of John away as easily as I would shake away a black and white image on an Etch A Sketch pad. But it was no use. He was sticking around for a while. Using the shotgun for support, I lifted myself up off the floor, hobbled to the stove. I opened the valves on all the burners without lighting the flame. The gas began to pour into the room.

Next, I went into the bathroom, grabbed a couple of towels. First I stuffed the end of one towel into the bullet hole in the wood door, sealing it up. Then second towel I stuffed into the jagged hole I made in the picture window, making that as air tight as possible. About-facing, I grabbed hold of the bedspread, yanked it off the mattress, and carried it to the bathroom door. Closing the door, I spread the blanket on the floor so that it completely covered over the narrow horizontal space between the bottom of the wood door and the plastic saddle. The room was now sealed off and filling with gas, fast.

"You've got a pair of steel ones after all, Hollywood," Cattivo said, from where he sat on the bed, sipping from my pint of whiskey. *"But you're still a fuck up. You know, none of this had to happen. All you had to do once my head was blown to smithereens was call 911, and confess the whole thing. No one saw you pull the trigger. You could have laid the blame squarely on my wife, and that alone would have got the gears turning in the mind of Detective Miller. Especially now that Miller knows she's been shacking up with my partner, Carl. Trust me, Hollywood, the woman is poison. Looks what she's done to you? You looked in a mirror lately? You look like forty miles of chewed up roadbed. And jeeze, that foot? It's really starting to smell bad. My guess is that before this thing is over, you're gonna lose the mofo."*

Dead Cattivo stole another sip of the whiskey, then made with his two hands like he was starting a chainsaw. He made a blade buzzing sound with his tongue pressed up against what was left of his mouth.

Once more, I tried to shake the asshole off. He was wrong of course. Maybe I killed the convenience store clerk in self-defense, but there was no way Miller or the Albany DA or God himself was going to see me as anything less than guilty in John's death. Not only was my DNA all over everything, I had motive and opportunity. All wicked characters in my scripts… characters who kill… require motive and opportunity or else they're just cartoon caricatures. Miller might be good to his word. He might actually stop for hard-rolls and coffee on the way back to Albany, but the only thing about to get chewed up and crapped out was my future.

Sitting back down on the bed, I slipped into my one boot, and put on my jean jacket. It surprised me how fast the small room was quickly filling with gas. But then why the hell should I have been surprised? The smell was intense and my eyes were beginning to water, my head growing light, a slight nausea settling in my belly. I nearly jumped a mile, bad foot and all, when the gas detector went off. The round plastic device was mounted to the popcorn-textured ceiling directly above the bed.

Grabbing hold of the shotgun, I slapped the alarm off the ceiling with the metal barrel. It landed on the bed, still blaring its ear-piercing squeak. I reached out for it, dropped it onto the floor, and crushed it with the shotgun stock. Still it squeaked. Bending at the knees, I grabbed hold of the now broken, disk-like unit, pulled out the battery, tossed it across the room.

"Ethan," I heard Miller bark through bullhorn speaker. "You okay in there? Something wrong? I hear an alarm?"

I eyed the air conditioner. I knew that at any second, its unit would start back up and at the same time, throw off some sparks that would ignite the gas and light this place up along with me inside it. I needed to get the hell out now. But I was also aware of this: once I opened the door and slammed it closed behind me, the vibrations from the wood slab connecting with the wood frame would also send a stream of sparks shooting out of the unit.

Shotgun in hand, I went to the door, opened it until the chain caught.

"I'm coming out, Miller," I yelled.

The troopers and cops took aim.

"Hold your fire!" Miller ordered.

I looked at him but remained in the room. Ever so gently I closed the door again.

"*So this is it?*" the dead cop said from the bed.

I glanced back at him, at his bloody face, and messed up head.

"What's it?" I said.

"*The moment in the movie when the fugitive makes his dramatic escape. When you run your ass out of here and try like hell to get away. You know, like when Harrison Ford jumps off that dam in The Fugitive, or when Butch Cassidy and Sundance try and shoot their way out of that spot where the Bolivian army has them pinned down. Come to think of it, ole' Butch and Sundance didn't make out too well. With all them guns pointed at them, they didn't have a chance.*"

251

"I got a chance," I said. "I'm gonna live."

"*A nice burst of confidence, Hollywood,*" he laughed. "*Just remember what I said. You're already dead.*"

"Go to hell," I said.

"*Working on it,*" he said. "*From what I'm told they've got a nice one bedroom, one and a half bath apartment waiting for you there. No air conditioning sadly.*"

Fingering the chain, I slid it slowly off its track so that it dangled before my eyes. I opened the door, stepped on out into the heat of the bright summer day, the shotgun gripped in my right hand, the barrel pointed at the cracked concrete. I faced down the barrels on at least half a dozen firearms with rounds loaded into their chambers, every single one of them engraved with my name. Miller had positioned himself only about fifteen feet away from me in the dusty lot. He was standing straight and tall in his gray blazer, white shirt, and tan trousers, that automatic gripped in both his hands.

"You're making the right decision, Ethan," he said. "Now please drop the weapon."

"Butch and Sundance," I said, shifting myself so that I stood protected by the narrow piece of wall that separated the room's wood door from the picture window.

"Excuse me?" Miller said, a look of confusion masking his tight face.

"Some people think that Hollywood got it wrong. That Butch and Sundance actually got away in the end."

"That so, Ethan," he said. "I did not know that."

"Now you do," I said.

And then I slammed the door closed.

CHAPTER 53

THE explosion proved more powerful than I anticipated.

It knocked me on my belly to the immediate left of the door while both the door and the picture window on room 30 blew out in the faces of the state troopers and Detective Miller. Out the corner of my eye, I saw Miller go down onto his back, as the troopers dropped for cover behind their cruisers. The woods were barely a dozen feet away from me. Pulling myself back up onto my feet with the shotgun posing as a crutch, I made a painful limping run for them. It was my only chance for escaping the law.

By sheer force of will, I cut across the open lawn, shooting off two rounds at the cops as I hobbled, until I arrived at the woods. By the time Miller and the troopers lifted themselves up from off the gravel lot, I'd already disappeared into the trees.

CHAPTER 54

THE woods were thick. But that was a good thing for keeping me hidden from some pretty pissed off troopers. On the other hand, with my injured foot, the going was almost impossible. The pain was intense and shot up and down my leg in bursts of electric jolts as I pushed myself through the brush and briars, the branches on the trees slapping me in the face, making it sting, making eyes tear.

I heard sirens and loud voices over the relentless pounding in my head. I heard tires spinning out on the gravel surface of the motel parking lot. They had to know that I'd taken off for the woods. They must have seen me limping for the trees. I wasn't sure how much time I had until they snagged me, but it couldn't be very long. Turning the shotgun around so that I gripped it by the barrel, I used the stock like a machete, barreling through the thick stuff on my way toward the road.

After a minute that seemed like an hour, I caught sight of the road through the branches. Without hesitating, I pushed on through what remained of the brush until I made it to the ditch that ran parallel to the roadside. A car passed by then. And another. Coming from out of the south, sirens. The troopers were coming up on my position, fast. My only choice was to somehow hijack a ride or else make a run for it through the open farm field directly across the road. I climbed up out of the ditch, stepped onto the road and prepared myself to enter into the field on the other side.

But that's when I saw the dump truck coming toward me from out of the north.

The truck was moving at a good clip. Faster than the speed limit allowed anyway. Without question, that truck was my only hope. The sirens grew louder as I recognized the blue and yellow trooper cruisers speeding toward me along a sub-baked road that was topped with a transparent, liquid-like mirage that hovered over the yellow-striped blacktop.

I had one chance, and I took it.

Positioning myself in the center of the road on the parallel line-stripes, I turned to face the truck down. The driver slammed on the brakes, the dump truck's big wide tires screeching, burning rubber, its metal dump fishtailing sideways. I stood my ground knowing I couldn't move out of the way if I wanted to. I just didn't have the energy or the strength in my foot, or the rest of my body for that matter, necessary to make the move. The truck skidded maybe twenty feet, horn blaring, metal banging against metal, straining and tearing, exhaust blowing out black smoke, engine revving RPMs, gears crunching. Until finally the truck came to a stop only inches from my face.

The door opened and a tall wiry young man in a white T-shirt and wearing a straw cowboy hat, poked his head out.

"Are you fucking out of your mind?" he said, his eyes hidden behind mirrored aviator sunglasses.

I shoved the shotgun stock against my shoulder, planted a bead.

"Get the hell back behind the wheel," I snarled, my beating heart jammed inside my throat.

Behind me, the trooper cruisers were closing in, their red and white LED flashers bright even against the brilliant mid-day sun. I hobbled over to the passenger side door and, planting myself on my bad foot, hopped up onto the running board, opened the door, and shoved myself inside with a scream that might have cracked the windshield if it wasn't made of safety glass.

Up ahead, the troopers made a barricade by having stopped their cruisers in the middle of the road, positioning them perpendicular to the opposing roadsides. They exited the vehicles, weapons in hand, crouching down behind them for protection.

The trucker turned to me.

"That foot looks like shit," he said.

"So I'm told," I grunted.

"It's bleeding bad. Smells too."

I peered down at it. The Flex Seal hadn't worked after all. "I'm sorry."

"You're the one with the gun. What do you want me to do? Turn around, go the other way?"

I pumped a shell into the shotgun chamber.

"Blow through them," I demanded.

He just stared at me through those impossibly shiny sunglasses.

"That shit only works in the movies."

"I'm aware of that. So let's pretend we're shooting a movie."

"You serious?"

"Do it. Do it, please. Pretty please."

The trucker turned to face the road.

"Lord have mercy on my soul," he said.

"Action!" I said.

He shoved the floor-mounted stick into gear, then gave it the gas.

CHAPTER 55

THE big truck took on speed.

It jerked, bucked, and bounced. When the passenger side windshield exploded, I dropped down onto my left shoulder.

"Holy Christ they're shooting at us," he said.

"What's your name, son?"

"Walt."

"Walt, just keep on trucking."

I brushed the pebble-like shards of shattered safety glass off of me.

Sitting up fast, I swung the shotgun around, aimed it not for the troopers but the closest cruiser and triggered off a shell. The shot blew out a tire on the vehicle directly ahead of me as we closed in on it.

The troopers leapt off the side of the road like they were abandoning ship.

"We're gonna ram them!" the trucker screamed, his voice an octave higher than God intended.

"That would be the point. Don't stop!"

Grabbing the metal underside of the seat, I held on while we barreled through both cruisers.

CHAPTER 56

I DON'T know why I started to laugh, but I couldn't help myself. Maybe it had something to do with acting out a scene I might have written for an Arnold Schwarzenegger action/thriller and actually succeeding without getting ourselves killed or totaling the truck. Sometimes you gotta go with your gut.

"See, Walt," I said, raising myself up. "Just like a movie."

Even he had to laugh.

"Gotta admit," he said, as he bounced in his seat, "that wasn't entirely no fun."

He hadn't slowed down since we blew through the cruisers. His cowboy booted foot was still firmly planted on the gas, his right hand gripping the ball-head on the stick shift, left hand on the big wheel. As we came upon the motel, I turned to view the parking lot. I saw something very strange. I saw Detective Miller standing all alone in the middle of the lot. He had one hand shoved in his trouser pockets, almost casually. And with the other one, he was holding something up for me to see. It was the security tape cassette from the convenience store. The tape I'd tossed into the dumpster out back. He was wearing this big grin like, "Gotcha asshole!"

As we passed, he pulled his free hand out of his pocket, tossed me a quick wave, then made like a pistol with thumb and index finger, and pointed it at the security tape. The scene was at once odd and somehow frightening. He wasn't giving chase or taking aim at the truck with his sidearm. He just stood there waving at me like he no longer needed to go after me at all. Like my immediate future was already doomed with or without his efforts. And he had the whole thing on tape to prove it.

I turned toward the open road, and what up until now had been a wide smile on my face disintegrated like a bullet through an apple. Instead, my brain filled with cold realization. Maybe I'd just escaped the state troopers. But as far as Miller was concerned, I was already caught, already sentenced before a jury of my peers.

Like the ghost of John Cattivo said, I was already dead.

SNAPSHOT

SHE *holds Miller's hand all the way from the interview room to the front vestibule and the guard sergeant's desk. She insists her mother is coming for her. And when the weary middle-aged woman arrives to claim her daughter, she bursts out in tears.*

"Why don't you listen to me, Lana?" the woman cries, her long dark hair streaked with strands of stark gray that seem more like battle-scars than the result of the organic aging process. "Look what happens when you sneak out at night? You can get yourself killed."

Lana lowers her head, stares at the scuffed linoleum flooring, but in her young brain she runs through the faces of the men and boys she's killed over the years, beginning with her stepfather. She sees that funny look their faces assumed the moment they knew their throats were about to be cut not by a big bad man, but a beautiful, young, blonde teenager. How could they have been so stupid, so naïve, so trusting?

"You should listen to your mom," Miller says, releasing her hand. "She knows best. She loves you."

"I will," Lana smiles, shifting her now empty hand to her mother's trembling

hand. *"From this moment on, I will listen to my mom."*

Miller locks eyes on Lana's crying heart tattoo as she exists the APD building. It's a mark he will never forget for as long as he lives.

CHAPTER 57

BAD idea: riding a heavy-duty dump truck all the way into Albany.

I might as well ride a helium balloon back into town, a brass band playing in the whicker basket as I floated over the downtown sky rises and the asphalt roofs of the outlying suburban homes. I didn't want take the same route back that I'd taken out here, either. Nassau alone would be crawling with cops and troopers. Truth is, I didn't care about getting caught, necessarily. That wasn't the real issue here. The cops were going to catch up to me sooner or later. Probably sooner.

What I really wanted was to buy enough time to get back to Albany and to Lana and Susan. Once I managed that, I'd find a way to extract a confession from one or both of them. A confession wouldn't keep me out of prison, but it might keep me off Death Row. Hell, a full confession might allow me the leverage to strike up a deal with Miller, potentially reducing any charges he was dying to lob at me.

Of course, he'd have to believe me when I told him I acted out of self-defense when I hit the old clerk over the head with the shotgun stock. That might take some doing, and the talents of a savvy lawyer. Miller might be an Albany cop, but he wasn't stupid. If forensic and circumstantial evidence existed of my having acted in self-defense, he would not be blind to it. I had to believe that.

My only other choice would be to lie down and die now.

As Walt and I approached Route 90, the east/west highway that would lead me directly back into the city, I instructed him to take the entrance marked West Albany. But as soon as he got on the three-lane interstate, I made him pull over onto the shoulder to let me out. Funny thing is, he didn't seem all that excited and relieved over getting rid of me. Instead he pulled off onto the wide shoulder and turned to me with an expression best described as concerned. As though during the short time we spent together, we'd become solid friends.

"Listen Walt," I said, "I need something else from you."

He nodded.

"I need your clothes. The cops have a make on what I'm wearing."

He sort of looked himself up and down.

"I'm wearing jeans same as you," he said. Then, "I got an idea though." He reached behind the seat, pulled out a pair of overalls. "I wear these sometimes when I'm dumping fine sand. Stuff gets in your hair, your ears, your nose, your pores."

I locked eyes on the dark blue acrylic overalls.

"They'll have to do," I said, as I proceeded to slip them on, zipping up the front.

"I can take you where you're going," Walt said, after I was dressed.

"You definitely *do not* want to do that," I said. "The place will be crawling with cops. They'll shoot us on sight. You need to get rid of me and then head to the nearest police station. Tell them everything." I opened the door, grabbed the shotgun, gingerly stepped out onto the running board, all the time wincing in pain. "Remember, tell them everything. Don't lie or withhold. Tell them the absolute truth about how this little ride went down. They'll believe you and let you go."

He nodded, the brim on his straw cowboy hat waving up and down like a Japanese fan.

"It's been quite the adventure," he said, trying to work up a grin.

"Glad I could break up your day," I said.

"Take care of that foot," he said.

Stepping off the running board onto my good foot and onto the shotgun stock, which I once more used as a crutch, I closed the truck door. I stepped out of the way as he pulled away from the curb and proceeded back onto the highway. Turning, I moved away from the roadbed and hid myself in a patch of woods where I would wait until nightfall. I also turned off my cell phone to save the battery. Under the cover of darkness, I'd get myself back to the city for a final showdown with my two lost loves.

THE afternoon was filled with cop and trooper cruisers speeding up and down the highway, rooftop flashers lit up, engines revving. I wondered if I'd left my cell phone on for too long, and they'd been able to make out my general position as opposed to a precise one. It was like one of my movies. Here I was fighting for my life, and the world never seemed so alive, even if I did feel like I was about to die or, at the very least, lose my foot.

Resisting the urge to power the phone back up to call Lana and Susan, tell them I was coming for them, I instead began to wonder if I'd made a mistake by not allowing Walt to take me all the way into the city. Then I could have hidden somewhere in the mostly abandoned north side industrial section. From there it would have been a short walk back to Orchard Grove. I guess I wasn't thinking straight when I had him drop me off in the woods. Maybe gangrene had set in after all, and the fever that went with it was cooking my brain.

When darkness finally fell, I stepped out of the woods, made my way to the soft shoulder, set the shotgun out flat in the grass behind me so that it was hidden from view. Then I did something I'd never done before in my life. I started thumbing for a ride. I knew I was taking one hell of a chance by attracting a cop, but at this point, it was a chance I was willing to take. If a cop or a trooper did pull up, I'd have no choice but to retrieve my shotgun and point the business end at him, tell him to scram or else.

My physical troubles were worse than I first thought.

My foot was bleeding, bad. The throbbing was almost unbearable, my fever growing worse. All I wanted to do was get to the Cattivo house, extract Lana's and Susan's confession for their complicity in this whole mess, and it would all be over. I'd turn myself in to Miller who would get me to a hospital.

It took some time while the cars and trucks sped past, the drivers not giving me a second look, most of them not noticing me at all in the dark and what with me wearing dark blue overalls. Until finally, a passing truck slowed down, pulled over. Over my shoulder I saw the red taillights illuminate as the pickup came to a stop along the shoulder. Limping the few feet to it, I recognized it as an old Ford F150, color dark blue, just like my overalls. Something from out of the late 1970s maybe.

The guy driving it leaned over the seat, rolled down the window. He was young. Maybe thirty or so. He had a head full of thick blond hair that was partially covered by a skull cap that was more like a stocking cap since a good portion of it hung down against his back. Like the kind of hat a Rastafarian would wear during all seasons, hot and cold. Or a committed stoner. He also sported a blond mustache and an equally blond beard. He wore a thin leather jacket over a denim button-down shirt, the tails hanging out of the blue jeans.

"Hop in, dude," he said, smiling. Like picking up a total stranger trying to thumb a ride on a hot summer's night was the most fun you could have with your pants on. "Ain't you heard? There's some crazy killer out there. You shouldn't be walking all alone like that."

I climbed in, as carefully as I could. When I set the heel on my bad foot on the floor, I flinched from the pain.

"Ouch, dude," he said, his gaze focused on the foot, which was illuminated by a dull floorboard lamp. "I hope the other guy is worse."

"Cut it on some glass a while back," I said. "Stitches haven't completely healed."

I don't know why I felt compelled to lie. But I did it anyway.

"Feet can be like really tough ass healers," he said in his pseudo-West LA stoner twang. "Hey man, don't forget the seatbelt. Safety first and it's the law."

I went to grab the shoulder harness part of the belt. But since this was an old truck, there was only the waist belt. I put the belt on, tightened it around my mid-section.

The driver looked out the window onto on-coming traffic. Then, reaching out the open window with his left arm, proceeded to make an official left-turn hand signal. Satisfied that the coast was clear, he threw the automatic, column-mounted tranny into drive, and pulled out. After we'd been driving for a minute or two, he asked me where I was headed.

"Albany," I told him. It dawned on me then that for a stoner, the truck cab didn't smell at all like he'd been burning pot inside it. I grew pot in my backyard, sold it to several stoners, all of whom loved nothing more than getting baked in their cars and trucks.

"I can take you all the way," he said. "Fifteen minutes." He held out his right hand. "By the way, I'm CP."

I took the hand in mine. His grip was tight.

"CP," I said. "What's that?"

"Short for the real thing," he said. "Letters are just easier."

"Hi CP," I said, "I'm Jim Summers."

I thanked him for the ride then, and as I sat back against the old bench-style seat, I felt the tight bounce of the suspension, and wondered if my luck was changing, or if it even had a right to change. Maybe I was going to find a way out of this train wreck after all.

"You mind if I pop in a CD?" CP said as the lights of the city became visible on the western horizon.

"People still listen to CDs?" I said. "I thought millennials all listened to Sirius radio."

"I'm all about the retro, dude," he said.

When he suddenly reached under the seat with his free hand, he gave my heart a start. I thought he might come back out with a gun. Or a knife maybe. You had to be crazy to hitchhike these days. Even crazier to pick a hitchhiker up. CP said it himself. There was a killer out there on the loose.

But he didn't produce a weapon. Instead he held a plastic CD case in his right hand while still gripping the wheel of the truck with his left. He set the case onto the empty seat between us, opened it one handed, pulled a CD out that had the words, "The Best of the Clash" printed on it. He slid the CD into a player that had been mounted under the dash as an afterthought. Before the first song came on, he forwarded the CD to a song he wished to hear more than any other.

As I listened to the ascending tom-tom buildup, I began to recognize the song. The drum roll finished in a crash of cymbals and an explosion of guitar and bass. "Breaking rocks in the hot sun," sang the gravelly voice of the late great Joe Strummer. "I fought the law and the law won… I fought the law and the law won."

CP sang along, slapping his fist to the catchy beat.

"Interesting choice of music," I said. My gut started speaking to me. Whispering, poking, prodding. My whole body tightened up, like something more was going on here than just an innocent stoner going out of his way to give me much needed ride into the city. Part of me wanted to slam him on the side of the head with my fist, then jump out of the truck. But my gut screamed at me to keep my eyes open, my mouth shut, and my hands and one good foot ready for anything. The important thing was that he was taking me into the city. Once I was within a reasonable distance from Orchard Grove, I could jump out at a stoplight and simply disappear into some non-descript cookie-cutter housing development. It wasn't much of a plan, but it was the only plan I had seeing as I was no longer in possession of the shotgun.

I no longer had the means to blow him away should push come to violent shove.

Minutes later we entered onto the north/south Hudson Riverside arterial that would take us into the North Albany suburbs. The Clash sang "I Fought the Law" non-stop. As soon as the song finished, CP would hit the repeat button, taking the tune from the top, like he was trying to pound it into my head.

"You must really like this song, CP," I said after a while.

"Yeah," he said. "Me and my coworkers listen to it all the time. It's kind of like our adopted anthem."

Coworkers…

He shot me a look over his shoulder, along with a wink of his eye.

"What's your line of work?" I said. "You don't mind my asking."

He cocked his head while turning onto an exit ramp that hooked up with the road that would connect us directly with Orchard Grove after about a mile. That's when he reached into his jean jacket, pulled out a small leather wallet-like object. He flipped it open, revealing a badge.

"I serve and protect," he said, as he pulled off the white wig and skull cap, along with the white mustache and beard, revealing a trim black mustache and goatee. "Surprise! Surprise!" he said in his best imitation Gomer Pyle.

"CP," I swallowed. "Carl… Pressman."

My heart went still inside my sternum.

"And you, motherfucker," he added, "you killed my partner, John Cattivo."

CHAPTER 58

SURE I was fucked. Totally, absolutely fucked. But I also had a choice. I could either sit there and allow him to take me into custody. Or I could go after him claw and fist. Disable him, then jump out of the truck, make a run for it. Or maybe run wasn't the right word for it. Hobble, limp, crawl, was more like it.

I was just about to choose the latter when he returned the badge to his pocket and drew his service weapon, shifting it into his left hand so he could more easily point the barrel at me while he steered with his right.

"Go ahead," he said. "Make my fucking day, Forrester. Try and jump me with that rotten stinky foot of yours. I'd love the excuse to blow a hole in you so wide I could drive my pickup through it. And trust me, ain't no one in the APD gonna care if you bleed to death. Doesn't matter if Cattivo was an ugly prick. Now it's personal."

Joe Strummer sang, "...*Killed my baby and I feel so sad, I guess my race is run...*"

Maybe that's what I should have done from the get-go. As soon as I realized that Lana and Susan had double-crossed me, I should have grabbed

269

one of Cattivo's guns and shot them both on the spot. But then, where would that have gotten me but a free ticket to the state death chamber? At least, as things stood right now, I had a shot at redemption and revenge, no matter how slight.

I glanced into the eternal darkness of Carl's pistol barrel.

"How did you know where to find me?" I asked.

"I'm a cop. I've been tracking you all day. I finally caught up with Miller just after you ran off. Then I followed you in that dump truck. I saw you head into the woods, but you didn't disappear entirely. I was able to keep an eye on you through the trees with a pair of binoculars."

That explains why no other cops or troopers picked me up… They were tracking me all along by way of Carl…

"You could have come after me."

"It's easy to run and hide in the woods, even for a cripple like you. Ain't you ever read *Little Red Riding Hood* or *Hansel and Gretel*? I didn't want to risk losing you. I'm a patient man, so I simply waited until you came back out."

I recalled Miller smiling and waving at me in that motel parking lot. He knew I was riding into an ambush, never mind the state trooper roadblock I'd just busted through.

"What if I'd never hidden myself in the woods," I said. "What if I came all the way back to Orchard Grove in that dump truck?"

"I'm one hell of a cop fortunately," Carl said. "When it comes to tracking down killers like you, I'm prepared for any eventuality. It's what separates the men from the boys."

"Nailing your partner's wife behind his back separate you from the boys too?"

He laughed, but it was a bitter, scornful laugh. And he further backed it up by removing his hand from the wheel and backhanding me with it.

"None of your business, Forrester," he scolded.

"My apologies," I said, feeling the sting in my check and nose, hearing the bells ring in my head. Then, "Where are you taking me?"

"Home," he said.

"Why?" I ran my fingers under my nostrils and upper lip, checking for fresh blood.

"Payback," he said.

"Payback," I repeated.

"Yup," he said. "Rotten apple like you has gotta pay for his sins."

Then, shifting his pistol back into his right hand, he swung it against the crown of my head and...

CHAPTER 59

WHEN I came to, I found myself still seated in the pickup. It wasn't parked in my driveway next door, but in Lana's driveway instead. Something strange was happening at the front door to the single-story ranch house. A queue of neighborhood kids extended from the open door out onto the concrete landing, down the two steps, and out onto the asphalt walk. From where I sat in the passenger seat, now faking my unconsciousness, I spotted Lana standing in the doorway of the pleasantly illuminated home. From what I could also make out, she was handing out cookies from off a silver platter to the children who were scarfing them down as fast as they could get their hands on them. She was wearing an apron over a pink and baby blue dress, and her hair surrounded her face beautifully. It was as if overnight she'd become a happy domestic Holly Homemaker.

"Now there's a brave woman for you," Carl mumbled to himself. "Her husband isn't even cold yet and all she can think about is giving out cookies to the children of Orchard Grove."

"You're kidding me, right, Carl?" I wanted to say, but I didn't want him to know that I was awake.

Something wasn't right about the situation. Something other than the obvious. As an Albany cop, Carl should have been carting me to the APD and promptly booking me for two counts of murder. At the very least, it was his duty to call the bust in to Detective Miller who would have handled it from there.

But he was doing none of the above.

No official arrest was made. No Miranda's issues. No calling the bust in to his fellow officers.

Nothing.

Instead he gave me a pistol whipping and then drove me straight to the Cattivo house where, no doubt, the women were expecting him. Maybe they were also expecting me. My guess is that they all had something in store for me. What exactly that something was, I had no idea. But my gut was telling me to open the door and try to get away. That whatever it was Carl and company wanted from me, it wasn't going to be the least bit pleasant. But then, I was also aware that I'd never have another chance to contract a confession from Lana. A confession that I could record with my cell phone app and forward to Miller. In order to make it happen, I'd have to stand my ground and hang in there, regardless of the potential shit storm that awaited me inside that house.

I felt Carl's eyes shifting their focus back toward me. In turn, I closed my eyes back up.

Reaching out with his gun, he poked me in the ribs with it. I felt the sharp jab, but pretended to be dead to the world.

"Still out," he mumbled to himself. "Just as well."

He opened the truck door, got out, closed it behind him. Lifting the lids on my eyes, I watched him walk on past the dozen or so neighborhood kids, hop up the couple of steps to the landing, where he greeted Lana, kissing her on the mouth, like lovers do.

When the two disappeared, I unzipped the overalls, reached into my pants pocket, pulled out my cell phone, turned it back on. The battery charge indicated only fifteen percent, which meant I had maybe thirty minutes of power left at most. One eye on the front door, the other down at the digital screen, I thumbed onto Recent Calls. When I spotted Miller's phone number, I selected the Send Text Message option. A blank message screen appeared for me. For a brief second I considered sending him a text that detailed the precise location of my whereabouts and how I came to be here. But then something told me, not now. That I needed to confront Lana and Susan first before I involved the cops. Otherwise, my one chance for extracting the confession would be destroyed.

What I did manage to do, however, was proceed to applications, one of which was a voice recorder. I waited for Carl to show himself at the door again, and then I pressed Record, praying that the phone battery would last long enough for Lana to say what I wanted her to say.

Carl was making his way back out of the house when I shoved the cell phone back into my jeans pocket, the voice recorder still running, and zipped the overalls back up.

When he opened the passenger side door, he stuck his gun in my face.

"Well good morning, Carl," I said. "How long have I been asleep?"

"Get out," he said. "In the house. Now."

"You mean like in there? Isn't my wife, or soon to be ex-wife, in there?"

"So to speak," he said. "But sadly, she won't be seeing you or anyone else for a long time." He grabbed me by the collar. "Let's go, asshole."

He yanked me out of the truck so that I went down onto the driveway on my face. He grabbed me once more, yanking me up with his sheer brute strength. I had no choice but to balance awkwardly on my bad foot, sending a wave of searing pain throughout the swelled, bleeding flesh, and up and down my leg. I screamed, scaring the kids. But that didn't stop Carl. He pressed the pistol barrel against my spine and pushed me forward. Through the waves of pain, I tried to make sense of what he was talking about with regard to Susan. Why wouldn't she be seeing me or anyone else for a long time?

As we approached the startled kids who were gathered at the door with the cookies in their hands and chocolate all over their lips, he said, "Party's over, kids. It's late. Get back home before your folks wonder where you are." He was hiding the gun for obvious reasons. For a second, I thought about shouting out to the children that the man behind me had a loaded gun pointed at my back. Maybe that would have diffused the situation, but it also would have wrecked my plan.

The kids dispersed, scattering like rabbits across the front lawn on their way back to their separate Orchard Grove homes. Opening the screen door, I limped into Lana's house, while Carl closed both the screen and the wood door behind me, locking the deadbolt.

Lana was standing in the middle of the living room to the right, her arms crossed over her chest, her face pale and frowning. She no longer looked like Holly Homemaker, even if the house did smell like freshly baked cookies. Instead she looked like the anxious but angry as all hell mother of some little boy who'd run away from home the night before after being sent to bed without any supper.

"You've been quite the bad boy, Ethan," she said, working up a sly smile. "So how does it feel to go from writing about killing people, to actually becoming a killer?"

"I wouldn't know," I said. "But maybe you can tell me."

I felt the pistol barrel slap me upside the head, sending visions of stars across my eyeballs and a sharp, skull-piercing pain throughout my brain. For a brief moment, I lost my balance.

"Don't talk until you're asked to talk," Carl said.

"Yes, you should listen to the police," Lana said. "Right now, they're the best friends you have in the world. What's that tell you?"

"You tell me," I said, my head ringing.

"It means you're all alone. You haven't got a soul on earth who loves you."

She poured herself a glass of sparkling wine from a bottle that had been put on ice earlier inside an old silver bucket. She sipped it, and then set the glass back down onto the glass-topped coffee table.

"I just love apple wine, Ethan," she said. "Did you know that my stepfather had plans to introduce his own brand of apple wines prior to his sad disappearance? He was going to name them Lana's Lovely Apple Wines. Name them after me."

"Has a nice ring to it," I said. "Too bad all the trees got cut down."

She pursed her lips. "Yes, sad isn't it. But then my mom and I could never have run the farm without him. He was the workhorse and the apple master." She picked the glass back up, sipped more wine. "But that's neither here nor there. Now where were we? I believe we were discussing your many homicides over the past couple of days."

The recording app on my phone… I could only hope it was picking up all our voices.

"Maybe we should talk about yours," I said.

Carl jabbed me against the spine. Hard.

"Now, now," Lana said, brushing back her long, blonde hair, her blue eyes glowing in the lamp light. "Killing an old man in a convenience store. Tsk. Tsk. How could you do something so deplorable, Ethan Forrester? And that job you did on Susan." She shivered, like a cold breeze just passed through the living room. "Absolutely barbaric."

My heart sank into my stomach. What the hell was she talking about? Then, out the corner of my eye, I caught sight of something else that was sitting on the coffee table behind the decanter. The Maxwell House Coffee I'd buried outside in the pot patch, the mud and dirt still partially caked to its sides, the plastic lid removed, and the cash all gone.

"Where did you get that?" I said, pointing at the can. "And where's Susan? Where's my wife?"

Carl poked me again, sending a shock up and down my spine. "Sorry about the can, Ethan, buddy. But you see, that pot garden you got out back is illegal as all hell, and part of your restitution is lining our pockets with a little petty travel cash." I turned and was able to catch a glimpse of the mustached and goateed cop shooting a look at Lana. "Isn't that right, baby?"

"You're the apple of my eye, Carl," she said. But she didn't seem in the mood to converse with her dead husband's partner. My gut spoke to me, told me she was using him as much as she used me. Then she said, "Obviously pot plants and money aren't the only thing Ethan feels compelled to bury in the soil." Stealing another sip of the apple wine. "He's an absolute animal. Aren't you, Ethan?" She smiled when she said it, approaching me with her right hand held out, her torso still wrapped in her flowered apron, her legs exposed, her feet in brown leather sandals, that heart-shaped tattoo and the blood that dripped from it drawing my attention more than her face.

She stopped just inches from me, ran her open hand softly across my stubbly face.

"You were such a delicious mistake," she said, sighing. "I'm so sorry

276

things turned out so badly for you. For Susan. You should never have allowed jealously and pride guide your emotions. And, by the way, you should curb that drinking of yours. It's the whiskey that turns Doctor Jekyll into that frightening Mister Hyde."

In my head, I ran through the events of the previous night. Getting drunk on Jack, grabbing hold of a French knife, carrying it with me to the Cattivo's back deck. I saw myself opening her back sliding glass doors. That's where the memories ended, however. But then I was reminded about the voice recorder on my phone. How it should have been picking up every word of this conversation, which thus far had produced nothing that could be construed as a confession on Lana's part. Now was the time to coax her into telling the truth. For me. For Miller.

"You wanna know something, Lana?" I said, forcing a laugh. "I really had no idea you were setting me up to take the fall for John's murder. I had no idea you *and* Susan were setting me up together, making me out to be the patsy. I believed you when you told me John was going to kill you over your affair with Lurch here." Shooting another glance at Carl. "Speaking of Lurch, my guess is you're fucking him over, same as me."

He jabbed me with the pistol once more. But this time, I braced myself for it.

"Why don't you shut the fuck up, Forrester," he barked. "What Lana and I have together is special. It's real love, just like John Lennon used to sing. Isn't that right baby?"

"Yes, Carl," she said. "Terrible thing what happened to Mr. Lennon. Too many guns in the world, don't you agree, Ethan? My life is full of guns and lovers."

I looked into Lana's face. "Tell me, how long have you and my wife been lovers?"

She glared at me with eyes that could melt diamonds.

"Long enough," she said.

"Lana," Carl said. "What's he talking about? You and Susan were good friends. What's he mean by lovers?"

"Shut up, Carl," she said. Then, her eyes locked back on me. "Don't look to me for an apology for what happened with Susan. From what she told me, you entered into a love affair with your work long before she even considered drifting. Your world is yourself, your typewriter, your pathetic movie scripts, and that bedroom window where you spent hours watching me sunbathe. You allowed your marriage to fall apart, and your home to be foreclosed upon. You had no love left for Susan or you would not have fallen hopelessly in love with me."

I felt my chest tighten. She wasn't saying what I wanted her to say. What I needed her to say. "I guess Susan did a great job of hiding her hatred of me. Even when she was making love to me. I can only assume that I'm not about to leave this house alive. So why not open up to me, Lana? Did you or did you not tell my wife to help you plan the murder of your husband, while laying the blame squarely on me? Or was the idea exclusively yours? Tell me, please. What have you got to lose?"

She drank some more apple wine, smiled. But she wouldn't open up. She wouldn't talk, as if she knew full well that I was recording this conversation. Even now... even after all that had happened over the past few days... she still looked as ravishing as ever. Her eyes were wet and deep and beautiful. But I knew that deep in her heart and soul, she was rotten to the core.

"Does it matter who came up with what plan, Ethan?" she said, after a time. "What matters is that he's dead and that you have blood on your hands because of it. They're all dead. Go outside to your secret garden, and see for yourself. Go see what you did before you ran away under the cover of darkness so early this morning."

They're all dead...

I wanted to scream because she wasn't admitting the truth. She wasn't talking. And why wasn't Susan in the room? If they were all dead, did that mean they killed my wife? I felt sick to my stomach and my head was spinning. Still, I had to get her to talk. I had no choice but to explore another angle.

"So why cart me back here?" I said, my voice raised a decibel so I could be sure the voice recorder app picked up my every word. "Why does this distinguished member of the Albany Police Force, Carl Pressman, have a gun pressed up against my spine? Why isn't he taking me downtown for booking and processing according to the letter of the law? Why did he hit me over the head with his weapon? Why did he kidnap me?"

Bracing myself again, I waited for the jab. It came hard and swift, stealing my breath away.

"Your word against mine, Forrester. And surprise, surprise, guess who the police are gonna believe? Me or a cop killer? A murderer of helpless old men? A sick man who mutilates his wife and tries to make it look like Lana did it? You're a mad man. A menace. That foot must be full of gangrene and it must have poisoned your blood stream, pal."

My heart, what was left of it, sank even deeper.

"What the hell are you talking about?" I barked. "I haven't laid a finger on my wife."

"Tell that to a judge at your hearing," Carl said. "That is you live long enough to have a hearing."

My foot throbbed and I felt the weight of the cell phone in my pocket. Maybe Miller would call me now and I could quickly answer the phone. "Pressman's gonna kill me!" I would scream. That would put a damper on whatever they had in store for me. Even though my plan to extract a confession was quickly going south, I tried to look on the bright side. My verbal sparring with Lana, and my equally verbal observations would have to count for something. So would Carl's reaction to them. It would at the very least implicate him in Lana's overall deception. My observations, Carl's reaction, and the fact that Lana had demanded an up close and personal audience with me after her husband's murder might be all I needed to prove that a conspiracy to kill John existed long before I asked him to demonstrate a classic cop suicide for me.

"We need a little something from you, Ethan," Lana said, setting down her glass, then raising the same hand, once again caressing my cheek.

"Why should I give you anything?" I said bitterly.

She removed her hand from my face, took a step back.

"Because you don't have a choice, now do you?"

"What exactly is it you want?"

"I need you to commit one final murder in your long string of murders."

CHAPTER 60

"CARL," she said, "would you be so kind as to escort Ethan to the gunroom where he will break into the cases, steal a weapon, load it, and attempt to shoot dead a helpless, grieving widow?" She giggled like this was all a child's game to her.

"Sure thing, baby," he obeyed.

Again, that pistol shoved against my spine. But suddenly, the pain didn't matter. Because Lana finally said something that would without question, implicate her in a conspiracy to set me up for murder, and I had it recorded on my cell phone app. That is, my phone was still working.

"*Baby*," I repeated with sarcasm, limping across the vestibule toward the room. "Hey Carl, looks like you're the next contestant in Fuck 'em and Kill 'em by Lana Cattivo."

"Shut up, cripple," he said, jabbing my shoulder with his fisted free hand.

"Not very PC of you," I said. "I'm telling Obama."

Entering into the gunroom, I could see that it had been cleaned. No more brains, blood, and hair stained the slider window or the wall behind Cattivo's desk.

"Now," Carl said, open the closet, pull down a box of 9mm rounds. Got it?"

As ordered, I went to the closet, slid the wood door open. I found one of the boxes of bullets stacked on the closet shelf, and pulled one down.

"Set the box down on the desk," Carl demanded.

I did it.

"What next, Carl?" I said, sensing for the first time that although the cop knew what he wanted to ultimately accomplish with me inside the gunroom, he wasn't entirely sure how to go about it. Here's how I scripted it out in my mind: he would make it look like I fled the police out in the country, then managed to evade his highway surveillance of me while somehow making my way back to the city, and eventually to Orchard Grove where I broke into Lana's house. I immediately made my way to the gunroom, smashed one of the cases, stole a weapon, loaded it, then used it to shoot Lana or Susan or Carl or all three of them. Attempted to shoot them, that is. But in order to make the plot viable, he'd have to stain everything with my prints, just like Lana managed to do less than forty-eight hours ago when she handed me the very .45 caliber bullet that would plow through her husband's head.

Leaning my left hand on the desk to take some pressure off my right foot, I looked into Carl's eyes. They were wide and slightly out of focus. His face was tight, his lips in deep frown position.

"What's wrong, Carl?" I said. "You look confused. Confused and nervous."

"Quiet, Hollywood," he said, wiping sweat from his brow with the back of his hand. "That's what my partner used to call you, right? Hollywood? Well tell you what, *Hollywood*, stop leaning on that desk and put a foot through that glass on the case to the right."

Bracing myself for more pain, I approached the case on the right.

"You mean this one?" I said. "You sure about that, Carl? The case housing the pistols? Or should I go for the gold and break open the case with the machine guns? If I were going to script a mass murder, I would go for the more-fire-power kind of scenario. But then, hey, that's just me. Mister Hollywood. But this is your show, Carl. The Lana, Susan, and Carl murder show."

"Shut your trap, Forrester!" He was shouting now. Losing control. Perhaps for the first time, he was beginning to realize the gravity of what Lana was asking him to do. Commit murder on her behalf. As a cop, it would go against his very nature, no matter how much he loved her, wanted her, needed her. I'd been in the same position just a short time ago. I was Lana's slave.

"Tell me, Carl," I said, tossing him a look over my shoulder. "Before I go ahead and start this thing, tell me something. Why are you doing this? You know what Lana's all about. You've seen what she can do to people, men *and* women. She's not exclusive to any one person. She fucks who she wants and then she fucks them over. She is a pathological case if ever there was one. How is it you don't believe you'll end up just as dead as I'm about to be? As dead as John is, and maybe even my wife? What have you got to gain by doing Lana's dirty work? I mean, this can't be out of respect for John. Even you've admitted how much you hated him. Is your obsession for her that bad?"

He blinked his eyes and cocked his head, almost like he didn't quite understand the question. Or perhaps he understood it all right, but was deathly afraid of the answers. But then, if anyone understood his obsession, it was me. Keeping the gun poised on me, he turned in search of Lana, as if she would provide the correct dialogue for him. But she was standing out in the hall, her hands gripped into tight fists, her lips pressed together. Suddenly she didn't look so beautiful. Now she just looked cheap and evil.

Carl turned back to me.

"So what if I did hate John," he said. "He was still a brother. Now you have to pay for what you've done to him."

"For what I was set up by Lana to do, Carl," I said. "Let's at least be honest and get it right. And of course, it's not up to you to make me pay for anything, is it? It's not your place any more than it's God's place. It's entirely up to a court of law. You're just following a script prepared for you by Lana. Or maybe you're just convinced that you're doing this for John. My guess is that, had John lived, he would have killed you. Killed you and Lana both for fucking each other behind his back… for breaking that secret code you cop partners share. Now why don't we do the right thing and stop this nonsense before someone else dies? Why don't we place a call to Miller?"

In my pocket I now had the voice recordings that would at the very least, get me off for the charge of murder in the first. Now was the time to bring in

Miller. I had to at least try to convince Carl of that. An impossible task to be sure. But I had to at least try.

The hand that gripped the gun was growing unsteady. But Carl's finger was still on the trigger. Out in the hall, Lana looked on pensively.

"Let's get this over with, Carl," she said. "Time is wasting."

He said, "If I call Miller, Hollywood, and have you arrested, you might end up getting off. Me, I could never allow that. Not now. We're in too deep."

"Carl!" Lana barked. "Now!"

More voice recording evidence for Miller to listen to. If only I would live long enough to play it for him.

"I see," I said. "So that's what this is all about. You're in this thing too deep. Lana has you by the balls. I know too much and now, like Susan before me, I have to be eliminated. That's how this works, right? Just remember, you're just moments away from your own elimination, pal."

His eyes blinked more rapidly now, his Adam's apple bobbing up and down in his thick neck.

"But you honestly don't believe that you're going to die do you, Carl?" I went on. "Maybe Lana has promised you something, haven't you, Lana? Maybe she promised you a life of living together. You could sell the house, move out of town and live on John's pension and insurance money. Because after all, there's more than a million dollars there. Sound familiar? It's exactly what she promised me before she revealed the plan to kill John by faking his suicide. Maybe you'd even retire early from the force, sweeten the deal by adding your pension to the mix. But all you've got to do is show your loyalty to Lana by getting rid of me first. You do that, you destroy the potential body of evidence that can prove, without a doubt, that Lana organized her husband's murder."

The sweat was pouring into his eyes, and he wiped his brow again with the back of his hand. His face was flushing redder and redder by the second.

"How many times I gotta tell you to shut up, Forrester?" he said. "How many fucking times?"

"Have it your way, Carl," I said. "I'll shut up. But since you're going to kill me anyway, at least answer this. Are you really in love with Lana? Or is it just a case of lust? Think carefully now, because there really is a difference. But before you nail the coffin shut on yourself like I have, you not only have to ask yourself that very question. You need to be brutally honest about the answer." I smiled. "Love or lust, Carl? Which is it? Love or lust?"

He thumbed back the pistol hammer.

"Break the fucking glass on the fucking case," he said. "Do it now."

"I'll take that as lust," I said. Then, turning back to the case that housed the pistols. "This case here, Carl?"

"Yeah, that one for Christ's sakes," he said, waving his gun with one hand and wiping a new layer of sweat form his brow with the other. "Hurry up about it already."

Inhaling a second breath to quell the pain in my foot, I balanced myself on its heel, then raised up my good foot and kicked the glass in. It shattered while I shrieked in agony.

"Jesus," I said, exhaling the breath. "You'd think a guy like Cattivo would have used safety glass to house his arsenal."

"Grab hold of the automatic in front of your face," he demanded. "The Smith & Wesson 9mm. Not the Colts."

Reaching out, I took the Smith & Wesson off the case wall, held it in my hand.

"Looks like my theory is balls on accurate," I said. "You want my prints on everything. You want to make it look like I worked my way back here to enact my revenge with one of John's hand cannons. But you're not actually going to allow me to load this pistol are you, Carl?" Then, locking my focus on Lana outside the door. "Is he?"

She peered down at her sandaled feet.

"This part I can't watch," she said. She turned, walked back into the living room and her apple wine.

"Way to go, Sherlock," he said. "Can't trust you with a loaded gun. Now stand back." He cocked his gun, aimed for my chest. "You don't need no stinkin' bullets, Hollywood," he said with a smile planted on his red face, and a droplet of sweat pouring down over his lips. "All you have to do is approach me in a threatening manner. I'm trained to recognize when my life is in danger, and I have the right to shoot you dead."

That's when I tossed the gun at his head.

CHAPTER 61

CALL it dumb luck. But Carl was able to evade the gun by shifting his head at the very last millisecond. At the same time, he took two quick steps forward and triggered his gun. The bullet grazed my left shoulder. I lunged at him, so that he reared back hard against the wall. Grabbing hold of his jacket, I held on while he pushed off the wall, propelling us both across the gunroom floor until we crashed into the case, the remainder of the still intact glass shattering. His gun fell out of his hand, hit the wood floor, slid, and came to stop by the open door.

He made a tight fist, punched my face, dropping me to my knees. He grabbed my left ear lobe, yanked on it so that I had no choice but to face upwards at him. He punched me again and again in the forehead, nose and mouth. Short sharp punches with a tight, hard fist that had the same effect as rapid-fire hammer blows. I felt my nose crack and my lower lip burst open, my head grow dizzy from a brain that was banging against the rigid sides of my skull. I knew I'd pass out if I didn't get free of his grip. Do it now.

My clear vision was fading. But out the corner of my eye, I saw the gun on the floor. Rallying my strength, I raised up my right hand, set it on his bloody face, and scratched at his eyes, trying like hell to gouge the eyeballs out with my fingertips. He screamed and released me, bringing both his hands to his face. I lunged for Carl's pistol, managing to grab hold of it with my outstretched right hand. But that's when I felt something sharp impaled into my bad foot.

The force of the act didn't register at first.

The pain that shot through my veins and nerves was so intense, so electric, so beyond anything I'd ever experienced, that all other sensory perception seemed to shut down entirely, like an overburdened power grid.

I dropped the pistol because I couldn't bear its weight in my now weakened state. Looking down at my feet, I could see that Carl had jammed a six-inch piece of glass into the top of my sutured foot. The knife-like glass had penetrated the Velcro strap on my walking boot, along with my skin and flesh. After a brief beat, I was able to retain enough clarity to work up a thunderous scream while I kicked at his face with the boot heel on my good foot. His head reared back and he seemed on the verge of passing out while the back of his skull collided with his upper spine.

Sitting up, I did what I knew I had to do. I grabbed hold of the glass and yanked it out of my foot, then brought the blood-smeared triangular point down fast into Carl's thigh.

He yelped like an injured dog, while once more I went for the gun. He turned himself around onto all fours, came at me with his mouth baring bloodied teeth. Aiming the barrel for that mouth, I pressed the trigger. There was an explosion and his head popped like a blood-filled water balloon slapped against a brick wall, his torso dropping dead weight onto my legs.

The gun was still gripped in my hand as it rested in my lap. I knew I should have been looking for Susan. What if she were still alive? Locked away somewhere in the house? In the basement maybe? But that was just false hope.

I knew she was dead.

They had been telling me she was dead all along, and that I was the one who killed her. I just had no recollection of the event. And if I had killed her, I had no reason in the world to live any longer. Carl's piece was gripped in my hand and it was my turn to eat it. Opening my mouth, I raised the gun up, turned it upside down, and pressed the barrel against the roof of my mouth.

Closing my eyes, I slipped my slipped my thumb inside the trigger guard, just like John Cattivo taught me.

I was just about to depress the trigger when I heard the clatter of footsteps outside the gunroom door.

CHAPTER 62

LANA screamed.

I pulled the gun out of my mouth, once more rested it in my lap.

"It wasn't supposed to happen this way," she said, more angry than afraid. "You were supposed to die. We couldn't take the chance on you testifying. That's what Carl told us. You had to be disposed of for good."

From down on the floor, I readjusted the gun in my hand, wrapped my hand around the grip, pointed the barrel at Lana.

"Where's Susan?"

"You know where Susan is."

"No I don't. Now where is she?"

"Far away from here. Let that be your first clue. You only have to go so far as your secret garden if you want a second clue. But then, you know all this don't you? You're the one who did it."

My body felt like it was burning up. Drowning in fever.

"How can she be far away?" I insisted, pressing my thumb on the hammer, cocking it back into firing position. "I thought you two were in love? What does her disappearance have to do with my pot patch?"

"Figure it out for yourself, Ethan."

"Maybe I should just shoot you now and be finished with you forever."

"You're not gonna shoot me," Lana said, working up the kind of smile she would assume when handing out cookies to the neighborhood children. "You're much too in love with me for that. Every man and woman I've been with since I was twelve years old has been hopelessly in love with me and they have all paid the ultimate price. You're a slave and once a slave, always a slave, Ethan. Now put the gun down and we can talk this through and then get the hell out of town. We still have a shot at being together. What do you say? Let's just pack our bags and make our way south to Mexico. We go now, no one will ever catch us."

I looked into her blue eyes.

"I lust you," I said.

"Excuse me?" she said. "What's that mean?"

"I lust you… I hate you."

I waited until her smile faded entirely from her sweet face before I pulled the trigger.

CHAPTER 63

LANA dropped like a stone. She landed hard onto her chest and face. She began to convulse and tremble like there was something trying to escape her dead body besides her soul.

Maybe it was the devil who was trying to escape, if you believe in that kind of thing. Or maybe it was just her badness. Her evil core. Whatever it was, I could only look at her until her muscles stopped moving and she exhaled a final poisoned breath.

CHAPTER 64

RAN.

Didn't matter that my foot was bleeding out or throbbing with blasts of sharp pain. At this point, I felt like gangrene had settled in for good, infecting my blood, infecting my mind. I didn't care. I just needed to get to that pot patch. Susan wasn't anywhere to be found. Lana said that I had done something bad to her and that my first clue was the pot patch. Carl also said I'd done something horrible and that I had to pay for it. The convenience store clerk said that I killed them all. But I had no recollection of doing anything bad.

No memory whatsoever.

I shoved Carl's automatic, barrel first, into my pant waist, and exited the house onto the back deck. From there I made my way through the fence gate. My heart raced, my foot pulsated in bursts of agony and blood. My entire body was on fire. As I made my way in the darkness down the narrow alley created by the parallel fence exteriors, I began to make out the sound of sirens. Without a shred of doubt in my mind, I knew it had to be Miller and his men coming after me. He'd already called me once before and I hadn't answered.

He must have known that eventually, Carl would pick me up and arrest me. But it didn't go down exactly as planned. Carl wanted to pick me up all right, but didn't want me arrested. He only wanted me dead so he and Lana could live together forever.

What it all meant was that I had only a minute or two to check on the patch, to prove to myself that Lana was lying… that I had nothing to do with Susan's disappearance. Once I did that, I would get the hell out of Orchard Grove. When I was a safe enough distance, I would send Miller the sound recording I'd made of Lana and Carl as they tried to kill me. It wouldn't prove that I had nothing to do with John's fake suicide, but it would shift most of the guilt to Lana. We'd all share in the guilt even if most of us were dead, or fast on our way to getting there.

I came around the fence to the small patch of woods, and in the moonlight I made out the spot where the coffee can had been extracted from the earth. I also made out something else. Another area beside it that had recently, as in mere hours ago, been disturbed so that the ground was no longer covered in dead leaves and varieties of vegetation. The area I speak of could not have been more than a couple of feet by a couple of feet, and it rose up out of the ground like a miniature burial mound.

All life seemed to drain out of my body then. What replaced it was inevitability. The ice cold realization that perhaps Lana and Carl had been telling the truth after all, and that my memory had indeed failed me, either because of the whiskey or simply a form of selective memory that can only be achieved after an event so violent and disturbing, the conscious brain can't possibly process it.

I no longer felt the pain in my foot, no longer cared it if was leaking an oil slick of blood. I only needed to know what exactly had been buried inside that mound. Hobbling through the brush and onto the patch, I dropped to my knees like a penitent man. I brushed away the dirt and dug with my hands until I felt a cold, round, semi soft object. Like a pumpkin covered in a sticky liquid. When I brought my fingers to my face, I smelled the unmistakable iron-like aroma of blood.

I put my hands back on the pumpkin and felt something soft, lush, and gentle.

Hair.

Tears began to fill my eyes, the pressure building behind my eyeballs as I dug around the hair, until I uncovered a small portion of face and a single eye. I dug in my pocket for my car keys and the small LED laser light attached to the keychain, and I shined the light on the face and saw that the hair was dark. Brunette. I shot onto my backside, because I knew now what I was looking at without having to see it in its entirety.

"Oh my sweet Jesus," I said, the first of the tears streaming down my face. "Sweet Jesus in heaven."

I shifted onto my knees and brushed more of the dirt away and I could see that the head had been severed at the neck. Shifting myself, I vomited onto the loose dirt and fell back onto my side. I recalled the previous night when I'd gone to Lana's home armed with a sharp French knife. I saw myself standing outside on the Cattivo back deck, the knife gripped in my hand while I listened to the sounds of Lana and Susan making love in the bedroom at the other end of the ranch home. In my head I saw myself going to the sliding glass doors, saw my hand taking hold of the opener, saw myself sliding the door open…

But that's all I recall.

All I recall, that is, until I woke up in my bed, my hands covered in blood from the small cuts on my palms and fingers. Or so I could only assume. Had I actually made my way into the Cattivo house, crossed over the dining room and the kitchen, and entered into the master bedroom and killed Susan after catching her making love to Lana? My Lana? Our Lana? Had I been filled with a jealous rage not only at seeing the two of them together in bed, but knowing they'd been plotting against me all along to take the fall for John's murder? Were there two sides to my personality? The movie maker artist and the cold maniacal killer? I was all too familiar with the artist, but I'd never been introduced formally to the maniac until now. Until last night.

"Oh sweet Jesus," I repeated as I pulled myself up onto my knees, then up onto my feet. "I killed Susan. I… killed… Susan."

…Or did I? I'd been drinking Jack Daniels. Jack Daniels makes me crazy, violent. It makes me black out…

As the tears fell, dripping off my chin and onto the raw earth, I did my best to cover up the shallow grave with dirt and dead leaves. Then, returning to my feet, awkwardly and out of balance, I began to make my way back through the brush, and around the fence perimeter to the Cattivo driveway.

CHAPTER 65

CARL'S truck was still parked in the driveway where he left it earlier, the keys still inserted in the column-mounted ignition. Opening the door, I shoved myself inside, turned the key, fired the engine up. For a beat or two, I stared out the windshield onto my new neighbor's home-sweet-home, until I shifted my gaze onto my own home only a few feet away. They were the kind of neighborhood homes that would be a dream for a young couple just starting their new life together. I was there once myself. Me and Susan.

Unzipping the blood and mud stained overalls, I reached into my pocket, pulled out the mobile phone. I saw that it still had power even if the battery life indicator was now in the red. Once I got to my studio in the city, I'd charge it back up. But for now, I also saw that the voice recorder app was still operating. Thumbing Stop, I then hit play just to make certain I'd succeeded at recording everything that went down inside the Cattivo house of horrors since I'd arrived there less than a half hour ago.

"Well good morning, Carl. How long have I been asleep?"

"Get out. In the house."

I hit stop, then went to texts. There was a new text from Miller and also several unanswered calls from him.

"Where are you, Ethan?" the text said. "You can't run. Let me come for you."

"Carl is dead," I texted in response. "So are Lana and Susan. They are all dead."

I hit Send and waited for a reply. It came within seconds.

"I must bring you in. You know that. Stay where you are."

"Not yet."

I thumbed Send once more, then turned the phone off, shoving it back into my pocket. Looking down at my foot, I could see the small puddle of blood pooling on the floor under the gas pedal. Setting my left foot on the brake, I shifted the truck into reverse. Backing out of the driveway, I could feel the sharp throb shooting in and out of my foot, and I could smell the rotting flesh, and feel the fever burning in my head. I had no choice but to suck it all up while I made one last drive through Orchard Grove back to my studio in the city. It would be one hell of a rough drive, but a drive I had no choice but to make.

I was all alone now.

The last slave of Lana Cattivo left alive.

THE PRESENT

I'M dying.

Serves me right I suppose. For now I sit at an old wood desk that's positioned only a foot or two from the front door to my downtown writing studio. I see my pale, scruffy face framed inside the mirror that hangs on the wall by a sixpenny nail. My smartphone in hand, I have it hooked up to the charger I store here and which is plugged into the wall.

"That's all there is to say, Miller," I say, speaking into my smartphone voice recording app. "There's nothing left to tell. Only questions remain, the major one being, what happened to Susan's body?

"But then, I can only assume you're probably at the Cattivo house as I speak. That you've seen the bodies of Lana and Carl Pressman lying on the gunroom floor. Have you located the rest of Susan's remains? Have you located her head in the pot patch out back? Did you find the knife that killed her? Was it a French knife?

"I still have no recollection of doing something so brutal and unspeakable to her. How is it possible I could take a knife to her like that? Sure, I woke up with blood on my hands, but there was no garden dirt on me that I remember.

297

Is it possible that I didn't kill her? Is it possible that I dropped the knife onto the deck outside the sliding glass door, like I remember? That Lana heard the back sliding door open and close, and when she came outside to inspect, she saw the knife and was overcome with a sick idea? Maybe, in the end, she decided the only way you and the rest of the APD would truly believe I carefully planned her husband's murder was by my leaving behind yet another body. The body of my wife. It would be a crime of passion. A murder committed by a man who was out of his mind with rage. By killing her in the most inhuman of ways, you wouldn't find it very hard to believe that I was also capable of taking out Detective Cattivo.

"Even the placement of the head would not have been an indiscriminate move. John knew all about my pot patch and he'd threatened on more than one occasion to use it against me. He knew I was selling weed in order to make ends meet. I was about to lose my house after all. He was aware that financially, Susan and I weren't making it. That in mind, Lana could have easily drugged Susan by slipping something into her drink, then cut off her head, burying it in the pot patch, all the time knowing full well that you would have no choice but to accuse me of the obscene crime. Add in the killing of the convenience store clerk and the run-in with the troopers down the road from that motel, and you've painted a picture of a crazed killer on the loose. A man who, in another life, achieved a degree of fame in Hollywood, but who'd fallen on times so hard, his brain snapped.

"I guess I can't be entirely sure how it all went down, but that seems as good a theory as any. Anyway, where I'm going, I guess God will be the judge. Or the Devil. But promise me something, Miller. That when I'm finally gone and you recover the rest of Susan's body, you will also make an attempt at searching for evidence that will exonerate me of her death. I can't be sure of what you will find, if anything, but it might just be enough to let my soul off the hook. After all, eternity is a long time to fry.

"Sirens. I hear sirens, Miller. Is that you coming after me down here in the city? Are the sirens I'm hearing outside my door meant for me? Let me look. I don't even need to get up out of the chair to crack the front door open a few inches.

"Okay, I see you now. I see you standing outside my building, protected by the opened door to your unmarked cruiser. I also see six or seven blue-and-whites parked diagonally in the middle of the road, their rooftop flashers igniting the black sky. I see cops armed to the teeth. It's a perfect ending, set up exactly the way I'd script it.

"Wait, what was that? The call for me to come out with my hands in the air. You want me to exit the door, climb the three steps to the sidewalk, and surrender myself to the law. Then you'll insist that I drop to my knees and lie down flat on my chest, face down on the hot summer-heated macadam, hands outstretched over my head.

"It's all over for me… for us, Detective Miller. It's all she wrote. Pun intended. So here's what I'm going to do. I'm going to pull out Carl's 9mm, and release the magazine. Pulling back the slide, I'm releasing the one-chambered bullet so that no bullets remain in the gun whatsoever. If only John Cattivo had checked his gun in the first place to see if it were loaded, none of this would have happened. But when you look at the empty gun in just a few short minutes, Miller, you'll see proof positive that even if I am guilty of shooting Cattivo in the head, I'm not really a murderer.

"I'm standing now, Miller, heading outside. But I'm taking my phone with me so I can record for posterity what will be my final moments. I'm opening the door wide and looking up through the stairwell, I see you standing only a few feet from me out in the road. You're bathed in flashing light, your hands gripping your sidearm. I'm heading up the stairs, the gun in my hand. I'm aiming the gun directly at you, Miller.

"Muzzle flashes. You're shooting at me. Bullets… against flesh and bone… but I don't feel them… I don't feel… any pain… Detective Miller. No pain at all… I see only darkness…

"Nothing but eternal darkness…"

Albany Police Department
(Preliminary) Incident Report

Case No. 1324-08232015

Date: 08/23/2015

Incident: Scriptwriter Ethan Forrester, 50, was shot and killed early this morning at approximately 1:30 AM outside his Swan Street writing studio by the author of this report who, at the time, was acting in a manner consistent with the conditions set forth by the "use of deadly force."

Forrester's death occurs on the heels of four related homicides, all of which transpired within the span of 48 hours and at the same location: 26 Orchard Grove in North Albany (see attached coroner's report for specific ETD and manner of death for each).

The four homicides are as follows:

-Susan Forrester, 48, of 24 Orchard Grove in North Albany: death by asphyxia and decapitation.

-Lana Cattivo, 46, of 26 Orchard Grove: shot with 9mm caliber semi-automatic handgun to the face at close range.

-Albany Police Detective, John Cattivo, 41, of 26 Orchard Grove: gunshot wound to head with .45 caliber handgun. Note: wound might have been self-inflicted, although evidence also points to Forrester having pulled the trigger.

-Albany Police Sergeant, Carl Pressman, 35, of 45 Fairlawn Avenue: shot with 9mm semi-automatic handgun to the face at close range.

Case Summary: At this time, all evidence, both circumstantial and physical, indicates Ethan Forrester conspired with Lana Cattivo to murder Detective John Cattivo. Forrester's testimony points to the fact that he asked Cattivo to demonstrate precisely how a cop "eats his piece" on behalf of research for a new movie script he was allegedly writing. While Cattivo agreed to the demonstration, he had no way of knowing that hours prior to the event, a live round had been placed in the magazine either by Forrester or Lana Cattivo. When cocked into the chamber, the single round created a "hot," and therefore potentially deadly handgun.

Forrester had been conducting an affair with Lana Cattivo for an undocumented amount of time. Forrester's wife, Susan, had also been conducting an affair with her simultaneously, even though both husband and wife were unaware of one another's illicit activity until hours prior to John Cattivo's death.

It might be interesting to note that a partial manuscript was discovered on the dining room table beside a manual typewriter in the Forrester home. The five pages describe an illicit affair between a next-door neighbor and the wife of a prominent banker. In the story, the two plot to kill the banker and collect not only his fortune but also his insurance payout. One can only wonder if fiction were reflecting reality in this manuscript as there is no question in my mind that Ethan Forrester conspired with Lana Cattivo in the fabricated suicide of her husband.

Regarding the death of Herbert Wylie, 73, the convenience store owner/clerk in Nassau (Columbia County): My professional opinion on the matter (and this can be corroborated by the Nassau Sheriff's Department), is that Forrester acted in self-defense when he issued a fatal blow to Wylie's head with a shotgun stock. Therefore I have not listed the death amongst the homicides. I believe the security videocassette tape which was recovered inside a dumpster outside the convenience store will conclusively back this theory up.

Questions also remain about how and why exactly, Albany Police Sergeant Carl Pressman engaged Forrester in an altercation at the Cattivo household, which resulted in the police officer's death by gunshot wound to the face (It should be noted for the record that Pressman's body was discovered with $5,000 cash on his person. Cash that can be traced directly to Ethan Forrester). While it is my professional opinion that Forrester was acting purely in self-defense when he shot Pressman, I have included the latter's name amongst the homicides because of his complicity in the overall plot to murder John Cattivo (see transcript of Forrester's semi-audible mobile phone recording, also attached).

Based on the testimony of sources inside the APD, I am also convinced now that Pressman was also conducting an illicit affair with Lana Cattivo. Perhaps Pressman's feelings for Lana combined with the knowledge of her sleeping with Forrester (and several others), provided the motive he needed for attacking the scriptwriter with lethal intent.

The question of how and why Susan Forrester died in a brutal beheading is naturally foremost on this detective's mind. I wish I could report that in all my years as a police officer, I've never come across so gruesome a murder, but that would be inaccurate. During the five-year period between 1979-1984, I, as a young APD detective, was placed in charge of investigating a series of murders/beheadings, all of which occurred in the North Albany area. All the known victims of the so-called "North Albany Mauler" were men. However, they ranged in age from early teens to one man who was in his late forties and the principal at a now defunct public grammar school.

In August of 1984, Lana Strega, then 15, allegedly escaped the killer in an attack that took place down in the wooded area of the Albany Riverside Corning Preserve. I personally interviewed her at the South Pearl Street APD moments after she was rescued and taken into police custody. At the time, I noticed that she bore a unique tattoo on the ankle of her left leg. A heart that cried tears of blood.

I have not seen a tattoo like that printed on that part of a woman's body, since August of '84. Until now that is, when I examined the most recent crime scene at the 26 Orchard Grove Cattivo address (It should be noted that although Lana's husband had been working for the APD for two months at the time of his death, I had yet to meet his wife in the flesh, much less take notice of her left ankle. Nor did I ever have opportunity to see that John Cattivo also possessed an identical crying heart tattoo on his left bicep, since department regs call for a long sleeve shirt and jacket for all detectives). That the deceased Lana Cattivo bore the identical crying heart tattoo on the same ankle, led me to immediately believe that after thirty years, I had finally found my killer.

What I find disturbing in retrospect, is that the North Albany Mauler had not only been in my presence back in '84, but that I had her in custody. Only because she appeared to be a sweet young lady did I immediately discount any possibility whatsoever that she could be responsible for a dozen known gruesome murders and beheadings. In a word, she didn't match the profile. I thought of her as the one victim who got away, and nothing more.

Having stumbled upon the North Albany Mauler quite by chance, I firmly believe Ethan Forrester had nothing at all to do with killing his wife, Susan, despite the fact that the weapon utilized in the killing, a common kitchen "French" knife, was later located inside the Forrester household and contained only Forrester's bloody prints.

My opinion is that prior to Susan's murder, Lana Cattivo broke into Forrester's home, stole the knife, committed the murder, then returned the knife to its original location on the floor of Forrester's dining room. It's possible she avoided leaving her own prints on the weapon by covering her hands and fingers in latex gloves, although this fact has yet to be confirmed by forensics experts.

A note on motive: Police records show that back in 1979 and some years prior, Lana Cattivo, then Lana Strega, was the victim of repeated sexual assaults from her then stepfather, Alex Burns, who at the time, owned and operated the Burns Apple Orchard which is now the sight of the Orchard Grove residential complex. On October 1, 1979, a missing person's report was filed by the Albany Police Department after Lana's mother, Tina Strega, now deceased, reported that her husband had not been seen at home or anywhere else in the community for more than 48 hours. Something that was very odd for a man who ran an apple orchard and farm 24/7.

After a lengthy investigation for the whereabouts of Mr. Burns, nothing substantial turned up. It was during this time, however, that Lana revealed the truth about her relationship to the stepfather. Something that must have been very upsetting for Lana's mother who was no doubt grieving the abandonment and/or loss of her husband.

In the course of my limited research for this incident report, I was surprised to find that the grounds in and around Orchard Grove had not been thoroughly searched by the APD or anyone else at the time of Burns' disappearance back in 1979. But when my forensics team scoured Forrester's backyard marijuana garden for the remains of Susan Forrester's head, a convincing trail eventually led to the adjoining Cattivo property, ending at a single apple tree that apparently had survived from the old farm.

We were able to perform an excavation under this tree in a spot that had supported newly disturbed soil. What was revealed were not only the remains of Susan Forrester's torso, but also the skeletal remains of Burns' beheaded body, plus the partial remains of several as of yet unidentified victims.

These two bodies of evidence, and the manner in which they had been killed, taken together prove to this detective that, without a doubt, Lana Cattivo acted alone when she slaughtered Susan Forrester, just as she had acted alone, and no doubt out of a "justified" vengeance, when she killed her stepfather and eleven other Albany residents between 1979 and 1984.

It is my further opinion that in killing Susan Forrester with a knife belonging to Ethan Forrester, Lana Strega Cattivo was attempting to further implicate the writer in the murder of her husband John, while at the same time, making it appear that he acted alone.

But did he truly act alone?

It should be noted that John Cattivo's two front teeth were broken off just prior to his receiving the fatal gunshot wound to the roof of the mouth. If he were demonstrating a suicide for Forrester, why would he shove the gun into his mouth so hard the barrel would break his teeth?

My view is that Forrester, acting out of panic, forced the pistol into Cattivo's mouth, and assisted him in pulling the trigger.

May God save and rest all their souls.

This concludes my report on the matter of "Orchard Grove," File No.1324-08232015.

Please note that no formal bench warrants or indictments are to be issued. The $5,000 cash collected at the crime scene will be issued to charity once released as evidence.

Chief Homicide Detective, Nick Miller, APD

August 23, 2015

Action Taken: Not Applicable. All suspects deceased (see above).

ABOUT THE AUTHOR

Winner of the International Thriller Writers Thriller Award and Shamus Award for Best Paperback Original in 2015 for *Moonlight Weeps*, Vincent Zandri is the *New York Times* and *USA Today* bestselling author of more than twenty novels, including *Everything Burns*, *The Innocent*, *The Remains*, *Orchard Grove*, and *The Shroud Key*. He is also the author of the Shamus Award nominated Dick Moonlight PI series. A freelance photojournalist and solo traveler, he is the founder of the blog *The Vincent Zandri Vox*. He lives in Albany, New York.

Visit him online at
www.VincentZandri.com
or on Twitter at
@VincentZandri